The

Merlin

Stones

By Gerry Woodhouse

Published by

LANTERN TOWER

An Imprint of Melrose Press Limited
St Thomas Place, Ely
Cambridgeshire
CB7 4GG, UK
www.melrosebooks.com/lanterntower

FIRST EDITION

Copyright © Gerry Woodhouse 2008

The Author asserts his moral right to
be identified as the author of this work

ISBN 978 1 906561 12 3

Printed and bound in Great Britain by:
CPI Antony Rowe, Chippenham, Wiltshire

FSC
Mixed Sources
Product group from well-managed
forests and other controlled sources
Cert no. SGS-COC-2953
www.fsc.org
© 1996 Forest Stewardship Council

The plot for this book came into my dreams whilst I was asleep on a coach in Germany.

I couldn't have put that dream into words without my wife's unfailing interest and patience over the last six years.

The Merlin Stones is dedicated to you, Rita.

I hope you enjoy the character who bears your name in the book.

Thanks to Karen for her ongoing encouragement. Also to Kevin and Peter. Their pertinent humour kept me going. Thanks to Austin Kehoe for his appraisal and trust in what has been written.

Vain Satan aspired to defeat the invincible God,
To set himself in heaven, as the one deity,
Satan, and his band of angels failed
And were hurled headlong from the Heavens,
To live in eternal damnation, but
Satan swore to rule the Heavens, once more.

CHAPTER ONE

In the Year of our Lord, Two Thousand and Seven.

I CAME TO MY SENSES with the stench of death trapped in my nostrils. The images of mutilated, dying men battered at my brain, and all because of the whim of an evil deity, in his desperate bid to rule the heavens. The red mist permeating the passages of my mind gradually receded, just as warm sunshine burns through early morning pockets of fog. I allowed my weary eyes to open. It took them time to focus in the bright sunlight which streamed through the windows of the ruined castle that had once been my father's proud home.

My heart pounded at a frantic rate. It threatened to burst through the wall of my chest. Muttering a brief prayer towards the heavens, I thanked Him for being alive. Without thinking, I pinched the top of my leg to make sure that I was in the land of reality. The pain proved that I was awake. It made me wish that the events of the past few weeks could have been a dream, instead of the real thing.

My body was covered in sweat. It had soaked into the fabric of my clothing. The warmth of the sun created a perceptible cloud of steam, rising like mist into the chill morning air. The mental and physical agony must have been etched into my face. Painful spasms ebbed and flowed through every muscle in my tormented body. My mind engaged in agitated turmoil, even though the demons had long departed.

Unashamedly I wiped away the tears that trickled down my face. I caught sight of my father's handwritten manuscript

1

lying on the ground. A wistful smile tugged at the corners of my mouth. No one will ever believe what is written on those pages, even though I am the walking proof of his words.

I thought about the girl. She should have been with me this morning. I was struck by the realisation that she was no longer a part of me. The girl is only a memory in the pages of time. I pictured her auburn hair, hanging in ringlets about her face, and those green eyes, which, with one look, had the effect of turning my whole body into warm jelly. It reminded me of how much I love her, and the immense happiness I have derived from her all too short presence in my life.

My love for her is so intense, that if she had asked me to die for her, I would willingly have done so. Such is the measure of the deep, unshakeable affection in which I hold her. I can't begin to think of a future without her.

The girl has gone, and the love we shared during our brief relationship is stripped from her mind. Her feelings for me have been blown away like chaff on the wind. I'm a complete stranger in her heart and mind. She's forgotten me, as if I had never existed.

I shivered at the images of what has happened during these past few weeks. But, at the end of our brief relationship, our happiness was blighted by a string of evil and moving events. I tried to summon up some inner strength, to help erase the memories of our relationship. It was a waste of time. How can I wipe from my mind the dangers, the passion and ecstasy that we shared during those few short weeks of light and darkness? Only my God knows where my future lies. At least he looks in favour on me for what I have done.

CHAPTER TWO

The 6th Century, in what is now Modern Day Wales.

I HAD TO ADMIT TO a certain fascination as the shimmering shapes slowly formed themselves into a picture. It was a clearing within a wood. The ground was covered in the brown debris of fallen leaves. A rude hovel stood at the edge of the wood, by a small pool of water.

Built from branches, and covered with moss and grass sods, the hovel was a crude attempt at some form of simple shelter. Sadly, it would never enjoy the status of a grade one listed building in future years. On the opposite side of the clearing stood a huge gnarled rock, covered in lichen.

A feeling of peacefulness bathed the scene. Birds twittered in muted sound, as the breeze played a rhythmic tune on the few autumn leaves still clinging to the mother trees.

This solitude was spoiled by a flurry of activity. Two figures stumbled out from the hovel. They were in violent argument. An incredibly ugly old man pulled a young girl into the clearing, very much against her will. He was unsightly and wrinkled, his back bent over by the ravages of time. Snowy white hair hung to his shoulders, and his beard stretched to his waist. The skins covering his scraggy body didn't do any favours to his over-ripened appearance. My first impression was of an elderly redundant Father Christmas, except that he wasn't acting very charitably towards the young woman.

She was a class act, a complete contrast to the wrinkled creature. It was hard to drag my eyes from her. White of skin, with flowing red hair, she was simply beautiful. My feelings for her were heightened by the scantiness of her clothing. I felt a movement in my groin.

What in heaven's name was this stunning creature doing in the company of the unbelievably repulsive old man? Perhaps they were father and daughter. If so, she favoured her mother's side of the relationship. I was deafened by the ferocity with which they shouted at each other. They spoke in a foreign tongue, but that didn't matter. I could understand every word they said.

She broke free of his grasp, and stood facing him, three or four feet away. A look of abject fear covered her face. The old buzzard stood his ground. He frantically waved his arms in the air, hurling a torrent of words at her.

Without warning, he moved towards her, a tirade tumbling from his lips. His spittle somehow managed to evade the confines of his beard, and was thrown in the air, giving the appearance of fine mist. His arms flailed like a windmill, fists clenching and unclenching. "Emuline! You have cheated me, and toyed with my emotions. Each time I penetrated your body, you swore that you felt love for me. Even though I am old, you told me that my body gave you the pleasuring of a younger man. And now I am the victim of your deceit. I find that all you want of me is the secret to my powers. You shall not have them."

Panic crossed her face. She shouted at him, her words tinged with menace and disdain. "Do not dare to threaten me. I too have mystical powers. You fool. Do you really believe I could have loved someone as old and ugly as you? You disgust me, Merlin. What has happened these last weeks is a ploy, set up by my husband, to get our hands on your stones. He is nearby, and will come if I call."

My ears pricked up at the mention of the old man's name. Who hasn't heard of him?

White beard took three faltering steps towards her. "I

4

will show you what I do to women who deceive me, you poisonous wench. I could strike you down where you stand." He snorted. "No, that's too easy. I will make you suffer instead. I called you poisonous, and poisonous you shall become. I will change you into a viper, so that you may crawl on the forest floor until you meet your death."

The woman's reaction was immediate. She pointed her fingers at the old man. He was visibly stunned by the fierce rush of words that spewed from her mouth: "Damn you for all time, Merlin. Ur tibo dyon vapo."

The effect of her words was nothing short of a miracle. Her frenetic ranting stopped him in his tracks. Merlin shouted in terror. He tried to run from the clearing. All he could manage was four steps before he came to a halt. He turned towards the woman. "My powers are great, but I cannot undo what you have done. I didn't mean the words that I spoke. I was angry. You know I would never harm you. I love you. Save me, I implore you. Remove your spell."

The woman tossed her head, and sneered. "Go to your prison, Merlin."

With one final effort he shouted at her. "This is the end of Merlin. You have overcome me, this day, but I will return. I am immortal. Mark my words, woman. I go to my prison, with the stones that you crave still in my possession."

His whole body stiffened, until there was neither movement nor sound. Merlin's body twitched. For a moment I thought that he was going to overcome her spell. He didn't. The animal skins covering his skinny frame disintegrated, and fell to the ground leaving him naked.

Whatever the witchcraft was, the effects took a swift course. Small cracks enveloped his body, and streams of red vapour seeped from a multitude of fractures. The old man began to break up, until his body disappeared from sight.

Where he had stood, a cloud of mist floated above the ground. It drifted, as if blown by a gentle breeze, towards the large rock, where it kissed the surface and permeated through the stony structure, until it was lost from view.

The look on the woman's face was fearsome. I conjured with the words that she had spoken. What they translated to wasn't important. It was their devastating effect which was most significant. The words were imprinted in my mind.

It defied any kind of understanding, that the female had produced a spell out of thin air, which had turned a powerful warlock into a puff of smoke and consigned him to the inside of a rock.

What had unfolded before me was the epitome of all my dreams. I had never managed to invoke anything like this, in my past dream world.

CHAPTER THREE

The 1980s, Onwards, in England.

HOW COULD I POSSIBLY HARBOUR feelings of jealousy toward that group of individuals whom I politely refer to as the 'have-it-alls'?

I haven't got an axe to grind when it comes to comparing their worldly goods with mine. Nor am I bothered by their qualities and achievements. Why should I be? After all, I am blessed with startling abilities that no other human being shares. And that includes the 'have-it-alls'. If I'd lived in the middle ages, the church elders of the day would have tried to burn me at the stake.

Nevertheless, I do envy one aspect of the 'have-it-alls' as they wallow in their endless bliss. Their enviable life-style has to be everyone's dream of contentment, as each day is spent cushioned in wall-to-wall, self-centred comfort and happiness. Life's lottery holds no surprises or incurs worries for them. Fate has already decreed that the cornucopian horn of plenty will succour their every whim.

There is another incentive in their heavenly existence. These revellers, in their feckless world, probably enjoy a sleep pattern totally uninterrupted by dreams. Why should they dream? Their waking hours are the very things that dreams are made of. I envy them for this.

I have never experienced such satisfaction, in the whole of my short life. My waking hours used to border on the realms of despair, until I tailored an escape route from the inevitable conditions in my life. My upbringing wove this despair. I turned to the land of dreams, and eventually harnessed their ethereal powers as an escape route from the hopelessness of my waking life.

My dreams have a happy theme, contrary to my childhood waking hours, which were unbroken misery. The great Prospero once said: 'We are such stuff as dreams are made of.' I couldn't have put it better myself. He must have been a dream weaver too. For as long as I can recall, my slumbers have been filled with dream images, right to that fateful day when I harnessed them during my waking hours.

I need to put things into perspective, if you are going to understand what the hell I'm talking about. All of mankind dreams during their nocturnal interludes. For all I know, even God dreams. If my humble conjecture is correct, at least He can make His dreams come true.

Some people remember the odd dream. Others recall nothing. We all dream, except the normal mortal has no control over their subconscious matter. Not wishing to put too fine a point on it, I am unique. God, or someone else, broke the mould on the day that I was born.

My mind possesses an unusual ability. When I wake up, I recall with vivid detail, every action, and every word, from my dreams. How fortunate, I hear you say. If you want this gift, then you can have it. I used to live two separate lives. One in my waking hours, the other during my hours of sleep.

My art of dreaming was up and running, before I tackled the hurdles of reading, writing and arithmetic. I began to spin dreams, before I stopped wearing nappies. When I was five I told my mother about these night encounters. She took me to task. "It's not healthy for a child to have fantasies." She couldn't have known how true her words would prove to be.

She took me to see our doctor. He couldn't see any problem in what was happening. "It reflects a healthy, enquiring mind.

There's no cause for concern." He patted me on the head, in that ingratiating manner that adults inflict on children. "He'll grow out of the habit. Something will come along to replace his dreams." He was spot on. Something else did replace my dreams, in later years. The doctor was wasted as a dispenser of good health. He should have been an oracle.

There are other things I can boast of when it comes to dreaming. From seven years of age, I trained myself to choose the fantasy that I wanted to dream. In my sleeping state, I always knew it was a dream. My self-service technique enabled me to control everything that happened in the dream, even to the extent of waking up when it suited me. My dream weaving enabled me to visit other parts of the country, and the world, to mingle with people. Dreams also provided me with fantasy, almost magic, powers, that don't form a part of the waking world.

My dreamland has its benefits. I never feel pain. If I drifted into sleep suffering from an ache, or the effects of an illness, the aching faded away as soon as I entered my dream world. Uncannily, the affliction had always gone when I awoke. The symptoms never returned.

My comments will open a can of worms. Dream psychologists, chancing on my words, will enjoy a good belly-laugh. "Nonsense," they'll cry, with derision in their voices. "The stupid boy is making this up. His theories fly in the face of what our scientific studies have proven, over many years. Greater minds than this impertinent youngster have been studying this subject for centuries. How long has this child been involved in the psychology of dreams?"

For the whole of my life, is the answer. The experts overlook one crucial factor. I hold the trump card. I haven't needed to study the subject matter. My gifts, in the field of dreams, are as natural as sliced bread. These powers were conferred on me by a deity.

You might think that I'm describing my dream spinning skills in a calm, offhand manner. Don't let this fool you. I didn't enter the world of dreams lightly. I learned as much as I could about my fantasies before attempting to control them. The same principle applies to everything in life. You wouldn't swim the channel without first learning to swim, would you?

In my tender years I read many books on the subject. My footsteps led me to the local lending library. The female trout of a librarian gave me an old-fashioned look, as I stood in front of her desk. I could barely see over the top. With great trepidation, I asked whether the library held a copy of 'Dream Worlds', by Doctor Ashton Raydon. I'd seen the book in a local bookshop window. My words brought a wry smile to her lips. With unblinking eyes and straight face, she shook her head in disbelief. Puckering up a look of disdain on her wrinkled face, she removed the spectacles from her bulbous nose. Her words were laced with sarcasm. "Does your father need the book to prop up the short leg on your kitchen table, young man?"

Her young assistant burst out laughing. The laughter was quickly stifled, as the young girl suffered an unspoken rebuke from the steely, frozen stare of her superior.

I plucked up courage, and countered her adultness in no uncertain terms. "No Miss. The table leg is already propped up with the 'do-it-yourself' book that dad borrowed from the library, last week."

Where I dredged up those words from I don't know. I closed my eyes, cringing in the expectation of a verbal explosion. It never came; I opened my eyes. She was glaring at me from behind her glasses. The severe looking blue eyes twitched. My cheekiness had harvested the desired effect. Her stern face unravelled itself, and the slit that masqueraded as a mouth, slowly unzipped. She turned to the young lady. "Go and get the young man his book. It's in the reference section under 'Mind and Body'."

She allowed me to sit in the reference room, so that I could take my time in studying the book. I encountered no further problems from her. On the many occasions that I called in at the library, she would pat me on the head. I forgave her for that. She referred to me as 'her little dreamer'.

That first book motivated my thoughts. One passage, in particular, caught my eye. Doctor Raydon sets out his definition of a dream in a very rigid way. His words are etched in my mind, and I quote: 'A dream is nothing more than a series of images, ideas and emotions occurring involuntarily to the mind, in certain stages of sleep.'

His definition doesn't apply to me. What better means are there to disprove someone's theory, than by my own practical application? My dreams are certainly not involuntary. They are deliberately planned, and spontaneous.

Other books set out the popular belief that dreams are a portent of something that will happen in the future. This idea didn't appeal to me. How can you dream about something that will happen in the future, when it is not yet a figment of the mind's eye? That is unless it is an implanted thought from some outside agency, such as God, or the Devil. Only I know the answer to that one.

I was spurred on in my efforts to infiltrate and dominate my dreams. I honed and fine-tuned my mental processes, to unlock the door to my imagination. If I had known that I'd been blessed with an unnatural gift, I would have been tempted to abandon my dream world, there and then. It might have saved me a load of tears and trouble. I had no way of knowing that in my adult years, powerful latent talents would surface in which my mind played no part.

The powers that I possess don't come as part and parcel to mankind, for which I thank God. Not these days, anyway. Centuries ago, some of my gifts would have been as common to the human race, as walking down the street. Even in the twenty-first century, each of us possesses a soul, or bodily essence, through which we are quite capable of channelling a unique range of powers, emanating from our creator. The mind boggles at the routine talents which would have been in common usage, in past centuries. Mind reading, telekinesis, thought transference, extra sensory perception, raising the dead, magical spells and hands on healing, to mention a few. These secrets were long lost to humankind, until I discovered that I held the key to unlock them.

The original purpose of these powers was to create goodness around us, until the system became corrupted by evil men. Witches and warlocks were routine, possessing powerful magical abilities. They've vanished as well. At least, I thought they had. You must realise that these essential skills remain dormant in our minds, waiting to be germinated. All you need is the key to unlock them.

I'm nearly twenty seven years old. My future lies over-heavily in the lap of the gods. In committing my recollections to the light of day, I won't blame you if you don't believe them. There's no point in providing proof of my powers. It's your good fortune that I believe in the Christian God, otherwise you'd be cringing under the shroud of an evil deity.

As I write these words, it's a beautiful autumnal October day, in two thousand and seven. A story is always written for a reason. My excuse is a manic desire to share the images of my life with mankind, especially the last few weeks. In seven days' time, on 31st October, I am taking a step into the unknown, whatever that might be. It's a crumb of comfort to me, that I have left a written account of my life, so far. If I get back, I intend to share my experiences with humankind, by writing a book. I will have to change names, and locations, for reasons that will be appreciated, when my book is published.

I was christened Kitchener Milner, but I'm known as Kit. I first saw the light of day on 25th of December, nineteen hundred and eighty, in the beautiful market town of Linmere, which nestles in rural Hertfordshire, on the border with Buckinghamshire. Some wag once described Linmere as a cemetery with street lights. My parents lived in a rented semi-detached property, on the outskirts of the town.

Every minute of those early years is imprinted on my mind. I even have a clear image of the day I was born. From a point of darkness I passed into light, with the soft, moaning sound of the wind wafting in my ears. The smell of wood smoke filled the air. My eyes alighted on a beautiful lady, dressed in flowing white robes. Her love-filled eyes devoured me, as she held me in her arms. She planted a gentle kiss on my cheek and rocked me from side to side, as she chanted a gentle lullaby. This loving interlude was suddenly broken. I was snatched from her arms by someone in a hooded cloak.

The woman cried sorrowfully. With a pleading voice she implored my abductor to return me. "Give him back to me. He's my son. The baby belongs to me, not his father."

I remember crying my eyes out. Her face wasn't the face of the woman who brought me up. It nestles clearly in my memory, along with everything else that's ever happened to me. I used to think it was my first dream. Perhaps that's where it all started.

I asked my mother about my birth. She was reluctant to talk about it. Then she relented, and laughed. "You were far too impatient to get into the world. You couldn't be bothered to wait for me to get to hospital. I gave birth to you in a roadside cottage, in front of a blazing fire." She clammed up, and told me not to ask silly questions. The subject was never mentioned again. Her story explained the smell of wood smoke. But what about the other lady?

I clearly remember my father dying when I was two. He was killed by a hit and run driver, who was never traced. My mother raised me on her own. She didn't go out to work, but we never lacked the creature comforts of life. I craved for her motherly love, but she always put up an invisible barrier when it came to the affection department. Her love and affection were destined to be channelled elsewhere, to my total exclusion.

When I was ten she met a man called William Grodam. He used to come round to our house, once or twice a week, when the three of us would have tea together. After tea, my mother always sent me upstairs. "Off to your bedroom, Kit, I want to speak in private with Mister Grodam. It's grown-up talk."

My feelings for William Grodam were non-existent. I wanted him to go away, and never come back. Their relationship blossomed during the next twelve months. One day, my mother dropped a bombshell. I knew it was something that I was going to hate, when she kissed me on the cheek, and held my hand. She hadn't done that for years. "Kit. We have something to tell you. Mister Grodam has asked me to marry him, and I've accepted. He's coming to live with us. Won't that be great? You're going to have a new father."

14

Mister Grodam hovered in the background, a smug look on his spotty, bloated features, which weren't helped by a hare-lip. I wasn't happy, but my feelings didn't count. They went ahead and tied the knot.

Grodam started throwing his weight around hours after the wedding. He caught me roughly by the ear, and stuck his piggy features into mine. The smell of his breath caught at the back of my throat. I felt sick. "Listen to me. I won't say this again. Your mother's looked after you for ten years. Now she's married, and it's my turn. That's the way it's going to be, and don't you ever forget it." He looked across at my mother, and blew her a kiss, before shoving his face into mine. I could see the sweat on his deformed lip. "If I had my way, you wouldn't be here at all. So from now on, keep out of my way. I don't want to see you in the same room as me, or else you'll know it." He grabbed at my throat and whispered in my ear, so that mother couldn't hear. "You won't be around for very much longer, you little arsehole. I'll see to that."

I shivered. It sounded as if he was threatening my life. He let go of me, and raised his voice for the sake of my mother. "You will always be respectful, if our paths do cross, and refer to me as Mister Grodam. Do I make myself clear, you little runt?" He twisted my ear. I bit my lip to stop the tears from coming. My mother stood there, her head inclined to one side, staring at him with a look of hero worship. He snarled at her, "The boy's going to take his meals in his bedroom. You have no objection, do you?"

She clasped his hands and kissed his twisted lip. "Of course not, William. I'll see that he doesn't get in your way." My spirits sank to a new depth, at her abject rejection of me. She grabbed me by the arms, and shook me. "I'm not having you upsetting your stepfather. When he's in the house, you'll stay in your bedroom, like he said. Don't you ever let me

15

catch you in the same room as Mister Grodam. Get to your room, now." I scurried out, with the blow from her hand ringing in my ears.

I formed my opinions of Mister Grodam. He spent most of his time in bed. That aside, he was as work-shy as my father had been industrious. In a high pitched whining voice, his distorted words frequently reminded my mother of all the good reasons why he couldn't work. "It's this wretched club foot of mine, Matilda. The pain doesn't let up. The doctor says there's no cure for it. I'll be an invalid for life. I keep getting these pains in my chest, and stomach. For all I know, I'm on the verge of a heart attack. You'll have to care for me, Matilda, and raise some cash. We can't live on my benefit money." These mutterings were followed by groans and more moaning. "Things can only get worse. I have to be brave, and face up to the truth. I'm going to spend my days sitting in this chair. It's the best thing for me, you know, rest, and plenty of it. That's what the doctor reckons." At this point his voice took on a threatening tone. "You do understand, don't you, Matilda? You don't think I'm making this up, do you?"

Mother always agreed with him. "Don't torture yourself, William. Of course you can't work. You're a sick man. There are ways and means of raising enough cash. We'll get by. Leave things to me."

There *were* genuine reasons why he couldn't earn an honest living. He hadn't got the time, or the inclination. His days were spent ogling television. He was an avid worshipper of anything made from hops, grapes, barley or tobacco. He'd have given Bacchus a good run for his money. His unsavoury habits were financed by successive Chancellors of the Exchequer. Like all Chancellors, he tended to overspend. My mother was forced to give him money, to feed his obnoxious habits. On the rare occasions, when she was stupid enough to

16

refuse him his beer and tobacco money, he beat her.

He wasn't fussy who was on the receiving end of his fists, or his club foot. Mister Grodam battered me more times than I care to remember. I always knew when a beating was on the cards. My mother's sobbing, and the stomping of his club foot on the stairs, heralded my punishment time. My mother could never bring herself to comfort me.

One strange trait always followed my beatings. I'd wake up, the next day, with no bruises or pain. My stepfather, on the other hand, always suffered excruciating pain all over his body. Mister Grodam never learned. He was a glutton for punishment, and didn't heed the lessons from this form of self-inflicted injury. I continued to be treated to his fisticuffs.

Things took an unsavoury and frightening turn one evening. He burst into my room to give me a thrashing. Things didn't pan out that way. He twisted one of my arms behind my back. I yelled out in pain. He put his mouth to my ear. The distorted speech had gone. It wasn't the pain that worried me, but what he said, and the way he said it. I had never heard his voice take on such a gentle timbre. For a moment, my pain was forgotten. His words soothed me. "Listen carefully, Kit." It was the first time he had called me by my name. "Don't be afraid. I don't enjoy hurting you, and hearing you cry. What I am doing is out of necessity. It's a part of your learning process. Things will get worse, before they get better. But, don't ever give up. Heed what I say. I will protect you from real harm."

The calmness of the moment was broken. He twisted my arm further up my back. I cried out in agony. His acrid breath sought out my ear. The distorted speech had returned. "It's all over for you, you little toe-rag. I've had my belly-full of you. I am going to finish what I came for."

He was a complete bastard. He'd deliberately tried to disarm me with sweetly chosen words. He pulled me through the bedroom door, to the top of our stairs. He hissed at me. "My only mission in life, young Milner, is to get rid of you. I don't care how I do it, but something that looks like a nasty accident will do very nicely. Say goodbye, boy. You're going to fall down the stairs, and break your bloody neck. If that doesn't finish you off, then it will have to wait until the next time. Nobody will believe I pushed you, you miserable little prick."

Fear plucked at my heart. I hadn't done anything to warrant his beatings, and now he wanted to kill me. I felt angry. He wasn't going to throw me down the stairs, if I could help it. I sank my teeth into his hand. It was his turn to scream. I squirmed out of his grasp. What happened next wasn't planned, and had nothing to do with me. He swore, and grabbed at me. I threw my arms out to ward him off. Mister Grodam was transfixed, rooted to the spot. His eyes bulged with fright. I could see that he was doing his best to move, but couldn't. The look of fear in his eyes turned to wretched panic. I took a step towards him to see what was happening. Only God knows why, but I wanted to help him. Words can't explain what happened next. My right hand moved around and around of its own accord. He started to revolve on the spot, like some giant top. My left hand pointed at him, and he was gone. He plummeted down the stairs, his body crashing against wall and banisters, before ending up in an untidy heap, at the bottom.

He was still in the land of the living. His moans were testament to that. My mother rushed in from the garden and screamed. "For goodness sake! What's happened, William? Are you hurt?" He continued to groan. She saw me standing at the top of the stairs. A questioning look crossed her face.

"What do you know about this, young man?"

Grodam interrupted her. "It's alright, Matilda. It wasn't the boy. We were having a nice friendly chat, when I lost my footing. You'd better call the doctor. I think I've done myself a mischief."

My mother shouted at me. "Get down here, and give me a hand to get your stepfather into the lounge." I did as she asked. As I put my hands on him, he looked me in the eyes. Sweat was trickling down his face. He was scared to death of me. He suffered a second setback. The smell of waste, excreted from his bowels, hung heavily in the air.

We managed to cart his great baggage of flab into the sitting room. Mother laid some newspaper on the settee, before we placed his soiled backside on it. The doctor was called. He diagnosed severe bruising, plus a couple of broken ribs. My stepfather was confined to the settee for six weeks.

I had a strange dream that wasn't planned that night. A voice in my head told me I wouldn't be troubled again by Mister Grodam. I still took the precaution of wedging a chair against the bedroom door every night. There were no more beatings from Mister Grodam.

I know what you're thinking. Kit Milner should be put in a straight-jacket and locked away. Not only does he control his dreams, but he hears mysterious voices in his head. I make no apology. That is how it happened.

During those unhappy years, I took refuge in my dream world. There was nothing to hold me in the home. I developed hang-ups and fixations, and acquired an attitude problem towards adult people in general and members of the opposite sex, in particular. I was part of a dysfunctional family unit, and it was playing havoc with my life.

There was one chink of light. My home situation didn't affect my school work. Ongoing school reports spoke of a bright child, in both academic and sporting fields, possessing a vivid imagination and blessed with a sense of humour. I was popular with my school peers, but found it impossible to form one-to-one relationships. I managed to share a loose-knit rapport with one classmate. He had a sense of humour, similar to mine, and was prepared to listen to me without condemning me as completely off my trolley. He was the only one I shared my dream experiences with.

I was offered a scholarship to the local Grammar School. Mr Grodam wouldn't hear of it. "We can't afford to send him there," he shouted at my mother. "If we do, he'll only get above his station. The next thing you know he'll be wanting to have his meals with us, and inviting people home. I'm not having him showing me up."

The chance was lost. It was just as well. I'd have been mixing with boys from a better background than my own. Kit Milner would have drifted rudderless in a sea of class distinction, before ending up shipwrecked on the rocks of inequality. I'd have drowned in the process.

I left school at sixteen, sporting a spotty complexion and facial bum-fluff. I had no idea where my job prospects lay. No obvious skills lurked within me, bursting to get out. Mister Grodam called me into the kitchen one Monday morning. With cigarette dangling from bottom lip, and a glass of beer in his hand, he put his two penny-worth in. "Get out and find a job, you lazy sod. If you think you're going to loaf around at home, you've got another think coming. You can't expect me to keep you fed and watered." He flicked his cigarette ash in the sink. "We need your money to make ends meet. You know bloody well that my old body won't let me work. Don't hang around, then. Bugger off, and find a job. And don't bother to come back until you do."

Linmere is a pleasant Georgian market town. It is blessed with all the usual market town trappings. Two fish and chip shops, a church, a chapel, three Chinese takeaways, and more than its fair share of public houses adorn its acreage. One other landmark mustn't be overlooked. It was to play a major part in my future. Linmere had once boasted a bustling cattle market. The last animals were auctioned and led to slaughter years ago. The only reminder was the rusting metal pens, memorials to the sheep, pigs and cattle that had passed through the market on the way to the slaughter house. These premises now housed the auctioneering company of Brine and Cherry.

It wasn't until many years later that I realised that fate was guiding my feet, as I walked by their premises, on that cold Monday morning. I was an unsuspecting pawn in a conspiracy plotted by providence. It had been intended that I should be there at that precise moment in time.

My attention was caught by a piece of paper pinned to Brine and Cherry's notice board, flapping with delirious rapture in the bitter, swirling wind. The convulsive movement of the paper annoyed me. I snatched the notice from the board, screwed it up and with undisguised venom, threw it into the gutter. The wind had other ideas. A blustery gust seized the paper, and clawed it into the air. It swirled round like a demented demon, before coming to rest in my open hands. The notice was as immaculate as the day it had been pinned to the board.

A gentle breeze nuzzled my cheek. I shivered at the stirring of a distant, precious memory. It reminded me of the gentle kiss that the unknown lady had planted on my lips, on the day I was born. My feelings of confusion were forgotten as I read the words printed on the sheet. 'Intelligent young man wanted.' I read on. Brine and Cherry were anxious to secure the services of someone to assist in the business. What a stroke of luck this was. A soothsayer would have been more truthful, saying that it was meant to be.

Any job would suffice, so long as it provided a weekly pay packet to placate Mister Grodam. I walked into the office to offer myself for the position. I couldn't believe it when a grey-haired lady told me to take my coat off and get stuck in. No questions were asked, no application form filled in, nor was any obstacle put in my way. As far as the company were concerned, it wouldn't have mattered if I had been a Martian. It was too easy.

Don't run away with the idea that it was my outstanding personality and magnetic charm that landed me the job. I found out, some months later, that I was the only person who'd bothered to apply for the job, even though the notice had sat on the board for more than three months.

The job wasn't intended for anyone else. The forces of destiny had dragged me, by the pubes, to the doors of Brine and Cherry. I didn't have an inkling at the time. Why should I?

The work didn't stretch whatever talents I possessed. But, it did offer one positive factor. I didn't need to come into close contact with people. This was just as well. My self-confidence was at an all-time low. At sixteen years of age, on the verge of a new calling, I had as much chance of believing in myself as our football team has of winning the European Cup.

I learned more about the company in the first few weeks. Messrs Brine and Cherry, the founders, were no longer on this earth. They were hovering on angel wings, looking down on their bygone business from some great cattle market in the sky. The present owner was a Martin Henderson. Not only did he pull the business strings, but he functioned as head auctioneer. He had set up the business with the intended aim of selling general merchandise. It didn't take me long to find out what that involved. His auction house sold all manner of flotsam and jetsam. It didn't seem to matter that most of the stuff was crap; Mister Henderson applied the well established premise that mugs will buy anything, so long as the salesmanship is pitched at the right level and the auctioneer is under-generous with the truth.

Despite this he came over as an affable man. He looked well over sixty, but was in his early fifties. Standing over six feet tall, with an upright military stance, a shock of curly grey hair sat comfortably with his ruddy complexion and twinkling blue eyes. He'd have been a handsome man, in his younger days, but his looks had been squandered to an over indulgence on fatty foods and alcohol. His double chin and over-capacious stomach were dead give-aways.

In those early days, our paths rarely crossed. He was aware of my existence, but there was no reason why he should form a close working relationship with me. That suited me. All my time was spent in the auction rooms, under the beady eyes of one Arthur Horne. He swaggered about the premises, glorying in the title of head porter. Arthur was a shrewd man of indefinable age. As thin as a broom handle, he gave the impression of possessing as much brain power.

From my first day, I was placed under his wing. He told me, with a straight face, that he was a director. That was true. He directed, and I did the work. Most of the time, he could be found in the 'Robin Hood' hostelry, next door, whilst I sweated my guts out. I had to learn the ropes quickly if I was to survive in his company. The first two years were routine, even boring. More than once, I was tempted to leave. I could have earned much more anywhere else. It never happened. Fate had shackled me to Brine and Cherry, without having the courtesy of telling me.

When he wasn't drinking at the 'Robin Hood', Arthur Horne taught me the basic facts about the business. Martin enjoyed a financial working relationship with several local solicitors. Suitable backhanders in their back pockets ensured that the effects from the estates of deceased persons were channelled into our auction salerooms.

Martin also auctioned goods that had been recovered by the police, being the proceeds of burglaries and house-breaking forays. Looking at some of the tat, I wondered why the criminals had gone to the trouble of stealing it in the first place. They were either short-sighted, desperate, or both. It also explained why the victims had never bothered to claim their property back from the police.

My duties revolved around the preparation of the sale entries. I had to make sure they were positioned in their rightful places in the various sale rooms. Being a big lad, I always clicked for the job of carting the heaviest pieces of furniture around. Arthur had this habit of whining, as he wiped his nose on his sleeve. "You're a growing lad, young Kit. You need the exercise to toughen you up. I can't do the lifting these days, what with my state of health. You'll thank me when you're older. Mark my words."

What a load of cobblers. Have you lifted a Victorian wardrobe, or Georgian dining room table, lately? This humping round was bound to produce hernia problems, in later life, as well as ruining my latent sex-life. Arthur was the living testimony of my forward vision. He was the proud possessor of a huge double-hernia. You could see how big it was, from the bulge in the front of his trousers.

He always wore a poker look on his face. We didn't know if he was joking, or not, when he said that sex hadn't figured in his life for years. And that wasn't the end of it. Arthur told us that his wife had moved into a separate bed. I wasn't surprised. There wasn't room, in a double bed, for him, his wife and the truss.

Mind you, what am I going on about? I am eighteen years old, and have never been out with a girl, let alone have sex with one, whatever sex is. My work colleagues hadn't rumbled me. In their eyes, young Kit was a real stud, and every woman's dream hunk.

I couldn't claim job satisfaction, but was reasonably happy in my lot. The job took me out of the parental home. That was important. Mister Grodam kept out of my way, although it was obvious that he hated me. We developed an understanding of mutual trust. I didn't trust him, and he didn't trust me. I loathed the man. He was a bully-boy, and I suspected he was still knocking my mother around. I wanted to help and protect her, not out of love, but out of a sense of duty. She wouldn't let me. That showed how much we had grown apart. I can't believe that I put up with my home life for as long as I did. Somebody must have brainwashed me.

Life took on a fixed, monotonous routine. It was equivalent to jumping through a hoop, except that with every jump, the hoop got smaller and smaller. I was stuck in the proverbial rut. The further my feet trudged along the rut, the deeper the furrow became. It didn't take me long to realize that the rut would soon become too deep to climb out of. When that happened, the game was up. I would be trapped forever, a prisoner of my manic disbelief in myself.

CHAPTER FOUR

1999, and Onwards.

SOMEBODY ONCE COINED THE TIRED comment that time goes quicker when you're happy. It's not true, time speeds along, even when you're miserable.

The spots on my face have given way to healthy skin, as my hormones settled down. I've grown a moustache and beard, giving me a debonair look. It hasn't helped me to find a girlfriend. More worrying were the admiring glances I received from certain men. Who could blame them? When you're not cavorting with the opposite sex, you tend to send out the wrong vibes.

Girls find me handsome. Standing tall, with dark, wavy hair, and vivid cornflower blue eyes, I ached to reciprocate the posturing female overtures that came my way. My confidence department wasn't up to it. A mental barrier stopped me from dallying with their affection, or anything else of theirs, for that matter. Not once did I doubt my masculinity. I certainly wasn't gay, no matter what that genre of non-masculinity might think. I braved the agony of a tattoo on my arm, hoping it would demonstrate that unsoiled male genes flowed through my veins. The artistic work wasn't going to cause Rolf Harris sleepless nights. It was nothing more than a simple bolt of lightning, spearing the initial letter 'M'.

The tattoo was an impulsive whim, which I hoped might give me the self assurance to joust in the love stakes, with an understanding woman who could tolerate a man with little self confidence, and totally lacking in personality. It made me feel better, until I spotted a girl with an armful of tattoos, as well as sporting six rings through her nose, and a chain hanging from her lip. She was smoking a cheroot. Life wasn't dealing me the right cards.

Another two years of my doldrums slipped by. It was just after my twentieth birthday that life decided to pile on the agony for me. It didn't slap me in the face. It stuffed me. The situation brought more anguish into my life than I have ever suffered before.

On that never to be forgotten morning I was humping a brute of a seventeenth century coffer around the sale room. Arthur Horne put his head round the door. "Kit. You'd better put that down, before you do yourself some serious damage. Martin wants to see you in his office. Now, Kit. Not tomorrow."

I'd never once been summoned to the inner sanctum during the whole time I'd worked here. My mind raced to think why he should want to see me. With a total lack of enthusiasm, I made my way to his office. A car was parked outside. Through his office window I saw a man talking to Martin in animated fashion. The frantic conversation ceased as I knocked on the open office door. Martin's deadpan face told me that something was horribly wrong. I was proved right when he walked across and gave me a hug. With a modicum of embarrassment he excused himself. I was left alone with the unknown man.

He was the harbinger of bad news, personified. "Sit down, Kit." I couldn't help but watch his Adam's apple, as it moved up and down in unison with his words. "I'm Detective Sergeant David Bruce. I understand that you live at…" he looked at his notebook "…14, Woodside Avenue, Linmere."

A cold hand grabbed at my heart. "What's the problem?"

He put his hand on my arm. It was my lucky day. Everybody wanted to touch me. He sat down. "There's no easy way of telling you this, but I've got some bad news. Your mother was found dead, at home."

The cold hand shook my heart from side to side. "She can't be. She was alright when I left this morning."

"I wish it was a mistake, Kit, but it's not."

My shaking head threatened to part company with my neck. "I can't believe this. What's happened?"

He raised his hand. "I know this must be a shock for you." He took his hat off, and laid it on Martin's desk. "The bad news doesn't end there. Your stepfather is dead."

It's difficult to describe my full range of feelings. I was devastated. But I didn't cry, nor did I break down. The full impact would hit me later. For a fleeting moment, I expected to wake up and find that this was a bad dream. I knew it wasn't. I didn't have nightmares, then.

Detective Sergeant Bruce tried to smile, but failed miserably. "You won't be able to go back home for a few days, Kit. The house is sealed off, whilst our forensic team check out the premises. If you've nowhere to go, one of my colleagues can book you into a local hotel; let me know if you want any help."

I was shaken out of my silence. "This can't be for real. Was it some kind of accident?"

"I'm sorry, Kit. I wish I could elaborate, but we haven't established what happened." He paused. "I'll have to take a statement from you, at some point." He consulted the notebook again. "I believe you are an only child." I nodded. "You'll be asked to identify the bodies of your mother, and stepfather." He thought about what he had said. "Someone will be with you. The identification will be made at the local mortuary. We'll let you know when."

I was determined to show some strength of character. "I'll be alright. Don't worry. What happens next?"

He looked relieved. "You're going to need some support, Kit. We have a specialist police officer, who'll be in touch with you. She's our Family Liaison Officer. Ask her anything that comes into your head. She'll get you through the coming weeks, and will update you with ongoing information about your parents' deaths. When our forensic team finish their investigation, your parents' bodies will be released for burial, following the formality of an inquest."

He put his notebook away, and looked me in the eyes. "It's some time away, but a coroner's court will be convened, to which the police have to report their findings. This will enable the coroner to come to a decision regarding your parents' deaths."

I managed to stop the tears that threatened to flood my eyes. A numbness took hold of my body. At least it blocked out the full impact of what had happened. I pulled myself together. "Are you sure there is nothing more you can tell me?"

He shook his head. "Sorry, Kit. You'll find out in good time. There's a lot of police work to be done. Don't forget to ask if you want any help with sleeping arrangements." He got to his feet. "I'll leave my card with you. This number will find me." He put a hand on my shoulder. "When will it be convenient to take a statement from you?"

"Any time tomorrow. I'm not sure that I can tell you anything that will be of help."

He put his hat on. "Don't worry. My questions will be simple." He wished me goodbye, and left me with my own thoughts.

There was a tap on the door. Martin stood there lingering on

29

the threshold of doubt and indecision. "Bad news about your parents, Kit. Don't forget, we are all here for you." The tone of his voice reflected the sincerity of his words. He fidgeted, and bit at one of his fingernails. "The sergeant mentioned that you've got nowhere to go, for a few days. Arthur Horne says he can help. Go and have a word with him, Kit, there's a good chap." He walked across, and patted me on the shoulder. "It's easy for me to say, but try not to let things get you down. If you need time off work, let me know."

On this day of personal tragedy, I had ventured into previously uncharted territory. I'd crossed a hurdle in my non-existent working relationship with Martin. Once I passed through the forlorn mists of the next few weeks, I was determined to give Martin my best shots at work. I shook his hand. "I'll go and find Arthur."

With heavy feet, I ambled into the main saleroom. Arthur was leaning on a broom. He put it down, and blew his nose. "Martin told me your bad news, young Kit. I'm sorry, mate." He took his flat cap off, and scratched at his sparse hair. "About your sleeping arrangements. Hope you don't mind, but I rang the missus. She says you're welcome to stay with us, until things sort themselves out. We've a spare room, and Mrs Horne isn't a bad cook."

I accepted his kind offer. His wife was kindness personified, and I glimpsed another side of Arthur which I would never have seen in the course of normality.

A lot of things happened during the next few weeks. I gave my statement to the police. The Sergeant asked some innocuous questions about my mother's relationship with Mr Grodam. Had they got money problems, what was the state of their health and did they get on together? I gave him what

I thought were honest answers.

I identified their bodies at the local hospital mortuary. They each reposed in a coffin, looking to all the world as if they were sleeping.

There was bags of media interest. A police representative issued a statement to the press, saying that following a thorough police investigation into the deaths of my mother and stepfather they were not looking for any other person in connection with their deaths. I was convinced that it was some kind of dreadful accident.

I met up with the Family Liaison Officer. Sergeant Aline Burch explained that her role was to help me to come to terms with what had happened. Nothing was too much trouble for her. I couldn't have coped without her. Sergeant Burch assured me that she would put me in the picture before any police information went public. Her kindly disposition, and the clever use she made of her words, helped me to offload some of the dark feelings inside of me.

My mother's body was released from the mortuary, and I made arrangements for her burial. Martin, Arthur and myself, were the only mourners. I also buried Mister Grodam. Nobody turned up at his funeral, including me.

After three weeks with Arthur Horne, the police said that I could return home. This was a blow, but I couldn't live with the Hornes forever. I'd made up my mind that I wasn't going back home to live. Martin came to the rescue. He offered me the empty flat above one of the salerooms. It was in need of some tender, loving care which was a blessing in disguise. It gave me something to occupy myself with in the evenings, which was more purposeful than wallowing in a sea of sadness.

A few weeks after the funerals, the Family Liaison Officer telephoned, saying that she wanted to see me. My heart fluttered when I opened the door to her. A slim, brown haired lady, with green eyes, she would have been in her late twenties. She'd been hand-picked for the job. Her agreeable personality had lifted me through the trauma of these past weeks.

She smiled, as I offered her a seat. "My reason for calling is to tell you that the date for the coroner's hearing has been fixed for the twenty fourth of May. Police enquiries are now complete, and the pathologist has given his report to the coroner. I want to talk to you about the hearing. The coroner won't be calling any witnesses. He intends to read a simple statement to the court, before confirming his decision on your parents' deaths." She paused. "You realise that the media will be present? If you feel uncomfortable with this, then you don't need to put in an appearance." She let her words sink in. "My advice is to meet things head on. Try not to let the hearing unsettle you. I'll be with you, to hold your hand."

"Thanks for the advice. I'll think about it, and let you know."

She got up to leave. I caught her by the arm. "Can I ask a question?"

"Of course you can. Fire away."

"What did happen to my mother and stepfather? It's been puzzling me for weeks. I've kidded myself that it was some kind of accident. If I'm to believe what some of the newspapers have been writing, then I don't fancy sitting at the coroner's hearing, and being confronted with things that I know nothing about. I thought you were going to be upfront with me. Can't you tell me?"

She didn't bat an eyelid. From the look in her eyes, I knew she was about to beat around the bush. "That's a difficult question, Kit." I saw her put her mental thinking-cap on. "You must appreciate that the police have procedures, which must be followed. I'll tell you what you need to know, nearer the hearing, so that you're not completely in the dark. It's not the answer you're looking for, but it will have to do, for now. Please try and understand."

I wasn't satisfied. She was playing the middle course, and trying to placate me. "I hear what you say, but I'm not stupid. I know what my stepfather was like. He used to knock the hell out of me, and my mother. He was a bastard. If he's responsible for what happened, then I've got to know. It's been eating away at me, ever since my mother died."

She looked at her watch. "I'm sorry, Kit, but we'll have to leave things as they are. I'll ring you tomorrow afternoon. We can have another chat then. I'd better be off."

Something snapped inside me. I pushed her back into the chair. I realised that I'd gone too far, but I didn't care. I grabbed hold of her shoulders and stared into her startled eyes. "You're going to tell me, whether you like it or not."

The frightened look vanished. Her green eyes glazed over. She sat there, in complete silence. On an impulse, I moved my hand, from side to side, in front of her face. Her head followed the movement. She was in some kind of a trance. I tested my theory. "Tell me what happened to my mother?"

The police woman's face came vaguely alive. Words tumbled from her mouth, in dull monotone. "The police were alerted by a neighbour, worried by the sounds of screaming and smashing furniture. The police made a forced entry into the house, and found your mother on the kitchen floor. She was naked. Your stepfather was lying, face down, on top of her. He was naked, too."

Anger and bitterness seeped through me, in equal measures. I stopped her flow of words. "Cut out the small-talk, Sergeant. Get to the point. What happened?"

"Your stepfather cut your mother's throat, with a kitchen

knife, after he had stabbed her repeatedly in the chest. Her head was severed at the neck. He then had intercourse with her. His semen was found in her body." Her tedious tones were in full flow. "The pathologist found a drinking glass on the kitchen floor. Traces of your mother's blood were in the glass. Over two pints of her blood were in his stomach."

I couldn't stop my tears. I wasn't helped by the total lack of feeling in the police-woman's voice. I asked her to stop talking, as I struggled to regain some vestige of composure. I clutched at my head, in an effort to rid myself of the maddening, dark images being painted in my mind. It was beyond me. I shouted at the woman. "How did my stepfather die?"

"He died as a result of asphyxiation, caused by choking on your mother's blood."

"What will the coroner's findings be? Is he going to tell the media what you've told me?"

"He won't go into fine detail. It's not a difficult decision for him. His assertion will be that Mister Grodam murdered your mother, after which he died an accidental death."

I'd heard enough, and clapped my hands together. She woke up. From her apparent composure, she had no idea what had happened. "I must be going now, Kit. I'll be in touch with you before the coroner's…"

I butted in. "Don't worry about that. I won't be going. Will you let me know what happens on the day?"

"Of course, Kit. That's fine by me. I'll telephone you, as soon as the hearing is over, so that we can get together. I'll see myself out."

I kept myself busy during the next few weeks. Sergeant Burch telephoned me, in the early afternoon, on the day of the coroner's hearing. "Hello Kit. It's all over. The coroner has come to a conclusion. Can I come over, say in about an hour, to explain things?"

She wasn't late. We settled down, and she got down to business. "My news isn't going to brighten your day. The coroner's verdict is that your stepfather killed your mother, before dying from accidental causes. The coroner was very meagre in what he had to say in court. Do you want some further detail?"

My reply surprised her. "No, I don't think so. I had a feeling that was what happened. I've got to put this behind me, and start living a normal life. I appreciate the help you've given me."

She smiled. "I'm glad to hear that. Is there anything else you want to know?"

"What about the media? I suppose it will be splashed across the front pages?"

She bit her lip. "Don't be surprised by what you read in the papers. Most of the reporting will be upfront, but a few of the tabloids might show an unhealthy interest. It will soon blow over. Give me a ring if you need any more help. I'll be seeing you."

I made a conscious decision not to watch television, or read the newspapers. Next day, it was Arthur who told me that the television news was full of the story, and the newspapers were spewing pages of newsprint on my parents' deaths. The bastard who had murdered my mother was satisfying everyone's lust for a good story. My feelings didn't matter. Like all media stories that hit the fan, I hoped it would soon go away.

It didn't happen that way. On Saturday morning, the phone rang whilst I was having breakfast. A very agitated Martin Henderson was on the other end. "Have you seen this morning's 'Daily Globe'?" I told him I hadn't. "The sods have published a front page story about your mother." His voice faltered. "Someone has leaked a story to them. It's a bit different from what the other papers are saying." The line went quiet. I thought he'd hung up on me. His deep breathing told me that he was still there. "It doesn't flatter your mother." I knew he was uncomfortable, from the way he laboured over his words. "You'd better get a copy, Kit." He rang off.

It was what he hadn't told me that worried me. I decided to check the 'Globe' out, and drove to a newsagent on the other side of town. A single copy of the newspaper lay on the counter. I bought it, and walked back to the car. The print dancing in front of my eyes mocked me with words that I couldn't, and didn't want to accept. Most of the page was taken up with a photograph of my mother. Goodness knows where they had dredged it up from. She must have been in her mid-twenties. It reminded me what a good-looking woman she'd been. The headline was a piece of gutter journalism. The large, black print screamed out a headline of claptrap rhetoric that any imbecile, without a brain, could have concocted:

'DECAPITATED VICTIM WAS IN THE CUT-THROAT BUSINESS OF PROSTITUTION'

The article trumpeted that 'this shameless woman had sold her body to all and sundry, and used her house as a brothel, right up to the time of her death.'

The journalist responsible for pillaging my mother's reputation asked what kind of woman could have exposed her son, in his tender years, to such a shameful occupation. He went on to totally destroy her reputation, skilfully leading the readership's imagination to a self-penned conclusion, that Mister Grodam had found out, and that was why he'd killed her. His final sentence made a mockery of the coroner's findings. It positively encouraged the newspaper's readers to agree with the journalist's own view of her murder. Who could blame William Grodam for what he had done was his implied conclusion.

Even if the story of prostitution was correct, it didn't excuse Grodam for stabbing my mother to death, cutting off her head, swigging her blood, and committing necrophilia. If she'd been seeing other men, I might have forgiven him for giving her a beating, but not a bloodbath and decapitation.

I wondered where this journalist had sourced his facts from, without the worry of a libel action from me. The answer was in the final paragraph of the hyped-up story. The person who so badly felt the need to tell this story to the world was my mother's sister. That came as a complete surprise. I didn't know that I'd got an aunt. My newly-found relation stressed that she and my mother hadn't enjoyed a meaningful relationship for many years, ever since she'd become aware of my mother's attraction for men. The next sentence made me weep crocodile tears. She'd searched her soul, and had decided to make a clean breast of things to the press.

Her reasoning was taken straight from the hypocrite's guide to life: 'In the interests of all concerned, and especially that son of hers, I feel it right and proper to bare my soul, and tell the world what my sister was really like. How her poor husband must have suffered.'

She was a bare-faced cow. For her own best interests was more like it. She'd been paid handsomely for betraying her kith and kin. I was glad that I'd never met this woman.

The newspaper assertions were something that I didn't want to believe. But, as hard as I tried, childhood signposts fell into place. I had to concede, with some reluctance, that her immoral earnings would explain why I'd never wanted for material things after my father died. My mother had never worked, and her benefit money wouldn't have stretched to the standard of living that we enjoyed.

A chilling thought struck me. If my aunt's story was true, then Grodam would have been a willing partner in my mother's nefarious habits. He would have known what was going on, because he rarely left the house. Grodam had shared her secret. He was a pimp who had encouraged her along the road of prostitution, to provide him with his beer and fag money. How curious that the newspaper hadn't touched on that side of the story.

Life continues to kick me up the backside. I've had an unhappy childhood, a psychopathic stepfather, a mother who seemingly sat on her greatest asset, plus an aunt who has derived financial pleasure from telling the whole world about my mother's secret life. She'd been prepared to accept Judas money, without considering the price to be paid, by me, for her lack of family loyalty. I feel so angry. I'm determined to put my rotten life behind me, and start living like a normal human being.

CHAPTER FIVE

The Year of our Lord, 2007.

THE YEARS FOLLOWING ON FROM my mother's death passed all too quickly. Another new year has reared its head, and two thousand and seven is upon me. Time does heal, but you never forget. The memories that I carried simmered beneath my level of consciousness.

Those years were spent toiling for Martin Henderson. For the first time, job satisfaction crept into my life. It had an important effect on me. I was determined to make the boss take notice of me. It wasn't easy. I took a load of knowledge on board to improve my work prospects. When the day-time job finished, so my pseudo-social pleasures came to an end. Every leisure hour was spent in the flat poring over books on antiques, with the ethics of religion and business studies thrown in for good measure. I became the proverbial book-worm. I surprised myself by signing on for an 'Open University' course soon after my mother's death. You could have knocked me down with a Victorian candlestick when I obtained a degree. The addition of BA to my armoury completely cancelled out my self-inflicted portrayal of being a BF.

The word 'socialising' still doesn't figure in my dictionary of life. Socialising means hanging out with people, and enjoying yourself. At the very best, I can be described as dull, boring, isolated, workaholic and definitely virginal.

The local cinema received the occasional visit from me. But always in my own company, except for one bad experience. I didn't have the nerve, or the know-how, to chat up the opposite sex. I've lost count of the number of times I tried to buck this trend. Life delighted in throwing the buck back at me. The fault lay in my mind.

My socialising might be a complete failure, but this was compensated for by improvements in my working life. My hard work eventually bore fruit. Martin Henderson called me into his office one day and said that he wanted me to be in charge of setting up the auctions, as well as carrying out my porter duties. He entrusted me to classify sale lots, and his confidence went so far as allowing me to value items for the sales.

Martin's auction house boasted three sale rooms. Two of the rooms sold what I politely term rubbish. They contained more crap than can be found in the 'Daily Globe'.

That left the third room, affectionately known as the 'posh room'. In this inner sanctum, we sell the best pieces of furniture, works of art, jewellery, silver and ceramics. These goods receive the most polished description in our catalogue. Dealers might see through our carefully crafted works, but even an expert can be tempted and led to a purchase, with honey-honed descriptions gilded with the very slightest of misinformation and all crafted together by the skills of the auctioneer.

General sales were held on Saturdays, except for every fourth Saturday, when we broke away from the crap sold at the general sales, and held our upmarket Fine Arts sale. Fine Arts is a contrived and somewhat over pretentious name for a sale which includes only our very best wares, preferably manufactured prior to the nineteen thirties. This sale attracts dealers from all over the country, tempted into our premises by the captivating up-market dialogue in our glossy catalogue, all dressed up with striking photographs taken from the most sympathetic angles.

It was during the early spring of two thousand and seven that Lady Luck smiled on me. Martin called me into his office one afternoon. He couldn't contain his excitement as he asked if I would like to take on the job of the assistant auctioneer, who was retiring in six month's time.

I rambled on a bit, going all around the houses in an effort to find a good reason for refusing his offer. He told me to shut up, sit down, and listen. His blue eyes twinkled. "For Christ's sake stop going on, Kit. The hard work you've put in these last couple of years hasn't gone unnoticed. I'm offering you the chance of a lifetime. You can throw your porter's smock away, and take on a real job." He threw his head back, and laughed. "At the rate of knots you're going, you'll be after my bloody job, next year."

How could I refuse? I donned my one and only suit, and started to understudy the retiring auctioneer.

The months sped on to late August. My new duties were a sheer delight, as I learned the special skills, and craftiness, that any good auctioneer needs. What's so special about an auctioneer? He carries a level of great responsibility. Not only is he extracting profit for the Company, each time he sells a lot, but he has to ensure that the seller's reserve price is met. If he sells below the reserve price, then the auctioneer might end up with Martin levering a Victorian three-branched candlestick up his rear end, sideways on.

September came and went, and October was upon us. Dates are an important part of our lives. Some are indelibly engraved in our individual minds. Friday and Saturday, the fifth and sixth of October, two thousand and seven, are imprinted on my mind. Those dates changed my life forever. They were the viewing and sale days of our October Fine

41

Arts sale.

The hairs on the back of my neck stand on end when I recall that Friday and Saturday. They triggered a chain of events which I would willingly have done without. When I woke on that fateful Friday morning, I felt in a buoyant mood. The hoar from an overnight frost lay on the ground. I smiled to myself. The saleroom would be like an icebox. We auctioneers appreciate that the combination of extreme cold, and the natural darkness in the old cattle market building, provide the ideal ingredients for selling antiques. Given these twin conditions, buyers are more likely to miss the goods that are damaged, chipped or cracked. Added to which, the cold can freeze your nuts off, which tends to speed the bidding process along, so we can all get home.

I strolled across to Martin's office. Wishing him a cheery good morning, I parked my backside on the radiator, next to his. He couldn't contain his enthusiasm at the unusually high quality of the lots in the sale. Most of the stock was genuine antique. We wouldn't have to hoodwink the punters for a change.

"Have you bribed someone, Martin? It looks a damn sight better than the usual tat we sell. Where's it come from?"

"You can cut out your caustic comments. We have been known to sell half decent tat. We must thank the late Reverend Julius Milner. Most of his effects have found their way into the saleroom, thanks to a solicitor friend who is handling his estate."

I carried on with my leg-pulling. It was that kind of day. "I suppose you had to bribe him? How else would they have turned up here?"

His fist whacked me on the arm. "Put a sock in it, Kit. It was a bad day when your name-sake died, but it was one hell of a day for us. I don't suppose the old boy was related

42

to you, was he? If so, there's a good chance he's left you something in his will. Perhaps his favourite commode. Toilet paper, slops, and all." He pulled a face. "Some people have all the luck."

"I'm a waif and stray, Martin. Reverend Milner isn't a part of my family tree. What do you know about him?"

He moved away from the radiator, and plonked himself behind his desk. "My solicitor friend tells me that he was the Rector of Lovington."

"Didn't he have any family to leave his things to?"

"A daughter was mentioned. His wife died some years ago. She was killed in a road accident. When it comes to the Reverend gentleman, that's a different kettle of fish. He was found with his throat slit. They reckon it was suicide."

I shuddered at the mention of his throat being cut. Martin covered his face. "Sorry, Kit. That wasn't very clever of me. I'd forgotten about your mother. I don't know why his effects ended up here, and not with the daughter."

We nattered on for another five minutes before Martin excused himself. "I have to go out, Kit. Check out the saleroom, and tie up any loose ends. I'll be back, mid-afternoon. See you later."

I made my way to the saleroom. The usual crowd of dealers were spread around the room, as well as some new faces. One person caught my eye. He didn't so much attract my attention, as demand it. Standing at five foot nothing, he must have weighed in at twenty stone, or more. As square as a centurion tank, he had short, jet-black hair, and sported a Hitler-style moustache. The moustache did nothing for him. It had looked better on Hitler. His podgy, pasty coloured face boasted several chins, hanging like a dewlap over his shirt. The poor sod had a hare-lip. I wondered why he hadn't had it sorted. His unsavoury appearance wasn't helped by a pair of weeping eyes. He kept dabbing at them with a handkerchief. A black suit, and dark overcoat, struggled to hide his resemblance to a stuffed elephant.

My eyes were drawn to him like a magnet. Something about his looks set off a niggling doubt, which hammered at my brain. I moved towards him, on the pretext that I was logging sale entries. I took another peep at him. The top of his head wasn't at all right. The reason impacted on me. It was his hair. What looked like a dead, black cat, sat on top of his head. Mr Big was sporting the worst wig I have ever seen. I shivered, involuntarily. It had nothing to do with the coldness of the room. Evil wafted from him, filling his airspace with an aura of malevolence.

The spectacle didn't end there. Attending him were two shady looking characters, clearly owning their own hair, but sharing the same sinister, gormless expression on their faces. They were dressed in mandatory dark suits and overcoats. Their size suggested that they were well capable of handling themselves. Looking at the state of their faces, they had been handling other people as well. Standing at well over six feet, they towered above the fat one. With hands pushed deep into their overcoat pockets, I wondered if they were hugging a cosh, or toying with a hand-gun. My gut feeling was to steer well clear of them.

I reproached myself for allowing this trait of over-imagination to get the better of me. It wasn't my fault. They reminded me of a thesis that I had written, during my degree studies, setting out the distorted Victorian beliefs of assessing peoples' professions. The Victorians invented a set of principles, in which they firmly believed, on their ability to place individuals into descriptive pigeon-holes, solely by examining the structure of their faces, and the way in which they bore themselves. If a man was unfortunate enough to have a broken nose, beetle brows and cauliflower ears, the Victorians argued that he couldn't be anything other than a criminal.

Time has proved that this concept is a little rusty in its application to life, but I had allowed myself to fall into the Victorians' trap. I was convinced that the criminal pigeon-hole fitted this trio, to a tee. They reeked of criminal activities.

I would rather have left them to their devices, but I couldn't resist watching them. The fat one became visibly excited when his eyes alighted on a davenport desk. He waddled across to it, as fast as his stumpy legs would allow. He removed every drawer, squatted on the floor, and peered into the drawer recesses. Not content with that, he pulled a torch from his trouser pocket, and shone it into the desk's interior. He pushed the last drawer back into place, breaking wind as he struggled to his feet. A smile, akin to that of the Grim Reaper, lit up those pallid features. He pointed at the desk, patted it, and muttered a few words to his henchmen. They nodded their heads in unison, as cheesy smirks spread across their faces. The fat one pointed towards the door, and they sauntered out of the saleroom in close convoy.

I ambled across to the davenport. It was a beautiful example, made during the eighteen eighties. For the benefit of anyone who has never had the pleasure of gazing on this style of desk, it is named after a certain Captain Davenport, who wanted a portable writing desk to take with him on his military campaigns. In its compact state, it is a desk of heart-warming beauty. A genuine davenport will always attract good money. Whoever was lucky enough to buy this desk wouldn't have much change left out of fifteen hundred pounds.

A davenport has a hinged lid covering a recessed well,

with four drawers built into its right hand side, matching four dummy drawers on the left hand side. At the top rear of the desk is a raised, hinged, lidded box, stretching across the whole width of the desk. The desk is supported by the real and dummy drawers, with two barley twist legs at the front, with the whole contraption standing on four porcelain castors.

I allowed my fingers to trace a path across the beautifully polished walnut, savouring the patina which can only build up with age. Weepy eyes had got to me. I removed the drawers, and peered into the dark recess. I wasn't sure what he was expecting to find, but if he knew his davenport desks, he might be looking for a secret hiding place. My brief search revealed nothing. I wasn't disappointed. Some hidey holes are harder to find than others.

The davenport had caught my eye when it arrived on the premises. It was in a class of its own. I allowed my hands to continue caressing the willing surface of the wood, as my fingers revelled in its smoothness. My raptures were rudely shattered by a painful blow on the shoulder. Rubbing the afflicted area, I turned round to see who was responsible. Three people confronted me, each with the same malevolent look on their faces. It was Mister Blobby, and his two associates. He wiped discharge from his eyes and looked up at me. His breath settled on my face. I detected the halitosis lurking on it. It smelt as though something had died in his throat, and was slowly decomposing. I looked down at the wig, speculating whether the white flecks were dust, or built-in artificial dandruff.

One of his sledgehammer fingers beat a tattoo on my chest. His words were slurred, because of the hare-lip. "Keep your hands off that desk. If you're thinking of buying it, forget it."

He smirked at his goons. They sniggered for his benefit, then stared at me with uncompromising, unsmiling eyes. His attitude was belligerent. I didn't need a brain to realise he was looking for trouble.

I returned his stare, and ignored his rudeness. "I'm not intending to buy it," I squeaked. With a quick cough I recovered my vocal chords, and continued in a voice more suggestive of my manhood. "It's a lovely piece of furniture, deserving a good home."

His weepy eyes bored into mine. "It is going to a bloody good home, you twat. Mine."

His voluminous chins rippled in unison to his laughter, the dewlap swinging from side to side. Mister Five Foot Nothing swaggered on the spot, smiling in a self-satisfied manner. The fat one was making a complete arse of me, in front of the other viewers. He was beginning to get up my nose, and I'm not referring to his halitosis.

My left brain lobe reminded me that I was a big, beefy chap, well able to look after myself, but warned me that if I carried on with this train of thought, then someone was going to get hurt. My central brain lobe was adamant it would be me. The right hand lobe asked what the bloody hell was going on? This wasn't the kind of behaviour expected of me.

What I hoped would pass as a look of authority settled on my face. I stretched to my full height, and glared at him. My right brain asked me, again, 'What the hell are you playing at?' I laid on my most convincing auctioneer's voice. "The ownership of the davenport is not a foregone conclusion. There will be other people wanting to buy it. The auctioneer will take your bid, along with any other bidders, tomorrow."

My words were a waste of time. Smelly breath stood his ground. A look of total scorn framed his face. He turned to his lapdogs, and attempted a larger-than-life impression of me.

"I say, old chaps. Just listen to him. How delightful that the auctioneer will be prepared to take my bid tomorrow. Is he putting us in our place, or is he putting us in our place?"

He glared at me. It made me feel as if he was staring at a piece of human excrement. Turning his head, he nodded to the thug on his left. The henchman's reaction was immediate. For his size, he moved quickly. Before I could react, he grabbed the lapels of my jacket, and pulled me towards him. His body and mine were moulded into one. The thug's face was barely an inch from mine. His breath smelt of second-hand lasagne. For a moment, I thought he was going to nut me. With bloodied eyes bulging from their sockets, and his spittle raining on my face, he berated me. "Listen, knob-head. Billy Grodam is going to buy that desk. Got it? If I have any more backchat from you, I'll cut your bollocks off."

It felt as if a thunderbolt had struck me. It had nothing to do with the physical threats, nor was it the caustic words that stunned me. My reaction processes were stopped in their tracks by the revelation that the fat slob with the attitude problem was called Grodam. This latter day Genghis Khan bore the same name as my late stepfather. They even shared the hare-lip, as well as the unhappy knack of inflicting misery upon people. There must be thousands of people on this planet named Grodam. Tough. That didn't enter into the equation. It was a shock to my system to hear the name. My thoughts turned to my mother, and the brutality and demise she had suffered at the hands of William Grodam. How could I forget? I detested the name. The past had come back to haunt me. I was being threatened by another Grodam. I didn't like it one bit. My hackles started to get very jumpy and agitated.

The tough guy let go of my jacket. He went through the well-worn charade of brushing my rumpled lapels with his hands, then he slapped me on either side of the face. In a final gesture of contempt, he put his hands on my chest, and pushed me away. He smoothed his hair, pulled his tie straight, and grinned for the benefit of the tub of lard who went under the name of Billy Grodam.

The few dealers left in the room were watching the unfolding saga with mouth opening amazement. None of them showed the slightest willingness to help me. My brain raced. How should I handle this situation? With diplomacy, was the stock answer. Sod that. I didn't have a reputation for fisticuffs, but I felt light-headed with white anger. I was unwavering in my resolve to take the fight to them.

This wasn't the Kit Milner that I'd come to know. So what? This piece of low-life was called Grodam, and he was threatening me. That was the crux of my anger. For years, I'd carried a picture of my mother begging for mercy, before my stepfather hacked her to death. Someone was always going to pay for what she had gone through. That moment had arrived. I moved towards the gorilla who had just abused me. I kneed him in the groin, and hit him on the point of the jaw for good measure. He collapsed, like a sack of potatoes, in a noisy moaning heap. The sound of his suffering filled me with untold pleasure.

The other two were frozen into stupefaction, sharing the same look on their faces. Before the second thug could react, my left fist exploded into his midriff. As his body jack-knifed forward, my other fist caught him flush on the point of his jaw.

I'm not sure who was the more dumbfounded, Grodam or me. Damn how he felt.

My fist hurt like buggery, but my deep rooted anger dissipated in the heat of my physical interlude. Grodam moved away as I stepped towards him. From the look of hate on his face, I knew I was dead meat. My days were numbered. What I had done would be avenged; another time. He wouldn't give me the chance to defend myself. His attack would be launched from behind my back, without any warning.

The odious little man spent the next few minutes swearing and kicking at the two aching heaps on the floor. Wheezing and grunting, the goons dragged themselves into a standing position, rubbing their sore parts. Grodam looked me up and down, and opened his mouth to speak. He didn't get the chance. I shouted, at the top of my voice. "I should ban the three of you from the sale, except that I doubt if you'd take any notice."

I wagged a finger at my mouth. "Watch my lips. Any aggravation tomorrow, and I won't hesitate in calling the police. You'd better leave, before I ask the police to come and settle the matter now."

Grodam's face turned red, as he struggled to hold himself in check. The two henchmen moved towards me. Billy Grodam raised his hand. "Not now, boys." He pointed a finger at me. "Our business isn't settled. You're a bloody dead man. We'll be back tomorrow. Billy Grodam always gets what he wants. Watch your back, and keep your door locked. My boys will be around to see you, soon."

Three murderous stares were thrown at me. It was like looking into a crystal ball, and seeing my death sentence. They turned on their heels and walked out of the saleroom, leaving the onlookers in a state of stunned silence.

The spell was quickly broken. Everyone flocked across to me, jabbering amongst themselves. Out of the corner of my eye, I saw Traffy Taffy Evans, one of our regular dealers, moving in my direction.

He wasn't nicknamed 'Traffy Taffy' for nothing. He was

a lovely Welshman, who suffered from permanent flatulence. He wasn't fussy where he dropped his soundless time-bombs. Traffy Taffy was the original bum-boy, before that other genre rewrote the English language. His name is written in the annals of dealer folklore, especially the day when he managed to clear a complete auction room.

On a bad afternoon, it was a stroke of good fortune that I'd seen him coming. I made a desperate attempt to retreat from his advance. A wardrobe impeded my escape, giving him the chance to trap me. My nostrils twitched, and twitched again. I didn't detect any offensive airwaves. "I hope you're not messing with that lot, Kit. They're bloody nutcases."

I snapped at him. "What do *you* think? Do you normally hit people that you're having business dealings with? For god's sake, you Welsh twat. I've never met them before in my life. You seem to know them. Who the hell are they?"

Traffy put his head on one side, and gave me an old fashioned look. He stood his ground contemplating, or something worse. I twitched my nostrils. The air was untainted. "Never seen them here before, Kit. But I've come across them, elsewhere. They're bloody psychopaths. You know who the square shaped villain is. The other two are his cousins, Alfie and Reggie Grodam. They're a bad lot. You had me worried. For a moment I thought you knew them." He winced. "That was before you decided to put the boot in."

"You've got it wrong, then, haven't you? They had every intention of beating the crap out of me. What else do you know about them?" I didn't give him the chance to answer. I detected a change in the air quality, and pushed past him to where the other dealers were standing.

Doris Goring-Hart, a ceramics dealer, put her hand on my shoulder. Doris wasn't popular with the other dealers. Her self-assumed haughtiness had prompted the regulars to change her name, behind her back. She was affectionately known as 'Doris Boring-Fart'. "Are you alright, darling? I met up with them, once." Her superior nasal tones put me on edge. "It was at the Lovington auction house, three weeks ago. The obnoxious threesome were there. The fat one was throwing his weight around. He was ferreting around every piece of furniture in the place. They didn't put in an appearance at the auction, thank god. Whatever they were after, wasn't there." She looked around, and lowered the tone of her voice. "The grapevine has it that the fat one fronts a bigger gang. His cousins do all the dirty work. Protection racket and rent-a-thug are their stock in trade. I was so relieved when they decided to leave."

Traffy butted in, and aired his knowledge on the threesome. "That's interesting Doris. Two weeks ago, I was in the Chapel Road saleroom. I was minding my own business, when I bumped into Billy, with his two minders. What I mean is, they bumped into me. I was giving a davenport desk the once-over. It really grabbed me, I can tell you. Grodam told me not to bid for it, otherwise yours truly would end up with a couple of broken legs, as well as other assorted injuries to keep my legs company. He scared the shit out of me, I can tell you."

Traffy noted the pained expression on Doris's face. "Sorry love. What I meant was, they scared me stiff. The little sod must have warned everyone else off as well. He was the only bidder, and bought the desk. It worried me, boyo, when I saw you with them standing by that davenport. It was so uncanny. I knew what was going to happen, before it happened." The Welshman clicked his tongue, and grinned at me. "Don't even think about buying that desk."

I glanced at my watch, "I've got a lot to do, folks. Just

forget what happened." I glared at Traffy. "Let's get one thing clear. I don't intend to buy the bloody davenport. If fat man wants it, then fat man can have it."

They sauntered away to continue their viewing, as if nothing had happened.

I carried on with my work. That wasn't easy. Billy Grodam kept breaking my concentration. It wasn't his physical threats that worried me. I didn't want any trouble at tomorrow's sale. I decided to make a clean breast of things to Martin. Someone was bound to tell him. I kept an eye open for him, whilst I pottered around. He rolled up at about five o'clock. It was now, or never.

Within five minutes I was in his office. The happy look on Martin's face clouded over as my story unfolded. At least, he allowed me the courtesy of telling him what had happened. He sat at his desk, strumming his fingers on the arm of his chair. But not for long. He exploded, "What the hell has come over you, upsetting my customers? Are you deliberately trying to ruin me? What's going to happen when that lot come back, tomorrow?"

He started pacing behind his desk, scratching at his head. The pacing ceased. "I am not bloody happy." The tone of his voice should have warned me of what was coming. "You've breached your contract. I should sack you, by rights. I must be mad, but I'm giving you the benefit of the doubt. Consider yourself lucky that you've still got a job. But, if those people make a complaint to me, or the police, it's on your head. You won't get any backing from me."

I wasn't stupid. He'd been sorely tempted to sack me. The only reason he hadn't was because it suited him. Martin couldn't do without me for the next couple of days.

He hadn't finished with me. "There had better not be a

repetition of what went on this afternoon. If there is, then you're out." He waved an arm at me. "Now, bugger off."

This didn't leave me in the best of moods. I made my way back to the flat, and calmed down with more beers than I should have done. It was just after six o'clock, when I made my way to the saleroom. Bidding goodnight to the last of the dealers, I got stuck into my last two tasks, before clocking off. I checked that Dick and Jeff, the night security men, were on site. Martin had gone against his natural habit of not spending the pounds, by splashing out a few thousand quid on a state of the art security system. As a second line of defence, he had employed the two security guys to lock themselves in the saleroom for the three nights before the Fine Arts sale, because of the particularly high value of the stock. Dick and Jeff were drinking coffee, and probably earning twice as much as me in the process. We traded some banter about them not falling asleep on the job, or inviting their mates in for an all night rave.

My last job was to secure the car park gates, before coming back to the sale room and locking Dick and Jeff in for the night. Leaving them, I pulled my collar up to shut out the cold night air, and strode across the semi-darkened parking area. A solitary light shone above the entrance to the offices. The only other lights throwing their welcoming glow into the car park, were shining through the saleroom windows.

The evening would have been as quiet as a church mouse, had it not been for the din of the security men's radio as it blasted out an indefinable garbage of music.

As part of my ritual, I checked for any stragglers. No one was around. I could see the outline of the gates in the faint light given out by the street lights. I started to close them. Sod's law prevailed. As I pulled the first gate across, a car engine came to life from the dark recesses on the other side of the car park.

Whoever it was, had been parked out of sight. The car moved slowly towards me. It had to be a dealer. He'd probably been chatting on his mobile phone, and lost track of time. I swore under my breath, and shook my head in frustration. The silly beggar hadn't got his lights on.

Pushing the gates open, I beckoned him to hurry along, hoping that he would switch his lights on. It crawled along, moving closer to where I stood. The engine suddenly burst into life, as the accelerator was pushed to the floor. The car's tyres screeched as they tried to get a grip on the loose gravel. The vehicle hurtled towards me. The driver switched his lights onto full beam, blinding me in the process. His intention became all too obvious. He wasn't intending to drive through the gates. I was his target. My feet were rooted to the spot. My back passage nearly evacuated itself in a moment of sheer panic. The car was almost upon me before my brain engaged first gear. With belated desperation, I threw myself out of the path of the charging monster. The effort was wasted. The side of the car impacted with my lower back, knocking me off my feet, and spinning me into the wire fence that ran down the length of the car park. The breath was knocked out of me, as I slid to the ground. In my state of shock, I was aware of the car racing through the gates, before stopping in the road.

I lay on the ground, barely conscious, in a crumpled, painful heap. My face was barely an inch from the ground, staring at the gravel. The thoughts running through my head were full of insignificant trivia. I made a mental note to tell Martin that we could do with another load of stones on the car park. And, what about having some security lights installed, so that I could see a potential assailant in future?

My lower back was in torment. I cried out from the pain.

I wondered why the security men hadn't come to help me. Then, to add to my worries, I felt a hand touch me on the head. A man's voice whispered in my ear. I detected the distinct smell of chocolate on his breath. "Don't worry, Kitchener, everything is working out fine. This is the first rehearsal. Ignore the pain, dear boy. Things will change. You'll come to no harm while I'm here. You're being watched over, as you have been for your whole life."

Who the hell was that? It wasn't one of my assailants, and surely the Archangel Gabriel wasn't guarding me? Forgetting my pain, I saw a twisted, funny side amidst my pain. A car had deliberately run me down, and someone had assured me that everything would be all right. In my disorientated state, I was convinced that my imagination was playing tricks on me.

This ridiculous train of thought was interrupted by the sound of running feet. Someone pulled me over onto my back, and aimed a violent kick at my thigh. There was a pause, before I was struck on either side of my face with a heavy object, swiftly followed by a number of heavy blows into my chest. Every smidgen of breath vacated my body. My lungs gasped for air. Panic took over. I knew what a fish out of water must feel like, as I found it impossible to breathe life-giving air into my lungs. My life flashed before my eyes, and I accepted that I was dying. I found time for a single, poignant moment of regret. I was going to die a virgin.

I opened my eyes for what I thought was the last time. The shadowy outline of my attacker towered over me. "Take that, you little arsehole." He gave me another vicious kick. His foot struck me in the upper left hand side of my chest. I gasped from the newly inflicted pain, and gulped air into my empty lungs. The acute hurting was unbelievable. But I was breathing, thank God.

My attacker must have been satisfied with the damage he had done. The assault ended. His footsteps beat a hasty retreat in the direction of the car. I heard him shout out, "I've done him over, Billy. He won't be going to any bloody auction tomorrow. The bastard won't be going anywhere, for a few months. Next time, I'll kill him."

It was the thug I'd kneed in the groin this afternoon. A car door slammed shut, and with squealing tyres, it sped off down the road.

My first attempt to move was a mistake. The spasms of pain jabbed at every nerve ending in my body. I fainted. When I came to, Dick and Jeff were fussing over me. One of them shone a torch in my face. It hurt like hell. My head felt as if it was filled with cotton wool, muffling the words they shouted at me. I shook my head, and regretted it.

Dick's words filtered through the fuzziness. "For Christ's sake, Kit, What's happened? We wondered where you'd got to. You look awful." He turned to Jeff. "This is your bloody fault. No wonder we didn't hear anything, with that radio of yours blaring out."

Unlinked words rolled in verbal disorder from my mouth. I wanted to tell them that a car had tried to knock me down. I wondered why my mouth wasn't working very well. It took an effort to raise a hand to my face; it was even harder to run the fingers over my swollen lips. My tongue explored the inside of my mouth, very gingerly. It didn't find very much. Where my teeth had once nestled snugly in the gums all that remained were gaps. I tried to count how many teeth were missing. I gave up at eleven. In my semi-conscious state, I scraped my fingers through the gravel, in a vain attempt to find the lost teeth.

Dick wanted to call an ambulance, and the police. Don't ask me to give specific reasons, because it wasn't obvious to me, but I pleaded with them not to. Between spitting blood, and howling with pain, I talked them into taking me back to the flat. I promised to ring the police in the morning. My slurred words must have been convincing. I was surprised when they made no objection.

"Whatever you say," said Dick.

They clucked round me, and managed to move me into a sitting position. I surprised myself by getting to my feet, albeit somewhat shakily. From the rasping pain hammering at my chest, I knew that my ribs were broken. Goodness knows what other injuries lurked inside my aching body. The lads helped me upstairs, where they plonked me on the settee. They returned to the saleroom, without a word between them.

I did my best to come to terms with the attack. It shouldn't have come as a surprise. Billy Grodam had warned me. It had happened sooner than I expected, and I wasn't prepared. My brain pleaded with me to check out the severe stabbing pains in my chest. I managed to undo my shirt, and drop my trousers. I looked a mess. My chest and stomach were covered in black bruises. Blood wept from several abrasions. The most agonising waves of pain centred in my chest. For a moment I though I was going to faint. I was tempted to call an ambulance. Some inner part of me turned the idea down. I couldn't believe what I was playing at. I was in desperate need of hospital treatment.

I staggered across to the wall mirror to check out my facial injuries. The mirror teased me. My reflection showed no sign of the damage that was causing such excruciating pain. One of my cornflower blue eyes winked at me, and a full set of teeth smiled away. I couldn't believe my ears when the reflection spoke to me. "From where I'm standing, you look a complete mess, Kit. But it won't last. This is a painful way to learn, but it's for the best. Go and sit on the settee, and make the pain go away."

I was nonplussed. With a feeling of inward foreboding, I allowed my legs to carry me to the settee. My ears, as well as my eyes, were playing tricks on me. I must be hallucinating. The kitchen door creaked open, behind me. I tried to turn round, but the pain made it impossible. Perhaps Grodam had come back to finish me off. It couldn't be. I'd asked the lads to make sure the front door was shut securely. I should have been the only person in the flat.

That same voice that I'd heard in the car park proved me wrong. "Don't panic, my boy. The mirror wasn't lying. I know that you're hurting, but time will heal you. You've always controlled your dream plots, so why not turn the clock back to the car park, to the moment before the car ran you down. You can change things, to your advantage. You've done it before. It's all down to time. When you wake up, your body will be mended, and normality will return. I'm sorry it's been painful, but you will have crossed your first hurdle, by using time." Nothing was making sense any more. Delirium had taken control of my mind, and the pain was dulling my thinking process. I tried to get up to ring for an ambulance. The effort was too much. In the distance, I heard the wailing tone of an ambulance. Or was it a police car? I wondered if those dozy sods had called the emergency services, after all.

What was I going to do tomorrow? Was there any point in telling the police what had happened? Would they believe me? Grodam was bound to have a ready prepared alibi, with witnesses to corroborate it. Tomorrow's sale concerned me the most. One thing was crystal clear. I wouldn't be taking an active part. I'd be in hospital. Martin would have to do without me. It might be months before I was fit enough for work, always assuming there was a job waiting for me. Would Martin be sympathetic of my situation? I wasn't convinced, especially after this afternoon's fracas.

As near as damn it, I was out of a job. And it was all down to a piece of lowlife called Billy Grodam. I fervently hoped that I would have the chance of paying him back for the damage he had caused in my life.

As I drifted into the sanctuary of painless sleep, I pondered on what the imaginary voice had said. Was there anything to be gained in dredging up, again, what had happened in the car park seeing that my injuries would still be with me when I woke up? Even so, I allowed myself to be drawn into my dream world game of changing what had happened, by using my dream weaving skills. Nothing was impossible in my dream world. In my years of dream spinning, I'd flown like a bird, moved objects by waggling my fingers, read people's minds, become invisible, and even made sick people better. What a pity I couldn't heal myself. I set my dream spinning thoughts into motion.

CHAPTER SIX

Friday Evening and Saturday, 5th and 6th October 2007.

M Y SLEEP PATTERN FOLLOWED A well trodden path. The wind wafted around me, as I slipped into my world of dreams. I walked across the auction house car park, to lock the main gates. The plot was clear. It had already happened. Grodam was hell-bent on running me down, after which a human gorilla would beat me black and blue.

My ears strained for the sound of the vehicle, above the noise of the radio, from the saleroom. A car engine came to life in the darkness. Move for move, it followed the pattern of what had occurred earlier in the evening.

The vehicle bore down on me at great speed. With measured deliberation, I sprang clear of its path, determined to keep my footing this time. The car sped past me. There was a dreadful crunching sound, as it struck the half-closed gate. It braked to a halt, and a rear door opened. The gorilla who had worked me over got out. I heard Grodam's frantic voice, "Get back in, you pillock. We must have woken everyone up, hitting that bloody gate. For all we know, Milner's calling the police. Get us out of here, Barry."

The door slammed shut, as the driver put his foot down on the accelerator, and roared off down the road.

The security guys hared towards me. Dick gripped my arm. "Are you alright, chap? We heard a horrible racket over the noise of the radio. What happened?"

"I had a little problem with a car. But it's done." I couldn't help laughing. This conversation was wasted space. All this was happening in a dreamscape.

Jeff looked at me, a puzzled look on his face. "I don't think it's funny. Who was in the car?"

"I don't know. I didn't get the chance to eyeball them. Thanks for your concern lads. We'd better get back, in case Martin decides to put in an appearance." I carried on the pretence, by walking back to the saleroom, locking them in, and returning to the flat. For a fleeting moment, I wanted to prolong the dream, if only to enjoy more pain-free time. I decided not to. The only people who live in their dreams forever are dead people. I flopped out on the settee, and closed my eyes. My body rushed through the tunnel of light that always ends most of my dreams.

I gritted my teeth against the waves of pain that would soon be hammering at my body. The minutes ticked by, and no agonising torment surged through my limbs. I tentatively felt my lips, and played the tooth counting game with my tongue. Every molar was resting in its rightful place.

When I looked in the mirror, a healthy face stared back at me. I unbuttoned my shirt. What I found didn't make sense. Correction. I made no sense of what I hadn't found. The cuts and bruises were gone. How was I expected to put into simple understandable thoughts what had happened? There was no logical reason, or was there?

Childhood memories stirred in my mind. Daytime aches and pains had always gone by the time I woke up next morning. I shook my head. How could a dream replace missing teeth and repair broken ribs?

On an impulse, I went out to check if the car had damaged the gates. The left hand one was a sorry sight. This presented me with a problem. A gate doesn't get damaged in a dream, and stay that way. There has to be an explanation for everything that happens in life. I toyed with the idea that the first cycle of events had been a dream, warning me what was going to happen. I rubbished the idea. Dreams don't offer a fortune-telling service, or do they?

I was sidetracked by the telephone ringing. "Hello, Kit Milner here."

"Good evening, Kit."

I was momentarily bemused. It was the same voice that I'd heard in the car park, and the kitchen, in my first dream, or whatever. "Who is this?"

The man laughed. "That doesn't matter, Kit. Let's just say that I'm a good friend."

I bridled. "Stop playing silly beggars. What do you want?"

"Calm down my boy. It's about what happened in the car park this evening."

I was tempted to slam the phone down, but didn't. The soft timbre of his voice was mesmerizing. I couldn't help but listen to what he had to say.

"I was there when it happened. The whole affair puzzles you, doesn't it? There is a logical answer. You've got to accept that neither of the incidents was one of your dreams. You changed what happened the first time, by varying the plot the second time round. Get it into your head. It's all about time, Kit. Think about it boy. Time is the key. You'll understand what it's all about soon. I'll be in touch. Goodbye."

I put the phone down, feeling agreeably soothed by the stranger, even though his words made no sense. He'd kept going on about time. I checked the mantle clock. It was twenty past six. Time wasn't making sense. I'd gone out to lock the gates just after six. By the time I'd limped back to the flat, and gone to sleep, it would have been about half past six. The second run had lasted just over fifteen minutes, and I'd been awake for five minutes. Using simple mathematics, it should be about ten to seven. I checked my watch. It agreed with the mantle clock.

I shoved everything to the back of my mind. I was shattered and had run out of explanations. I slumped onto the settee, and fell asleep. No dreams about cars, or mysterious voices, troubled me.

Sunshine streamed through the window when I opened my eyes. I felt unusually relaxed after last evening's excitement. A bath, a change of clothing and a fried breakfast completed my self-prescribed therapy. I checked the time. It was a quarter to nine. Today was Martin's big day. The auction wasn't due to start until eleven o'clock, but the car park was filling up. I wondered if Grodam had arrived. I made a mental note to keep out of his way.

My first chore was to brew a pot of tea for Martin. He believed that the caffeine settled his nerves. I joined him so that I could settle mine. He wasn't in a happy frame of mind. His face reflected his mood. "Isn't there something you should be telling me? What do you know about the damaged gate?"

I told him what had happened. I wasn't stupid. He would have checked with the security men. I didn't mention Grodam.

He sipped at his tea, a frown thrown across his face. "I hope it's got nothing to do with yesterday's nonsense in the saleroom."

A lie tripped out. "I think I disturbed someone who was up to no good."

I poured him another cup of tea. He visibly relaxed Perhaps the caffeine was working. "Get it repaired. What about the auction? Is everything ready for me? It's going to be a good day. I can feel it in my water. We can't go wrong with what we're selling."

I drained my cup, and excused myself. Things needed doing before Martin started banging the hell out of the gavel. The saleroom was packed. There was no sign of Grodam. I took a cursory glance at the davenport. The sooner Fat Man bought it, the better.

My fanciful thoughts were disturbed by a gentle 'dinging' sound. Jim Yates had this annoying habit of ringing every piece of ceramic with a teaspoon. If it didn't ding, he wouldn't dream of buying it. I turned round. My intuition hadn't deserted me. 'Ding-a Ling' stood there, cup in one hand, and a dirty teaspoon in the other. He sniffed, and looked at me in a derisory manner. "I know what you're thinking. Silly old sod." He tapped a nicotine stained finger against his nose. "Customers won't buy cups with bloody great cracks in them. They don't want their coffee leaking out like a bleeding colander." He wandered away, still muttering to himself.

Out of the corner of my eye, I saw Rick Adams shuffling around the tables displaying the smaller ceramic lots. Rick is the closest thing I've seen to a walking septic tank. His creased black overcoat had once prided itself on being a light fawn colour. A ragged muffler covered the collar of a dirty, threadbare shirt. Rick never wore shoes, preferring a pair of cut-down wellies. A pair of dodgy–looking trousers were tucked into them. He made a scarecrow look tidy. He was known as 'Dirty Rick'. The nickname had nothing to do with his state of dress, but the smell that wafted in his slipstream. I preferred Traffy's silent bombs to 'Dirty Rick' and that's saying something.

Traffy wandered over. A big grin spread across his florid face. "Hello, Kit. Are you wearing your steel toecaps, in case your mates turn up?" He walked away, with a few choice words ringing in his ears.

Not for the first time, I checked my watch. The sale was

due to start in thirty minutes. It was time to don my porter's smock. The usual porter was ill, and Martin had asked me to step in. I didn't mind.

Eleven o'clock arrived, and right on cue Martin mounted the rostrum. A stickler for tradition, he sported a red bow tie, and a sprig of heather pinned to his jacket lapel. Every auctioneer has a pre-sale ritual. Martin was no exception. He bowed to the crowd, earning himself a round of ribald applause. After another bow, Martin poured himself a glass of what looked like water, but was neat gin. Arthur once told me that Martin poured it over his cornflakes.

The auction started. I was kept busy, locating and displaying each lot. The furniture lots were sold at the end of the sale, so Grodam had plenty of time to turn up. Martin whipped through the books, prints, paintings, metal-ware and small ceramics. The auction was going well, with each lot selling above its reserve price. Martin's face turned redder and redder, beads of perspiration running down his jowls. He mopped at his face with a polka-dot handkerchief.

He galloped through the gold and jewellery, and followed them with the larger ceramics. The first of the furniture lots came up, and Martin raced through them. My heart fluttered when he came to the davenport desk. He offered it up for sale. I sauntered across to where it stood, and pointed to it for the benefit of the punters. The bidding opened at eight hundred pounds. Three dealers ran it up to twelve hundred pounds.

I started to calm down. Martin would knock the desk down at any minute and Grodam hadn't bothered to turn up. The main door, at the back of the room, creaked open. Billy Grodam strolled in. He'd brought more reinforcements today. He was backed up by four muscled gorillas. Billy stood at the back of the room, while his side-kicks sauntered to various parts of the saleroom. His eyes caught mine. An unpleasant smirk spread across his pallid features. He drew a finger across his throat, and pointed at me. His hands moved like someone driving a car, and he mouthed a silent obscenity. Uncannily the unease that I'd felt all morning, went away. A feeling of calmness oozed through me. He didn't frighten me anymore.

Martin sensed that the ebullience of the past few minutes had slipped away. He gulped down another gin, and wiped a dribble away from his chin. "Gentlemen, I am selling the davenport desk. It dates to about 1880. The last bid was for twelve hundred pounds. It's worth a great deal more. This desk is a beautiful example of its type." He filled his bottomless glass, and took another swig. "This is silly money for such a fine piece. I'm tempted to buy it myself, if another bid isn't forthcoming." For his health's sake, I hoped he wasn't winding Grodam up.

"Come on now, do I have another bid?"

Two dealers moved the price up to sixteen hundred pounds, at which point the bidding ran out of steam. Martin used all of his skills in a frantic bid to push the price up. His pleas fell on deaf ears.

My fingers caressed the surface of the desk. A sharp feeling of pins and needles shot up the length of my arm. I rubbed at my elbow. The self-help therapy worked. The discomfort vanished as quickly as it had come.

Martin was showing the first signs of stress. His voice took on a note of desperation. "I have been offered sixteen hundred pounds for this desk. We all know it is worth more than that. Who's going to give me another fifty pounds?" His frantic words drew no reaction from the sea of blank faces. "If there's no further bid, I intend to sell the davenport. Make no mistake about that." He blew his nose, and rubbed the garish handkerchief across his forehead. He looked round the room, willing one further bid. A look of dismay crossed his face at the lack of response. Martin raised his gavel, fully intending to take his paddy out on it. He didn't get the chance to bring it down.

Grodam came to life. "Sixteen hundred and fifty pounds."

Martin glared at him. "I am prepared to take your bid, even though you left it late." Grodam leered all over his chins. He stared at me, raised the middle digit of his right hand and rotated it. I got the message. I willed Martin to bring his hammer down. Fat Man could have his bloody desk. Martin went for the final countdown. "Can I assume that there are no further bids? If that's the case, then I'm going to sell this fine desk to the gentleman at the back of the room." He raised the gavel. "Going for the last time…"

Before the hammer could drop, someone shouted out: "Over here, Martin." It was another bid. Some twat had raised the price to seventeen hundred pounds. This was going to put the cat amongst the pigeons. Some idiot stood the risk of getting a right good thumping. I felt genuinely sorry for the silly beggar, whoever he was. My eyes swivelled around the room. Who'd have been so bloody stupid as to up the price? I needn't have bothered. Everyone's eyes were on me. I was the only one who hadn't noticed that it was my hand sticking up in the air. I pulled the offending arm down. What was I playing at?

Martin turned to me, an incredulous look on his face. His expression was topped by the thunderous look from Grodam. They weren't as surprised as me. You could have cut the silence with a knife, wrapped it in brown paper, and sold it at the next auction as rarefied air.

Martin accepted my bid. I use the expression in the loosest sense of the word on the premise that I hadn't consciously made it. "Well folks, we appear to have another late bidder." He glared at me, then turned his gaze to Grodam. "It's against you. Do I hear your bid for seventeen hundred and fifty pounds?" Grodam raised his hand. Only God knows what was working my arm. My hand rose in the air, countering his bid. Everyone eyeballed me. "I have eighteen hundred pounds. It's your bid, sir." Martin looked at Grodam. As did everyone else in the room.

Grodam moved the bidding to eighteen hundred and fifty pounds. He nodded to the goon closest to me. The pet gorilla's reaction was to sidle round behind me. Out of the corner of my eye, I saw him brush his fingers across the top of the davenport. He put his mouth close to my ear, and in a quiet voice explained the Facts of Life to me. "Listen you knob. Unless you want something really nasty to happen to you, don't make any more bids. Do I make myself clear, dick-head?" He let out a loud laugh, for the benefit of the crowd, as if the two of us were sharing a joke about the desk.

Grodam shot a threatening glance at me. Martin took his bid for eighteen hundred and fifty pounds. I thought of leaving the room, on the pretext of using the little boys' room. When I tried to move my feet, they wouldn't budge. The only part of me in working order was my bidding arm. The price for the davenport rose to two thousand two hundred pounds, in my favour. The goon, perched on my shoulder, carried on whispering sweet nothings into my ear. His last words made my future crystal clear. "It'll be a waste of time if you buy the desk. You won't live long enough to enjoy it. I'll cut you into little pieces, and feed you to my cat, you arsehole."

I knew I wasn't controlling my bids, but that didn't bother me, anymore. The vitriolic fervour from Grodam's goon sailed over my head. I had no idea what was happening. but I was enjoying the moment. It felt as if I'd been shrouded in a snug cloak, that nurtured me with contentment, and assuredness. I looked across the room at Grodam. Our eyes met. I winked at him. He was working up a sweat. His wig had worked its way over his forehead. He frantically pushed it back with both hands.

"I have two thousand two hundred pounds," purred Martin. "The bid is with Kit Milner. Do I hear a further bid from you, sir?"

A look of disbelief crossed Grodam's face. He stared at me, a mixture of fear, hatred and loathing patterned across his face. Froth flecked at the corners of his mouth, as if he were in the first stages of a fit. Martin broke the silence. "In the absence of any further bid, I intend to sell to Kit Milner."

Grodam mouthed an obscenity at me, raised two fingers at Martin, and walked out of the room, followed by his menagerie. Martin brought the gavel down with an almighty thud. "Sold to Kit Milner."

Everyone broke into applause. One person, in particular, clapped his hands, and yelled at the top of his voice. He stood at the back of the room, partially obscured by a large wardrobe. All I could see was a pair of twinkling eyes, a generous nose, and grey beard, peeping from the confines of his anorak hood. He waved at me. I had no idea who he was. I turned away. When I looked back, he'd gone.

Martin's impatient voice brought me back to reality. "What's the buyer's bidding number, Kit?" I gave him my personal number. He frowned, as he entered it onto his sales sheet. Martin carried on selling the remaining lots, before bringing his gavel down for the last time. He collected his papers, gave me a dirty look, and swept out of the room.

Most of the crowd melted away to pay for their purchases.

A few regular dealers, who stayed behind, were shocked that I had bid well over the odds for the davenport.

Doris Goring-Hart tapped me on the arm. "Who's the mug who paid that sort of money? He's got no idea of furniture prices. Must have wanted the desk badly. Is there a wad of money hidden away, inside?"

The dealers had a good laugh at my expense before wandering away to collect their lots. They'd have laughed even louder if they'd known that Kit Milner was the mug who had bid that kind of money.

The premises emptied during the next half hour. Martin walked into the saleroom, as I was about to lock up. The sour look on his face didn't bode well for me. "What's going on, Kit? I'm worried about the davenport. Who were you bidding for?" He didn't give me the chance to answer. "He's paid well over the top. Have you carried out your client's instructions to the letter, and will I be getting my money?"

I was getting a dab hand at lying. "Don't worry Martin. You'll be paid. Does my client have the usual seven days to cough up?"

He stared at me. "He can have the usual terms. One thing, though. The desk stays in the saleroom until I get my money. No cheques mind you. I want cash." He hadn't finished with me. "I'm not a fool, Kit. I saw all that nonsense with you and that obnoxious mountain of flesh you were bidding against. What was that big bastard doing, standing behind you? I'm not daft. This is to do with yesterday's trouble, isn't it? What really got up my nose was the fat one holding two fingers up at me. There'd better not be any more problems from that lot. Do we understand one another?" I nodded my head. Without another word, he walked out.

I locked up, and made my way back to the flat. I could still feel the aura of well-being, that had kicked in, earlier. One thing bothered me. I hated the thought of letting Martin down, but where was the money coming from to pay him? I was tempted to spill the beans. It would give him the chance of re-auctioning the desk, or offering it to Grodam, assuming that fat-boy was prepared to buy it at that price. Either way, Kit Milner would be signing on at the local Benefits Office, as long as I wasn't waylaid by Grodam's thugs.

What I didn't know was that I was about to cram more living into the next three weeks than I'd done during the whole of the last twenty six years.

After a spot of supper, I crept into bed. It wasn't surprising that sleep was hard to come by.

CHAPTER SEVEN

Saturday Evening, 6th October 2007.

SLEEP REFUSED TO SHROUD ME within its shelter. How could I sleep, with the whirling dervishes of inexplicable thoughts pummelling at my head? Avenues in my life, which hadn't existed a week ago, had been prised open, without any conscious help from me.

My experiences serve as a reminder that our predictable life patterns can be swiftly derailed, and replaced by a completely new lifescape.

At the end of the day, it depends on the particular highway of life that we travel, as individuals, and what happens when we come to a crossroad in our life's cycle. We all have the option of taking the left, or right hand turning, or travelling straight on. Whatever road our footsteps follow, we don't make that decision, ourselves. The choice can be laid at the feet of destiny, whatever destiny is. But who controls destiny? I'm the only person on earth who knows the answer to that one.

During the past few days, it has become increasingly obvious that my feelings and thought processes have changed. I no longer seem to have any manual, or mindful, control over the new horizons that are yet to show themselves. It doesn't worry me. I'm too busy basking in the warmth of my new found esteem.

My childhood and teenage paths left their mark on me. My spirit was ground down to a level where I didn't give a toss as to which direction my path led. I've never once looked at life's signposts. My eyes were always set on the ground, not even noticing what lay on the surface. Today, at the auction, a ray of sunshine burst through my clouds of doubt and uncertainty. I sighed to myself. Would my social life change for the better?

I recall, with a mixture of amusement and horror, the one and only time I had the temerity to ask a girl out and go through with it. I was about twenty one at the time. Goodness, what came over me? I was in a state of great agitation, as I stood on the threshold of my first encounter with the opposite sex. I asked her if she would like to go to the local cinema. With much fluttering of eyelids, she cooed and wiggled her enthusiastic agreement.

Don't get the wrong impression of me. I have a good rapport with people, so long as it's not in your face. Had I been an outgoing chap, I could have pulled any bird that I fancied. Whatever the young lady was expecting from me, by the time our date ended she obviously hadn't got it.

I'm getting ahead of myself. This bird was a fluffy, petite, natural blonde, with blue eyes. I've never forgotten her figure. Everything was in the right place, with a built-in abundance of it. She was wearing a skimpy, low cut dress, which revealed a lot of boobs at one end, and most of her thighs at the other. That dress left nothing to the imagination.

We sat in the back row, munching popcorn and drinking coffee. I honestly thought I'd cracked the social barrier. But, once the popcorn and coffee were finished, what was I supposed to do? I only had to look around me to find the answer, by watching the antics of other young people. They hadn't come to watch the film. Every couple was snogging like mad. And that included the men. But not the two of us. We sat, with space between us, watching the screen. My social chinks were beginning to show.

Halfway through the film, she let out a sigh of frustration. Her hand slid along my thigh. During the next few minutes, her hand massaged every part of my lower anatomy. There's nothing wrong with that, in a normal relationship. Sadly, I lacked the knowledge and confidence to react to her advances by putting my hands and brain into tandem.

I took the coward's way out. I told her I was popping to the toilet. She laughed, and squeezed my groin, probably thinking I was going to put some money in the contraceptive machine. I didn't bother to come back. For all I know, she's still sitting in the back row of the cinema, eagerly awaiting my return with a packet of three in my pocket. That was my one and only taste of socialising. I'd been frightened stiff, and resolved never to go down that road again.

These delicious thoughts clouded over. The grotesque Grodam came to mind. I accepted that our paths were bound to cross another day. I welcomed another run-in with him.

My roving thoughts turned to Martin. I owed him a lot of money. My instinct told me that something was going to turn up. As it happens, destiny solved that problem for me, but not in the way I expected. After an hour of tossing and turning, the thinking phase came to an end. Clouds of tiredness invaded my brain, driving all thoughts away. I beamed in an instruction for no dreams to disturb my slumbers. That was a big mistake. My dreams were about to become nightmares, and I was powerless to do anything about it.

CHAPTER EIGHT

Saturday Night and Sunday, 6th and 7th October 2007.

ANY HOPE OF DREAMLESS SLEEP went out of the window. My years of mind training had been wasted. I passed into the dream-world, to find myself sitting up in bed. The bedroom wall shimmered in shades of black and silvery white, threatening to explode into shapes and images. This was the first time, ever, that my dream images had been focussed on the wall.

I had to admit to a certain fascination as the shimmering shapes slowly formed themselves into a picture. It was a clearing in a wood. The ground was covered in the brown debris of fallen leaves. A rude hut stood at the edge of the wood, by a small pool of water.

Built from branches, and covered with moss and grass sods, the hut was a crude attempt at some form of simple shelter. Sadly, it would never enjoy the status of a grade one listed building in future years. On the opposite side of the clearing stood a huge gnarled rock, covered in lichen.

A feeling of peacefulness bathed the scene. Birds twittered in muted sound, as the breeze played a rhythmic tune on the few autumn leaves still clinging to the mother trees.

The solitude was spoiled by a flurry of activity. Two figures stumbled out from the hut. They were in violent argument. An incredibly ugly old man pulled a young girl into the clearing, very much against her will. He was unsightly and wrinkled, his back bent over by the ravages of time. Snowy white hair hung to his shoulders, and his beard stretched to his waist.

The skin covering his scraggy body didn't do any favours to his over-ripened appearance.

She was a class act, a complete contrast to the wrinkled creature. It was hard to drag my eyes from her. White of skin, with flowing red hair, she was simply beautiful. My feelings for her were heightened by the scantiness of her clothing. I felt a movement in my groin.

What in heaven's name was this stunning creature doing in the company of this unbelievably repulsive old man? Perhaps they were father and daughter. If so, she favoured her mother's side of the relationship.

I was deafened by the ferocity with which they shouted at each other. They spoke in a foreign tongue, but that didn't matter. I could understand every work. She broke free of his grasp, and stood facing him. A look of abject fear covered her face.

Without warning, he moved towards her, a tirade tumbling from his lips. His spittle managed to evade the confines of his beard, and was thrown into the air, giving the appearance of fine mist. His arms flailed like a windmill, fists clenching and unclenching. "Emuline! You have cheated me, and toyed with my emotions. Each time I penetrated your body, you swore that you felt love for me. Even though I am old, you said that my body gave you the pleasuring of a younger man. And now I am the victim of your deceit. I find that all you want of me is the secret of my powers. You shall not have them."

Panic crossed her face. She shouted at him, her words tinged with menace and disdain. "Do not dare to threaten me. I too have magical powers. You fool. Do you really believe that I could have loved someone as old and ugly as you? You disgust me, Merlin."

My ears pricked up at the mention of the old man's name. Who hasn't heard of him?

White beard took three faltering steps towards her. "I will show you what I do to women who deceive me, you poisonous wench. I could strike you down where you stand." He snorted. "No that is too easy. I will make you suffer instead. I called you poisonous, and poisonous you shall become. I shall change you into a viper, so that you may crawl on the forest floor, until you meet your death."

The woman's reaction was immediate. She pointed her fingers at the old man. He was visibly stunned by the fierce rush of words that spewed from her mouth: "Damn you for all time, Merlin. Ur tibo dyon vapo."

The effect of her words was nothing short of a miracle. Her frenetic ranting stopped him in his tracks. Merlin shouted in terror. He tried to run from the clearing. All he could manage was four steps before he came to a halt. He turned towards the woman. "My powers are great, but I cannot undo what you have done. I didn't mean the words that I spoke. I was angry. You know I would never harm you. I love you. Save me, I implore you. Remove your spell."

The woman tossed her head, and sneered. "Go to your prison, Merlin."

With one final effort he shouted at her. "This is the end of Merlin. You have overcome me, this day, but I will return. I am immortal. Mark my words, woman. I go to my prison, with the stones that you crave still in my possession."

His whole body stiffened, until there was neither movement nor sound. Merlin's body twitched. For a moment I thought that he was going to overcome her spell. He didn't. The animal skins covering his skinny frame disintegrated, and fell to the ground leaving him naked.

Whatever the witchcraft was, the effects took a swift course. Small cracks enveloped his body, and streams of red vapour seeped from a multitude of fractures. The old man began to break up, until his body disappeared from sight. Where he had stood, a cloud of mist floated above the ground. It drifted, as if blown by a gentle breeze, towards the large rock, where it kissed the surface and permeated through the stony structure, until it was lost from view.

The look on the woman's face was fearsome. I conjured with the words that she had spoken. What they translated to wasn't important. It was their devastating effect which was most significant. The words were imprinted in my mind.

It defied any kind of understanding, that the female had produced a spell out of thin air, which had turned a powerful warlock into a puff of smoke and consigned him to the inside of a rock.

What had unfolded before me, was the epitome of all my dreams. I had never managed to invoke anything like this, in my past dream world.

The bedroom wall continued to shimmer. The woman was rooted to the spot, worry covering her face. I wanted to take her in my arms and comfort her. My chivalrous thoughts were jarred by the sound of galloping horses. Three horsemen clattered into the clearing, sending a cloud of dead leaves into the air. They wore light chain mail and metal helmets. Each was armed with a sword, and carried a small round shield.

One of them dismounted. He was a giant of a man, standing well over six feet tall. A swirling black cloak covered his shoulders. He would have been handsome, had it not been for the gaping empty socket where his eyeball had once sat. A disfiguring scar ran the length of his face. He grabbed the woman by the arm, shook her violently, and shouted at her. "Where is he? Where's Merlin? Did our scheme work, wife?" She raised a hand. For a moment, I thought he was going to end up as a puff of smoke. He let go of her. "Did you entice the secrets out of Merlin? Have you taken on his magical gifts?"

An anxious smile played about her lips. "My Lord Madrog. The secret of Merlin's powers lay in the pouch that he wore about his neck. It contains his magic stones. I couldn't get my hands on them."

The man lost his rag. "I was ill at ease to let another man touch you, let alone ravish your body. You swore that you could unlock Merlin's powers. I have a mind to punish you."

He slapped her around the head. Anger flashed on the woman's face. "You have gone too far. With one word, I could turn you into a demented dwarf." Her voice was full of scorn. "Of course, I did what we planned. I fed him a love potion, when I thought the pleasures of my body had overwhelmed his senses. But I was too eager to snatch the stones. Merlin is a wily bird. He realised what I was up to. He would have harmed me, had I not banished him inside that rock."

Lord Madrog's manner changed abruptly. He embraced his wife, and planted a kiss on her lips. "You misunderstand me my Lady. You have done well. We have him imprisoned. On the morrow, you will use your skills to release him. Whilst he is confused, I will disable him. Then you can take the stones, and drink of his blood. His gifts of magic will be bestowed upon you." He knelt down, and kissed her feet. "I am your husband and servant my Lady." The scar-faced man turned to his two companions. "Sons of Madrog. Collect wood to light a fire. It grows dark, and the evening has a chill to it."

A huge fire burned in front of the hut. His sons piled more wood beside the blaze. The man spoke. "Your mother and I will stay here this night. She has a task to carry out tomorrow. Leave us, and return to camp. I will see you there on the morrow." The young men mounted their horses, and galloped out of view. Madrog took hold of the woman by her waist. "Come, wife. I have missed the pleasures of your body. There is much that must be done before you close your eyes this night." She took his hand, and pulled him into the hut.

I thought the dream had ended, until I heard a scream and the raucous sound of the man's voice. Madrog walked out of the hut, waving a sword above his head. His other hand clutched a round object. He walked towards the rock, and bellowed at the lump of stone. "It pains me that the Lady Emuline has failed me. But, no matter. Her magic will pass to me, as will your powers, when I manage to free you from your prison. Make no mistake, old man, I will prise you from that rock. It is your destiny."

He sheathed his sword, and turned towards me. An evil smile played round his lips. Madrog swung the thing that he held around his head. Manic laughter escaped his lips. He let go of the object. It hurtled towards me, spinning and turning in the air. On and on it came. It was going to hit me. I calmed down, and cussed myself. How could it? I was curled up in bed, watching dream fragments. This thought didn't comfort me. I ordered my subconscious to stop these bizarre images. Nothing happened. I sank into the confines of the bed, and pulled the blanket over my head to shut out the nightmarish visions.

A swishing sound echoed round the bedroom. I put my hands over my ears to shut out the disgusting noise. Something thumped on my feet. The impact sent a spasm of pain shooting up my legs. Everything went quiet. With some trepidation, I raised myself onto the pillow, and opened my eyes. The fire burned in the clearing, bathing the bedroom in gentle light. The dreadful man had gone.

Something lay on the bedcover. I couldn't make out what it was, until my eyes sent a message to my brain that it wasn't prepared to accept. I froze in disbelief. A pair of unseeing green eyes stared into mine. Lady Emuline's severed head lay at my feet, reposing in a state of still life, a frozen look of incredulity written across her face, begging an explanation for what had happened. Blood seeped from the base, where it had been cleanly struck from her neck. A trail of mucus trickled from her nose, emptying itself into a gaping mouth.

A feeling of revulsion gripped me. I had to get rid of the savaged head. I stretched my right hand out, and reluctantly clutched at the red locks of hair. I hurled the head towards the shimmering scene. It sailed through the bedroom wall, and landed on the edge of the clearing. It rolled across the ground, like some bizarre football, until it trickled to a halt.

My feelings of disgust for this dark dream were broken by the sight of the man coming out of the hut. He made slurping noises as he drank from a goblet. Red liquid dribbled down his chin. I retched. This madman was drinking what looked like blood. I vomited onto the bedcover, and asked why my mind was punishing me. Long hidden images, lurking somewhere in my subconscious, had been unearthed to create these vile scenes.

The man drained the goblet and threw it away. He belched, and let out a cry of satisfaction. It was a fleeting state of mind. His eyes alighted on the woman's head. He lashed at it with his foot. It flew through the air, spinning and turning like a soiled rag doll, before vanishing into the trees. He laughed, and walked back into the hut.

My whole sense of decency had been assaulted. The combination of wood smoke, mixed with the stench of blood, gore and vomit, lay siege to my nostrils. My head ached, and there was the added risk that I was about to lose control of my back passage. I tried to wake up. It was a squandered effort. More sounds floated from the clearing. I closed my eyes against these nightmarish scenes. They were prised open against my will. The madman appeared from the hut, dragging the corpse of the young woman. A trail of blood spewed out from the stump of her neck, as it bobbled across the ground. He pulled the body close to the fire, where he let her lifeless legs clatter to the ground. Lord Madrog fed more wood into the flames. With a measure of tardiness, he removed his leggings and undergarments. He knelt by the dead body, grasped the woman's clothing in his hands, and ripped them from her body. Madrog straddled the corpse, and pleasured it. He grunted with pleasure and got to his feet. Madrog looked down at the body of the woman. "You stupid witch. We could have ruled the world together, if only you'd wrested the secrets from the old man. You have paid the price of failure. I don't need your help in defeating Merlin. By drinking your blood, I have absorbed your dark powers. When the old wizard falls into my hands, I will rule supreme."

What I had witnessed had to be the work of someone in league with the devil. What kind of person could murder, and then commit necrophilia? I felt angry for allowing myself to get carried away. This was a nightmare, not reality. Then without any prompting, the penny dropped. I reproached myself. "You bloody idiot. You're responsible for this nightmare, Kit Milner."

The imagery for this dreadful dream had been planted in my subconscious years ago. It was the harvested crop from the germination of the seeds that were sown when the Family Liaison Officer had described the act of bestiality inflicted by William Grodam on my mother. Everything dropped neatly into place. Reality had come back to haunt me. If I'd been smarter, I would have cottoned on to the fact that Madrog was an anagram of Grodam.

What a fool I'd been. The truth didn't help. The hairs on the back of my neck stood on end as I watched the wall. The man wasn't content with ravishing a headless corpse; he was now sucking blood from the mutilated stump that had been her proud neck. I couldn't stop my bowels from defecating.

His mood turned to anger. "It's all your fault, woman. I possess your black gifts, but Merlin's magic should be flowing through my veins." Tears ran down his face. "How I hate you, you useless baggage." He dragged her body into the hut, and walked across to the rock. He bellowed at the inanimate object. "Your sanctuary will be a brief one, old man. There is a way to draw you from that accursed stone, but I must bide my time, until the means of your release is in my hands. Then I will snuff your life out, and drink of your magic." He mounted his horse and with a final shake of his fist, rode off.

I sat amidst the vomit and the products of my back passage, knowing how a rat on a sewage farm feels. I hadn't wanted to dream, but my subconscious had insisted on dredging up foul images from my past. I made another attempt to leave this cesspit of a fantasy. Good fortune did not smile on me. Another sound carried through the evening air. Merlin's voice spoke from within the rock, pleading in plaintive and cajoling words. "Is there anyone who can hear me? If so, I beg that you draw near, that I may speak with you. Do not be afraid. All I ask is a favour of you."

From somewhere in the forest glade, I heard the sound of a man singing. The sounds came closer and closer, until a young fellow strolled into the clearing.

Merlin started to shout. "Young man! Young man! Do not fear me. Draw near to the rock, for I have things to tell you. My words will fill your pockets with riches. Come hither."

84

The youth scratched at his head. "Who's there? Is this some kind of witchcraft?"

Merlin's voice encouraged him. "Do not be afraid. I can make you rich, if you come closer."

The man walked over to the rock. "How can I make my fortune?"

A cry of delight rang from the rock. "Thank you for heeding my request. I am an old man who has been trapped in this stone by a powerful witch. I only ask you to undertake a task which will free me from my prison one day."

The young chap pulled a face. His voice took on a note of caution. "What is required of me? If I am to be placed in danger, then I'll be on my way. I have no desire to get involved with a witch."

Merlin laughed. "Your life is not threatened. The witch that I speak of is dead. Your task is simple, but rewarding. If my offer appeals to you, then strike the rock with your sword, and pick up four pieces of the rock's chippings."

The man started to walk away. "I'd rather not. It's a trick to imprison me in the rock, if I'm not mistaken."

The voice of Merlin chased after him. "Don't go. Hear me out. There is no trickery, I swear. If you do as I ask, I will reward you, and your line, with treasures beyond your wildest dreams. All I ask is that you will come back and rescue me, in the future, when the time is right. You will face no danger in helping me." The voice took on a wheedling tone. "I promise you gifts without equal. Strike the rock, I implore you."

The tempting promise broke his resistance. He drew his sword, and hit the surface of the stone. Slivers of rock flew about him. He sheathed the sword, and picked up four pieces. The rock trembled. The words of an elated Merlin made the debris on the forest floor blow around the clearing. "Thank you young man. Go forth from this place with the stones. I will impregnate them with my powers. They will protect you from mortal danger, but you must always wear them on your person. Ignore my words at your peril. Should I not ask for your help to free me from my prison during your lifetime, then I charge you to pass the stones to someone you can trust, within your family lineage, to take on my mission. Speak the words that I have told you today to the person you choose. Stand before me and open the hand that holds the pieces of stone."

The young man did as he was asked. The voice in the rock recited a string of words. The effect was staggering. The jagged pieces of rock moved about in his palm, and gradually changed their shape, until four finely rounded stones lay in his hand "Put them in your pocket, young man. Remember well what I have told you. Before you go, tell me how you are named."

The man bowed to the rock. "I am known as Gerard the Traveller. I spend my days moving from place to place."

The voice of Merlin chided him. "You will be a traveller no more. Journey from this place, and find the settlement of Lovington, which lies many miles to the east of this place. There, you will put your roots down, and raise your family. Go, until the day I make myself known to you, or your kin."

The man nodded his head, and stuffed the stones into a bag. With a friendly wave to the rock, he started to whistle, and strode out of the clearing. The voice in the rock hadn't finished. "Listen and learn from what has taken place this day, for this is your destiny." The words were wasted. The young man had long gone. A further outburst disturbed the night air. The fragments of rock, littering the ground, vanished from sight.

The picture on the wall faded away. The nightmare had ended. A shiver passed through me. The fantasy had been too real for comfort.

I eased myself out of bed, and put my foot on the floor. A jarring pain shot up my leg. I frantically rubbed at the hurting, as my other hand scrabbled across the carpet to find what I'd trodden on. I picked up a small piece of stone. In a moment of sheer madness, I thought it was a fragment of the dream rock. I laughed. If I'd looked outside the window, I'd have seen pigs flying across the sky. I managed another laugh, and threw the fragment of stone into a dish on the chest of drawers.

After a shower, and a tablet for my thumping head, I settled down in the lounge. It was ten minutes past midnight. My body was crying out for sleep, but I didn't dare close my eyes, I wasn't going to chance another nightmare. I picked up a Fine Arts sale catalogue to read. It was a bad mistake. The battle with my eyelids was lost. I drifted into slumber.

CHAPTER NINE

Sunday, 7ᵗʰ October 2007.

T HE BLOODY WALL STARTED TO glow. I felt too weak to stop it. The flickering light was unwavering in its desire to run its course. I sighed with relief. The scene didn't have the semblance of a nightmare about it. A large house came into sight, standing in its own grounds. In long herbaceous borders flowers threw their heads up, bending in unison with the breeze. The house outshone the garden. Constructed in red brick with inlaid knapped flint stone, this was complemented by hand cut slates on the roof. A wooden sign, hanging in the porch, proclaimed that this outstanding residence was the 'Lovington Rectory'. I groaned. My brain was still dredging up latent images.

The house faded away, to be replaced by a brightly lit lounge. The room oozed good taste, from the impeccable quality of the furnishings to the exquisite water colours and oil paintings adorning the painted walls. A fire burned merrily in the Adam fireplace. The tongues of flame leapt up the chimney, in a futile effort to escape into the outside air. A mouth-watering mahogany over-mantle straddled the fireplace.

The floor was covered by a lavish Persian carpet. The furniture was Georgian, augmented by some choice pieces from the Victorian period. A Canterbury, stuffed full of sheet music, sat by the piano and a Victorian what-not reclined in another corner of the room. Its four shelves were stacked with silver knick-knacks and miniature figurines.

These were forgotten as I spied the davenport desk,

standing in the bay window. I got up, and walked across to the wall to take a closer look. There was a crescent shaped mark on the lid, where it had suffered some minor damage. It was the piece of furniture which presently stood in Martin's locked saleroom. I chuckled to myself. Here I was, making a complete idiot of myself, and not for the first time. I had tripped over my brain before it got into gear. All the furniture and fittings had been in our recent Fine Arts sale. The dream was a hangover from the auction.

The door on the far side of the room opened. A grey haired man came in. The poor chap had a deformed back, giving him the appearance of a hunchback. His face was dominated by a fine aquiline nose, that sat grandly in a gentle and kindly looking face. The whole appearance was completed by a pair of twinkling green eyes, and distinguished grey beard. The dream continued to feed on my world of reality. This was the man who'd shown such delight after my successful bid at the auction.

He moved over to the fire. Placing his hands in the waves of heat, he rubbed them together. He turned around, and presented his ample posterior to the flames, waggling his buttocks from side to side. Agreeably warmed, he ambled across to the davenport, and knelt down at the right hand side. He removed the bottom drawer. His head swivelled round towards me. He pointed a gnarled finger at the recess, and silently mouthed 'watch what I am doing' before sliding his arm inside. There was a clattering sound. He breathed a happy sigh as he pulled his arm out. A wooden box was grasped in his shaking hand. With the faintest hint of theatrics he opened it. He delved inside, and pulled out a brown envelope.

As he waved the envelope in the air, he pointed toward the drawer recess, as if to remind me where he'd found the hidey hole. I nearly fell off the settee when he spoke to me. It was the same voice that had whispered words of comfort in the car park, and spoken to me on the telephone. I pulled myself together. This was old hat. I was still drawing on figments of my subconscious. "It's behind the bottom drawer, Kit. For everyone's sake, make sure that you find it. If you don't, then we might as well give the whole thing up. It will prove that you're the wrong choice, and another failure." He pulled a face. "Exercise a degree of tolerance, if you want to find the box. Remember how I did it. You tend to be an impatient, naive young man, who takes a lot of convincing."

He put the envelope and box inside the desk, before sliding the drawer back into place. He struggled to his feet. Somewhat red of face, he glared at me. He tapped a finger on the side of his head. "Think again, young man. Get a grip on yourself, and start using your brain. You're not believing what you're seeing. I can't blame you. It's a big step to take. I'll be seeing you soon." He crossed himself, and left the room. The wall picture faded away, and I woke up. Was this night never going to end? I pondered on the latest dream, and the davenport desk. Was there really a secret box in the bottom drawer recess?

If Charlie Chang, the famous Chinese detective, had been sitting on the settee with me he would have quoted Confucius. Charlie would have poked me in the chest with his umbrella, and said: "Confucius, he say. Man who dreams of secret compartment in davenport, and ignores prompting of fate, deserves swift kick up backside. Best to go, and prove dream wrong. Better than sitting on settee, juggling with brain."

Nothing else was in the offing at this unearthly hour, especially sleep. What harm was there in popping down to the saleroom and satisfying the curiosity of a dream spinner?

I telephoned the security centre, to let the guy on duty know that I was opening the saleroom out of working hours. I gave him the password, together with a plausible sounding story for my early morning visit. My ears rang from the security man's last words. They are unprintable. Suffice it to say that he likened me to the offspring of a lady of the night, for having the temerity to wake him at such an unearthly hour. God help us if real intruders ever break into the saleroom.

I picked up the saleroom keys on my way out. It didn't take me long to unlock the door, flick on the lights, and de-activate the alarm. I found the davenport, and squatted by its side. I copied everything the old man had done in the dream, including the grunting. My arm slid inside the desk, probing for a secret panel. My fingers detected a piece of wood which hadn't been put there by the craftsman who'd made the desk. It stood proud of the original surface. I tried every imaginable manoeuvre to shift it. The damned thing wouldn't budge. My fingers probed, pushed and pulled it. Nothing happened. I concluded that it was an old repair.

I'd had enough of this charade. What in heaven's name was I doing in the saleroom, at half past one, on a cold frosty morning, kneeling on a filthy, concrete floor, trying to find a secret compartment, which didn't seem to exist? I hit the side of the davenport with my fist, angrily accepting that the dream was all make-believe. I shouldn't have been surprised. That is what dreams are. A cup of tea was a far better option than this clichéd attempt to create a miracle from the state of unreality. I dragged my cold feet towards the door.

The wind started to moan outside. It rattled the door and windows. For one moment, I thought it was going to blow them in. A cold draught swept under the door. It wafted about my head, and tickled the nape of my neck. I thought I'd lost my marbles, as my imagination ventured into the realms of silliness. For a fleeting moment, I heard the gentle strains of a woman's voice pleading in my ear: "Don't give up. Please try, for your sake."

On a whim, I opened the saleroom door, and strolled into the yard. The wind ceased blowing. The silence was deafening. I returned to the saleroom. With a sigh of frustration, I settled down beside the desk. For the umpteenth time, my fingers explored the dark inner recess. I began to share the same reluctance that a veterinary surgeon must feel as he pushes his arm up the backside of a cow.

My fingers tightened on the piece of wood that wouldn't move upwards, downwards or sideways. A shaft of inspiration touched the deepest recesses of my brain. Perhaps I shouldn't be trying to move it by force. I caressed the wooden protrusion, gently prodding every part of its surface. My frozen digits were like pieces of wax, totally unresponsive, and lacking any form of sensitivity. I was about to give up the ghost when my index finger lightened on what felt like a raised knot, in the corner of the piece of wood. I applied as much finger pressure as the confined space would allow me. The piece of wood sprang away, and fell with a welcome clatter into the bottom of the desk.

Amidst my elation I told myself not to get carried away. Accepting that reality situations are the very fabric of dream weaving, it didn't explain how a grey haired hunchback had shown me where the secret compartment was concealed. This was stretching incredulity to the limits. In that moment of fanatical imbalance, I swept these thoughts from my mind. The excitement of the hunt had become more important than the inconsistency of reasoning. My life was turning upside down, and I couldn't care less.

With stomach twisting expectancy, I removed a wooden box from inside the desk. It was hollow, with a hinged lid, like the one in my dream. Hardly daring to breathe, I opened it. Lying inside was a big, bulgy envelope. Spidery words were written on it. My heart missed a beat when I saw that it was addressed to me.

My Doubting Thomas side kicked into gear, submerging the foolish gusto that had prevailed a few moments ago. This was plain silly. My brain was asking me to take on board the impossible suggestion that a dream had been the means of finding this letter. Dreams can't solve life problems. Yet the envelope flew in the face of that theory. The commonsense factor honed in on me. What was the point of getting an envelope to me in this complicated way?

Why not use the first class postal service? It would have been a damn sight quicker, and cheaper. The whole thing smelt of silly buggers. Talk about going around the houses. What if Grodam had bought the desk? I wouldn't have got my hands on the letter. I had no plausible answers.

I replaced the drawer, locked the saleroom door, and retraced my steps to the flat. The envelope lay on the coffee table willing me to open it. For the moment, enough was enough. The last twenty four hours had already provided an excess of surprises, with no answers. Whatever was in the envelope would have to wait. If I was honest with myself, I was scared of what I might find. My body gave up on me. I fell into a deep sleep. There were no more dreams. I needed to recharge my batteries. The skirmishing was about to get under way.

CHAPTER TEN

Sunday, 7th October 2007.

I T WAS HALF PAST SEVEN when I woke. A quick shower blew the cobwebs from my mind. Suitably relaxed, I settled myself into an armchair, and prepared myself for the envelope. I acknowledged that normality had been turned on its head, but the prospect of opening it created a feeling of inner agitated speculation. It was the proverbial birthdays and Christmas rolled into one. I slit the envelope open. A letter, and a leather pouch, tumbled onto the table. I unfolded the letter. A key was taped to the bottom of the second sheet. I took a peep to see who had signed it. The scrawled signature of the Reverend Julius Milner spread itself across the bottom of the page.

Martin's sarcasm about the Reverend gentleman had settled in my mind. Supposing we were related. He might have left me something in his will after all. I just hoped it wasn't the commode and its contents. The letter was undated:

> '*Dear Kit*
>
> *I haven't called you Mister Milner, because I feel that I know you sufficiently well. You'll be puzzled by my boldness, seeing that you have never knowingly met me. By the time you read this letter, I will be dead. That doesn't mean to say that we won't ever meet. We will become acquainted, in the near future. To be more precise, we will meet in the past. I could tell you when, but I won't.'*

94

I read the paragraph again, trying to get my head around what he was on about. The words weren't making sense. I read on:

'Please trust, and believe in me. I implore you to accept that anything in life is possible, especially those things that seem totally impossible. My choice of words must be teasing you, especially as I already know how confused you are.

I hope it won't add to your confusion, but you are being groomed to carry out a quest. I was given the chance, but my mind and flesh were too weak. I am yesterday's man, Kit, a failure to the Milner family. That doesn't worry me. I am in good company. I am not the first Milner to have failed. I hope I will be the last.

Don't worry about it. You will be clothed in great powers. They will see you through this mission in life.

You should have some idea of what is involved from your recent vision about Merlin. Look in the leather pouch. There are people who will kill you, to get their hands on it. Wear the pouch and its contents about your neck at all times. It will protect you from your enemies.

You are wondering why I went to all this trouble to get the envelope to you. I hid it in my davenport desk, quite deliberately, instead of using a more conventional method of sending it. You have to prove that you possess the aptitude, and ability, to get your hands on this letter as a part of your test. This is only the beginning. Your preparation for the mission is a continuing learning curve.

In giving you the pouch, I have knowingly signed my own death warrant. It was a conscious decision that goes some way towards atoning for something I did, many years ago, that was in conflict with my religious views. I hope my maker will forgive me, when I meet up with him soon.

Strange things will happen to you in the next few weeks. You are a young man who was born with talents beyond your wildest dreams, even though you have not yet identified them. You will find out what they are, in good time.

Don't be afraid, even though the changes in your life defy logic. Your footsteps are being guided. You have no control over the path that you tread. Don't ever try and justify what is happening to you. A higher authority will make it clear, one day. Just concentrate on your task. That is all that is asked of you.

Take the key to the bank manager: he will give you something that you sorely need. His name and address are written at the foot of this letter. I know you will be contacting him.

Don't be concerned for me. You might even rekindle my life, one day.

Your friend, JULIUS MILNER.'

The letter made no sense, and wouldn't have done so in a month of Sundays. How could it, when it contained such wild, conflicting statements? The only part which struck a chord was the reference to my life being guided. I hoped that God had something to do with it.

I undid the leather bag. Three stones, the shape and size of small marbles, fell into the palm of my hand. They reminded me of the young man in my dream at Merlin's rock. I held one of them between my fingers. It felt cold. I was justified in believing that some benefit might make itself known, but no energy field surged through my fingertips, nor did Kylie Minogue appear, when I made a wish. I put the stones back into the pouch. Ignoring my lack of enthusiasm, I hung it around my neck.

Surrendering to an impulse, I pulled an encyclopædia from the bookcase. I looked up the reference to Merlin. The passage was short, and sweet. Merlin was a wizard who lived during the sixth century. It told of his escapades with King Arthur. The Arthurian Merlin had died in battle, fighting by the side of his King. His final resting place is unknown. No mention was made of Merlin being incarcerated in a slab of rock.

Was I expected to believe that my stones were connected with last night's dream? The implication was outrageous. The very idea that they'd been handed down through the centuries, for over fourteen hundred years, before ending up with the Reverend Milner, was absurd.

The Reverend didn't need to draw a veil of intrigue around his so-called mission. I knew it was all about Merlin being trapped in a rock. I enjoyed a belly laugh at the Reverend's expense. Merlin has been dead for fourteen hundred years. The idea of rescuing a dead man was a load of cobblers. It would have been easy to have dismissed everything as complete drivel, but I didn't. Things had happened to me that defied explanation. Whatever the key unlocked might make things clearer. That would have to wait.

Although it was Sunday, there was work to be done. I was still covering for the sick porter, and the Fine Arts sale had to be wound up by logging any unsold lots. I made my way to the saleroom and pulled my key out to unlock the door. That presented me with a problem. The door was already open; from the marks etched into the door jamb, it had been jemmied.

Why hadn't the alarm gone off? I was certain that I'd re-activated the alarm after my early morning visit. With the system reset, the sound of the alarm bell should have woken the dead. The security company would have alerted the police, as well as telephoning me and Martin. My phone hadn't rung, Martin wasn't on my tail, and the police hadn't knocked at my door.

A cold sweat covered my body. Had I forgotten to set the alarm? I pushed the door open, and looked around. Everything seemed to be in its place, except for the davenport desk. Lying on the floor, where it had stood, was a piece of paper. The message was short and sweet: 'Thanks for arranging to leave the alarm switched off, Milner, I've collected the davenport. Sweet dreams, Kitchener.'

Kit was in trouble, big time. The damn desk wasn't paid for, and now it had gone missing. The prospect of paying two thousand two hundred pounds for a brown envelope didn't fill me with joy. I fleetingly wondered if Martin's insurance company might cough up some compensation. I rang Martin. He sounded happy and relaxed when he answered the telephone. That slipped away as I fed him the news about the break-in. I had to mention my early morning visit, because I'd logged a call with the security company. He went ballistic. "You dick-head." He calmed down, momentarily. "What's the point of having a security system, if people just walk in and help themselves, you bloody idiot? I'll be over. Meet me in my office."

He turned up ten minutes later. "What were you doing in

the saleroom at that time of the morning? You had no right to open it up."

I was a mite tardy with the truth. "I was woken, in the early hours, by noises coming from the saleroom." I didn't mention Billy Grodam's letter. That would have incriminated me.

Martin gave me a withering look. "Don't try and bamboozle me with crap. You've dropped yourself in the mire. You had no right to turn the alarm off, for whatever reasons. You should have called the police." A look of derision crossed his face. "What was your real reason, I wonder? It's funny that only the desk was taken. For all I know, you stole the bloody thing yourself. I can't accept your dim-witted excuse about hearing noises. That's a load of old bollocks." He stopped for breath. "On top of all this, I had a call, last evening, from some obnoxious git called Grodam. He's threatening to report me to the Society of Auctioneers. He says you started a fight in the saleroom, and tricked him out of buying the davenport. I managed to calm him down. The little scumbag was pleased to hear that the davenport desk was safely locked away on the premises. At least, it was until you switched the alarm off." He wiped the sleeve of his jacket across his sweaty face. "You know more than you're letting on, I'm not wearing it."

What a twat Martin was. Fancy telling Grodam that the davenport was still in the auction room. It was an open invitation to steal it.

Martin fixed me with a steely gaze. "Your behaviour is something I can't accept. It's as well that I've seen the other side of you, before you became a full-blown auctioneer. You're finished here, and I don't care if you take me to the Industrial Tribunal. You can pick up what you're owed, next

Saturday. I'm going to call the police. Make sure you're around to give them a statement."

I tried to salvage my job. "You don't understand, Martin. Give me another chance."

"It's you that don't understand. Not only have you potentially damaged my business, but you've made me look a right prick. Because of your stupidity, every piece of furniture in the storeroom could have been stolen. Thankfully, for some reason known to you and the thieves, only the desk was taken."

I knew my timing was wrong, as soon as I opened my mouth. "Is the desk covered under your insurance?"

A look of disbelief masked his face. "You've got a bloody cheek. If you think my insurance company is going to cough up money for that desk, forget it. The desk has gone, and you're still responsible for paying. I'll give you until next Saturday to find the money. You can stay in the flat for another four weeks. If you're not fixed up elsewhere by then, too bad. You're out."

I started to protest. He picked up a paperweight from his desk, and hurled it at me. It thudded against the wall behind me. "You're wasting your breath." He turned his back on me, and stared out of the window. I walked out of the office.

My new found confidence bounded to the rescue, even though I was knee-high in sludge. I'd lost my job, but there were other things to do. I wanted to check out the Lovington rectory, that had figured in my dream. After that I was going to satisfy a long standing whim. Yours truly intended to spend the evening in a pub. There was also the little matter of calling into the rector's bank, but that had to wait until Monday.

I directed two fingers towards Martin's office, walked to the car, and drove to the Linmere Sunday Market. If Kit was going to socialise, then a new outfit was called for. I bought a pair of trousers and a casual jacket from a male stallholder sporting a limp wrist, and speaking with a lisp. I declined his offer to take my inside leg measurement, but let him talk me into buying a heavy metal-buckled belt to support my new trousers. He assured me it was all the rage, and guaranteed to pull someone. He didn't make it clear which gender he was on about.

I changed into the new gear, back at the flat, and set out for Lovington. Two hours later, I drove into the outskirts of the town. I aimed the car towards the steeple peeping above the town houses. Within minutes, I was parked outside All Saints' church. A sagging wooden sign pointed disconsolately toward the rectory.

A short walk later, I was lapping up a red brick and inlaid knapped flint stone frontage, with herbaceous borders of waving flowers. It was the house of my dreams, in more ways than one. I should have felt surprise, but didn't. I meekly conceded that my dream patterns had changed. Somehow, they had advanced towards the reality of life, leaving the brittle and meaningless unrealities of mind games behind.

I thought about knocking on the front door, but didn't. The Reverend Milner was dead. I returned to the car. It was a short drive to the town market place, where I parked the car.

I whiled the rest of the afternoon away, walking the narrow streets in the guise of a tourist admiring the crumbling buildings of yesteryear. The fine architecture held no interest for me. I was too preoccupied in taking stock of my situation, and wondering where it was going to end. I chanced on a teashop in the High Street. The door bell tinkled as I opened it. The interior left no doubt that this place dispensed tea. Endless shelves festooned the walls, each crammed full of decorative tea-ware. Hundreds of teapots sat to attention, their erect phallic spouts waiting to perform their man-made task. They were virgin teapots, every one of them. None was ever destined to conceive an infusion of tea leaves, or hold a tea bag in the womb of its body.

A grey-haired lady welcomed me. She turned out to be the owner. As her only customer, she lavished her full attention on me. I asked if she'd heard of the Reverend Julius Milner. She threw her hands up in mock horror. "Heard of him, you say. I'm a regular worshipper at All Saints'. He was a lovely gentleman. Wouldn't hurt a fly."

My question touched on a sensitive memory. She dabbed at her eyes with a paper napkin. "He did a beautiful sermon, that man. Always going on about our duty to help those less fortunate than ourselves." She blew her nose, and wiped another tear from her eye. I had opened her floodgates of verbosity. The woman rambled on, sharing stories of her wonderful man. "He was our rector for years. Julius was popular with everyone. We all loved him. His wife, bless her, died some time ago." Her face took on a grave look. "Then we lost him. It was so sad." She glanced over her shoulder, to make sure no one was listening. Her voice fell to a whisper. "There were suspicious circumstances about his death. The police were called in. The coroner decided he'd committed suicide." She tossed her head, and her voice regained its normal tenor. "We were so angry that anyone could believe such a cock and bull story. The rector would never have done away with himself. He wasn't that kind of man. Who would have wanted to kill him? He hadn't got an enemy in the world. We shall never know."

I pressed her, while she was in talking mode. "How did he meet his death?"

She pushed her grey hair back with her hands, and licked

her lips in anticipation of what she was about to say. "It must have been horrible for his housekeeper, finding him like that. He cut his throat with a kitchen knife." She swallowed noisily. "We couldn't understand why he'd want to do such a horrible thing. Mind you, having said that, we all noticed a big change in him during his last few months. The poor man seemed to have the weight of the world on his shoulders. He even lost his sense of humour. He never let on what was bothering him. It's all water under the bridge now." Her face screwed up, like a dried prune. "We've got a new rector. She's a woman." Her flow of words trailed off. I felt sorry for the new incumbent. She would never achieve the heights of popularity that the Reverend Milner had enjoyed.

I swallowed my last mouthful of tea. "He sounds a wonderful man. What did he look like?"

A look of uncertainty crossed her face. "Why do you ask?" I didn't get the chance to answer. The desire to tell me overcame her curiosity. "He was a fine looking man, my dear. Julius Milner had flowing grey hair, and a beard, and what you would call a gentle, happy face." She sat down at the table, and looked over her shoulder again. "I never married. Had I felt the inclination to do so, he was the man I would gladly have chosen for a husband." A glazed look took control of her face. She patted her grey locks into place, as if she expected the Reverend gentleman to walk through the door. I was momentarily forgotten. She got up and started to clear the things from my table.

I coughed. It brought her winging back to the land of reality. "Did the Reverend have any particular distinctive features?"

She gave me an old fashioned look "You ask a lot of questions. But not to worry, eh? We are not being disrespectful to his departed soul, are we?" The glassy-eyed look reappeared. "Special features, you say? He had the most magnificent nose. It gave me a shiver of pleasure, just to look at it." From the sheer picture of delight etched in her face, I thought she was having an orgasm, probably for the first time in her life. She recovered her composure. "It was kind of hooked, almost Fagin like. And the poor man had a hunchback, bless him." Her eyes moistened over. "I still miss his sermons and kindly words."

I sat there in my own self-contained stupor. Her description of Julius Milner fitted the old man in my dream to a tee.

Wishing the lady goodbye, I left the cosiness of the tea house and plunged into the darkness of a cold October evening. A light mist swirled down the High Street, adding a curtain of dampness to the chilly night air. I walked back to the car, knowing where my evening pleasures lay. It didn't take long to drive to the outskirts of the town, where I'd noticed a public house called the 'Rising Sun' earlier in the day. Its quaintness had appealed to me. I pushed the door open, and walked into a dimly lit interior. A vocation of vicars, and assorted ladies turned their heads and stared at me. The gentle hum of conversation fell flat. For one moment, I thought I'd trespassed into an Anglican General Synod convention. My short-lived enthusiasm was severely dampened. I was about to make a quick exit, when I noticed that most of the ladies sported stubble on their faces, and three of them had beards.

One of the ladies shouted at me in a beautiful bass voice. "Who have you come as? Are you the Bishop of Ely, in plain clothes?"

They all dissolved into laughter. One of the vicars walked across, and patted me on the back. "Ignore him. We're in fancy dress. The landlord though it would be a good idea to have a 'Vicars and Tarts' night, to drum up some extra business. Don't worry about your garb. Come and join the fun."

I did my best to swagger up to the bar, as the bishop might have done. This caused a hoot from the assembled mass. "Good evening. What will it be?" asked the barmaid. I couldn't see her face or anything else for that matter. She was swathed from head to foot in a burka. She might have been as ugly as sin, for all I knew. This apart, the sound of her voice brought a sensation of weakness in my knees.

I ordered a pint of the best bitter, and addressed the slit in the hood. "I understand the vicars and tarts, but what's your gear all about?"

She nodded towards the landlord. He was the most startling of all, sporting big womanly breasts, a reasonable pair of legs, all backed up with a ginger beard, and moustache. "Blame him. He thought I should provide a religious contrast. 'Let's be politically correct,' he said. That's why I'm wearing this one piece number, with a peep-hole." The girl sounded peeved. She turned away to serve one of the tarts.

I wandered across the room. The chap who'd spoken to me invited me to sit at his table. I was introduced to his assorted friends. It didn't take long for their infectious banter to seep into me. It had taken me twenty six years to socialise with people, and less than twenty six minutes to find how much I enjoyed it. I was gutted when the landlord called time. After much back-slapping and shaking of hands, I strolled out into the cold night air, shouting my final farewells. Pulling my overcoat tightly about me, I walked to where the car was parked.

A female voice shouted goodnight to someone. It was the young bar assistant. She was dressed in her normal attire, but too far away for me to get a good look at her face. If I'd met her in daylight, I wouldn't have known her, except for the voice. We were never likely to meet. What did it matter? The door closed behind her and the bolts were drawn. The sound of her heels clicked on the pavement, as she hurried off in the opposite direction, with her coat collar pulled about her ears.

The peacefulness of the night was broken by a woman's scream. The shrill sound floated down the road where the girl had gone. I spun around. In the light of a street lamp, two men were struggling with her. One had his arm around her neck, while he pulled at her body with the other hand. The second man snatched her handbag and started to rifle through its contents. A fusion of screams and shouting reached my ears. The pleading tones of the woman detached themselves from the hubbub of noise. "Help, someone! Anyone! Help me!"

She didn't get a chance to say more, as the man put a hand over her mouth. My first reaction was to knock the landlord up and telephone the police. I swore for being so dim. By the time the police arrived, the girl could be injured, or something worse. I tore towards them, my feet barely touching the ground. The thug manhandling the girl hit her across the face. Grabbing her around the neck, the toe-rag dragged her through the bushes. The other man stood with his back to me. He was too preoccupied in throwing bits and pieces from her handbag to be aware of my approach. My clenched fist caught him a heavy rabbit punch on the back of the neck. He grunted and fell to the ground, dead to the world.

I scrambled through the bushes, where the yob had dragged the girl. The gloom was lightened by the dappled rays of the street lamp shining through the leafless bushes. The man was astride the girl. She was putting up a fight, but it wasn't enough. Her harsh breathing showed that her physical exertion had drained her strength. Her coat, and most of her clothing, lay on the grass. The yob dragged at her underwear, ripping everything away from her body.

She pleaded with him. "Don't hurt me. Take my money and credit cards. They're in the handbag, with my mobile phone."

The words were wasted. His chilling throaty laugh filled the glade. "You can keep them, darling. I'm not after your money or mobile phone. Shut the chat. Just lie back and enjoy a shafting." The menace in his voice diminished, and took on a pleading tone. "I'm not going to hurt you. When I've finished with you, I'll take what we came for, and leave you alone."

He wasn't making sense. What was more important to him than money, and raping the girl? I'd seen enough. I tiptoed across to where they lay, and tapped him on the shoulder. He turned, and looked up at me, a stupid grin on his face. He'd expected to see his mate enjoying his handiwork. The grin vanished. My right foot caught him in the rib cage. He gasped for breath. Grabbing his hair, I whacked him on the jaw and pulled him off the girl. He slumped to the ground, labouring to draw air into his lungs. I know how he felt.

The girl lay there, with her legs stretched apart. She'd got no idea who I was. I could have been another rapist, for all she knew. She was naked, except for the remnants of her tights, which hung around her ankles. A pair of shoes adorned her feet, ridiculing her nakedness. I knelt by her side, hoping my words were pitched at the right level. "Don't worry. I'm here to help you. Do you remember me? I was in the 'Rising Sun' this evening. I was the only one who wasn't in drag."

The frightened look left her face. She sat up, hands loosely draped across her naked body in a futile attempt to hide her breasts. Modesty was forgotten. She held a hand out.

It shook as I grasped it. I gently helped her to her feet, picked her coat up and slipped it over her shoulders. She shivered violently. "You'd better have my coat as well. You'll freeze otherwise. Come on. Let's get out of here."

She let me drape it around her shoulders, and button it up. I pulled the collar up, and tied my scarf over her head, and under her chin, to keep her warm. The girl's body shook as she clung to me. She looked down at the groaning yob, and started to sob. I guided her through the bushes, onto the pavement. The other scumbag was still laid out. I took a tissue from my pocket, and pushed it into her hand. She dabbed at her eyes. Her sobbing ceased. She stared at me. Her hand touched my face, and the fingers stroked my beard. "I remember you." She went into verbal overdrive. "Thank god, you were around. I was walking along, when they jumped out on me. This wouldn't have happened if my car hadn't broken down this morning. I'm a bloody idiot. Why didn't I get a taxi, or ask someone for a lift? It's too late now."

The tears that threatened to vacate her eyes, dribbled down her cheeks. She covered her face with a hand. I tried to put her at ease. "Nothing else is going to happen to you. I'll protect you. It's all over." My good intentions were accepted. She put her arms around me, and snuggled into my chest. I gave her a squeeze. "Nobody will ever hurt you while I'm around." She went quiet. Perhaps I'd overdone the chivalry. I broke the silence. "Let's go." There was no response. I persevered. "Are you alright?"

My words penetrated her wall of silence. "My head hurts like hell. My legs and body don't feel much better." She shook her head from side to side. "This can't be right. I've been assaulted, yet I'm standing here with my arms around some bloke that I don't know. It doesn't make sense." Her flow of words ceased, momentarily. "When I spoke to you, in the pub, I felt that I'd known you for years. That's a daft thing to say, because I've never seen you before in my life." She stroked my moustache, then pulled her hand away. "I don't even know if I can trust you." She giggled nervously. "Did you mean what you said? Would you really protect me?"

My confidence was increasing by the minute. "If you'll let me, I will."

We'd forgotten about the thug who tried to rape her. As he crashed through the bushes, he yelled expletives at me. Releasing the girl, I turned to face him. His blustering didn't worry me. What he clutched in his right hand did. The knife blade glinted in the dim light. He moved the knife from hand to hand. His cockiness showed that he was no novice when it came to using the blade. "I'm going to kill you, you bastard. Then I can finish shafting the girl." He lunged towards me. I felt the impact of the blade as it struck me in the midriff. The girl let out a shriek. I didn't collapse in mortal agony. The youth let out a surprised grunt. He moved back a couple of steps. His mouth twisted into a meaningless smile. "You were lucky that time, arsehole. Now you're a dead man."

I stretched my hand out as he rushed me. I use the word rushed in the slowest sense of the word. The thug was hell-bent on ripping me apart as he moved towards me in slow motion. I waved a hand in front of my face. It moved through the air, at the speed that I'd intended it to. The girl was screaming, but the decibel level of the sound was like a fog-horn, as it translated into the language of slow motion, as the pace of time dawdled. Any sense of surprise was lost on me. It was another twist in my changing lifestyle.

Whatever was happening worked to my advantage. The knife crept leisurely towards my neck. At the rate it was moving, I could have shaved, and combed my hair, before it pierced my skin. With a feeling of malice, I grabbed his wrist, twisting it quickly and sharply. The bone snapped under my grasp. The knife slipped from his fingers, and floated like a feather towards the ground. My hand moved to his crotch. His flies were still unzipped after his encounter with the girl. I nestled his family jewels in the palm of my hand. It was too easy. I squeezed, and twisted his tackle in one movement. The effect was devastating. He floated to the ground like a sack of potatoes filled with helium gas.

The girl stared at the yob, fascinated by his cries of pain. She touched my arm at normal speed. "I thought he'd stabbed you. Are you hurt?"

I pulled my pullover up. The street light showed a deep scratch on the buckle of my new belt. "That was lucky. The buckle saved me." I put my arm around the girl. "I'll call the police to pick up these scumbags. After that, I'm taking you to hospital."

Her reaction wasn't what I expected. She pushed her face as close to mine as her height allowed. "Let's get one thing straight, I don't want the police involved. And forget about hospital. I'll be fine after a good night's sleep." She calmed down as quickly as she had blown her top. "Don't try and make me change my mind. I know what I'm doing. I want to go home. End of story." The knifeman groaned, and tried to get to his feet. My right foot swung into his testicles. He wouldn't be making love to a woman, with or without her permission, for a long time.

I collected her clothing, and put the scattered belongings into her handbag. The girl hadn't moved. She looked like a waif and stray, swamped by my overcoat. I held her hand, and walked her back to the car. Five minutes later I was parked outside her home, a smart-looking block of flats at the top of a hill. I helped her out of the car. She winced, but didn't complain. We walked up the steps to the front entrance. I gently pulled her around, and put my arms around her. "I'm worried about you. You should have let me take you to hospital."

She snapped at me. "Don't bring that up again. Forget it."

Her lack of appreciation annoyed me. I pecked her forehead, and let go of her. "Don't worry about my coat and scarf. I can pick them up tomorrow. You'd better take your bits and pieces."

A feeling of guilt clutched at me. My clinical insensitiveness was beyond belief, as I prepared to abandon her on the doorstep. For someone who had promised to look after her, my behaviour was outrageous. The girl pulled a face at the soiled clothing. Her eyes sought mine. She put her hand on my arm. "Would you see me to my flat before you go?"

How could I refuse? She squeezed my arm, and keyed a number into the security box. The door swung open, and we walked into a well-lit entrance hall. She pulled my scarf from around her head. It was the first time I'd seen her in the full light. The smudged mascara and lipstick couldn't hide her beauty. I melted at the sight of her eyes. Jade green irises bordered black pupils, topped by long curving eyelashes, above a face of fragile porcelain whiteness, with a full mouth rising over a delicate chin. Her prominent, high cheekbones gave an added dimension to her looks. My libido floundered in the bottomless depths of her beauty. A surge of unrequited love coursed though my body. I felt a tingling sensation in my groin.

She casually undid the ribbon holding her hair in place. A mass of auburn coloured hair cascaded around her face. It hung in ringlets over her shoulders. I shivered. She bore an uncanny resemblance to the woman that I'd seen in my nightmare.

The girl pointed to the lift and I ushered her in. She pressed the button for the top floor. The lift moved smoothly up the shaft, before coming to rest. The doors opened and we stepped out into a warmly lit corridor. She rummaged in her handbag for a key, and unlocked the flat door.

I wished her goodnight for the second time. The girl didn't say a word. She didn't need to. Her pleading eyes spoke volumes. Her tongue licked at her lips. She put a finger in her mouth, and nervously bit on the nail. "Don't go, yet. Would you like a coffee? You don't have to stay long." She stood there, her hands held out in silent invitation, willing me to accept the offer. If she needed my company that badly, who was I to argue? "Alright. I won't stay long though. You need some sleep."

I was rewarded with a big hug. She switched the lights on, and propelled me into the room. The door closed behind me. "Thanks. I feel safer with you around."

This was unreal. I was alone with a beautiful girl, and didn't know her name. I held my hand out. "It's a bit late in the day, but I'm Kit."

The girl took my hand in hers. I didn't let it go. She giggled. "I'm Anne Wood." She twigged that I was fondling her hand, and let out a nervous laugh. "We can't stand here all night holding hands, can we?" With great reluctance, I let go of her. Anne pointed to a comfortable looking settee. "Sit down, Kit. Switch the television on if you want. I'm going to have a quick shower, then I'll make the coffee."

She casually undid the buttons on my coat, slid it from around her shoulders, them removed her own coat. My mouth gaped open, at the same time as my eyebrows hit the ceiling. Anne was showing more than she had intended. She made a vain attempt to cover her breasts with one hand. Her other hand fled to her nether regions, but not before I'd glimpsed a dark triangular patch of auburn coloured hair.

The girl was a mass of confusion. She ran from the room, slamming the door behind her. A shrill note of apology floated through the door. This was followed by the noisy slamming of drawers, then complete silence.

I put my face close to the door. "Don't worry, Anne. I know it wasn't intentional." I tried to lighten things. "There's something you should know. I'm short-sighted, as well as being blind in one eye, and I'm not wearing my glasses."

The door opened. Anne walked out, suitably covered by a green dressing gown. The mood of discomfort had passed. "Thanks for being so understanding. I'll have that shower now. See you soon."

I sat on the settee, and looked around me. The terracotta coloured walls worked wonders with the thick pile tan carpet. The furniture had been chosen by someone with taste. The whole room oozed well-being.

The sound of rushing water drifted from the bathroom. I failed in my resolve not to think of her wet, naked body. I walked across to the window. The twinkling lights of Lovington were spread out below. I heard the lounge door open and turned away from the window. Anne walked into the room. The smudged mascara had gone. Her wet hair hung on her shoulders. Anne's choice of garment was a long, loose, wide sleeved green robe, drawn together with a black sash. I heard myself spluttering inadequate words. Something I said must have hit the target. She tossed her head and blushed. She glided over, and pulled me onto the settee. "About this evening, Kit. I'll always be grateful for what you did. If you hadn't been around…" She pulled a face, and didn't finish the sentence.

My tongue was tied in a granny knot. I managed to unravel it. "Try and forget what happened. I know that's easy for me to say. How are you feeling?"

"Much better. Thanks for seeing me home, and being so understanding."

Anne's face started to flush. She got up. "I'll go and make that coffee."

I followed her into the kitchen. "I'll do it. Show me where the things are. You should be resting."

She kissed me on the cheek. "Thanks. Coffee and sugar are in that cupboard. Milk is in the fridge, and spoons in the drawer, over there."

When I carried the coffee through to the lounge, she was asleep on the settee. I didn't want to wake her. I made her comfortable with a pillow and duvet from her bedroom. She stirred, and murmured my name. In the few hours that I'd known her, she'd had a devastating effect on me. I felt like a real person, not a nobody who had to take refuge in his dream world. I settled down on the settee, next to her. She slid towards me. I eased my arm around her shoulders, covered my legs with the duvet and made myself comfortable. I smiled to myself. I was about to sleep with a woman, for the first time in my life. It was an overrated pastime if this was what it was all about. I felt awash with happiness. Was I suffering from the symptoms of really caring for someone? If so, then I was happy to bear the spasms that flowed through my body.

Anne moaned in her sleep. It was weird the way our paths had crossed. The last couple of days had been abnormal, and that was putting it mildly. I'd been sacked, kicked out of my flat, and owed a lot of money for a desk that had been stolen. On top of that, there was the letter from a dead man, together with a bag of stones, hidden in the davenport desk.

Were the stones really a passport to great powers? I

speculated whether they had saved me from being bladed. And, did I possess the knack of slowing time down? A fly crawled across the arm of the settee. The insect was a godsend. I closed my eyes, and concentrated on slow motion. With some doubt, I opened them. Anne's breathing seemed to have stopped.

Her chest rose and fell in unhurried motion. I placed my hand close to the fly. It tried to take off, but only succeeded in making a deep droning sound. With no effort, I plucked it out of the air. I thought of normal motion. Anne was breathing freely, and the fly was frantically buzzing in its efforts to escape from my fingers. I let it go.

I'm not sure how I should have reacted to achieving the impossible. I wasn't shocked, or overwhelmed by surprise. Shaken is more like it, but strangely, I took it in my stride.

I put these thoughts on hold, as I backtracked to this evening. Why had my footsteps taken me to Anne's pub? If I hadn't been there, would fate have conspired for somebody else to have filled my shoes? Had she got a boyfriend? She wasn't wearing a ring, but that didn't mean anything. I was pushing the boat out too far, to even consider that the two of us might end up as an item. My eyelids began to flutter, and I fell asleep.

CHAPTER ELEVEN

Sunday Night and Monday, 7th and 8th October 2007.

I SHOULD HAVE DREAMED ABOUT Anne, but it didn't happen that way. The lounge wall lit up in iridescent mode. The prospect of another dream didn't appeal. I needn't have worried. There were no nightmarish scenes, only the outline of a church, boasting a magnificent steeple let into a Norman turret, with four smaller turrets supporting it. The main body of the building extended away from the steeple keep. The church was encircled by a well tended graveyard, with headstones standing in repose. A gravel path snaked its way to the main door of the building from a lych gate set in the wall that surrounded the church. A dilapidated notice board informed all and sundry that this was All Saints' Church, Lovington. The one notice pinned on it reminded people that the churchwardens were appealing for monies towards the restoration fund. I hoped that a new notice board was top of the list.

A man dressed in a cassock walked out of the church. I moved closer to the lounge wall to get a better look at him. He was bent over under the handicap of a deformed back. He was a younger version of the man that I'd seen in my dream. This was the Reverend Julius Milner. He looked in my direction and waved. "Come on over, Kit. I'd like to speak with you." I hesitated. He beckoned to me. "You are allowed to come across, you know."

I had reservations, but took a hesitant step across the floor and glided through the wall. My feet were firmly planted on the road in front of the church. I turned around, expecting to see the outside of Anne's flat. All I could see were bare trees, where winter had made itself known, with a layer of snow on their branches. Pungent smoke caught at my nostrils as it drifted out of the chimney pots of the Georgian houses at the far end of the road. This dream was unnerving. It was all too real. I stepped back onto the pavement as a car trundled past.

The rector called to me. "Hello, Kit. I told you we'd be meeting up."

"Why do I keep dreaming about you? This is becoming an obsession." I scolded myself, as soon as the words left my lips. This dream was nourished from events of the past twenty four hours. I crossed the road to where he stood.

"I hope things will become clearer by the time I've finished with you. I accept the fact that you are going to treat my words with scepticism." He spoke in a gentle reassuring tone. I was fascinated by his looks. That fine nose sat happily between a pair of green eyes. "Your world has been turned upside down these past few days, has it not?" He chuckled. "That's an understatement."

I humoured him. "You can say that again. You know a great deal about me. Yet, I know very little about you. You were older in my last dream, and sporting a white beard."

He slapped a hand against his thigh and laughed. "That is how I will age in future. I am Julius Milner, rector of the parish of Lovington. And you are Kit Milner." He took my hand in a firm grip, and shook it with vigour. "I know that you've found my letter in the davenport. I hope you're wearing the stones?"

My hand strayed to the pouch hanging around my neck. He nodded in satisfaction. "Take the contents of that letter seriously, no matter what you think." He clicked his tongue several times. "Let's clear up one thing straight away. This is not one of your childish, fabricated dreams. You have travelled back through the time zone to see me. Don't be concerned. I remember my own stubbornness to accept the truth.

My reaction was one of anger. I calmed down and let my hackles sink. Contentious disputes have never figured in my fantasies. "I'll stick to my conviction that I'm dreaming."

The Reverend pointed towards the church door. "So be it. Come inside, Kit. You must be cold, standing out here without an overcoat."

The medieval tiles resounded under the tread of our shoes. "Let's sit in this pew. One way or another, I have to convince you that you're not flirting with one of your mind games. Look around the church. It's going to play an important part in your future life."

It boasted a wonderful interior, with an angel ceiling, and a beautifully crafted wooden altar screen, which had somehow managed to escape the ravages of the Victorians. Reclining on the upper walls was a gathering of gargoyles. One in particular caught my eye. It was the spitting image of Billy Grodam.

He bit his lip and mused for a moment. "How best can I convince you that you are not dreaming?" He got up, walked across to a side-table, and came back with a piece of paper in his hand. "This is a bulletin for this month's Sunday services. It is dated February, 1994. When you return to your own time, or as you prefer it, wake up from your dream, read it. It will leave you in no doubt that you have travelled through time."

I tucked it into my jacket pocket, knowing it wouldn't be there when I woke up. Julius Milner's voice took on a graver tone. "I was in the auction house car park when that car did its best to run you down. It wasn't your dream spinning that gave you the chance to re-enact the attempt on your life. The second encounter with the car was down to time travel. You went back in time, and changed what happened the first time." He stopped to let his words sink in. "I was at the auction, when you bought my davenport desk. It wasn't your hand doing the bidding, as well you know. You were influenced into buying the desk so that you'd find my hidden letter."

I was warming to this new fangled dream experience. "It was a clumsy way of getting the letter to me." I allowed myself a smile. "I don't know how you managed to attend the auction. By that time you were…" I stopped. How could I tell him that he had cut his own throat?

"Don't concern yourself about that." I heard the rustling of paper as he took a half eaten bar of chocolate from his pocket. I refused the segment that was offered. He popped some in his mouth, and chewed noisily on it. "You were about to say that I was no longer in the land of the living. So be it. Most of us have to die at some point. The Lord calls us to his side when he is ready to receive us." He sucked on his teeth to savour the last threads of his treat. "I attended the sale by travelling forward in time. Time travel does work in both directions, you know." He patted me on the knee. "Don't tell me the details of my death. Or when it's going to happen. I was never tempted to use my stones as a means of checking out my future. And I won't use time travel as a means of preventing my death. The stones never sat easily with my religious beliefs. I'm not fortunate enough to possess the power of eternal life, not on earth anyway. Let death creep up on me, as it should do for every one of God's creatures." His eyes bored into my face. "None of us can avoid dying unless you're one of the chosen few. I will meet the obstacle of death at the due time."

I opened my mouth to put my two pennyworth in. He silenced me with his hand. "There are more vital matters to talk about before you go. Lovington will play a major part in your life. It's already started to. Your destiny lies here, together with your future happiness. There is so much you can achieve for yourself, and those around you. Don't throw it all away through dread of what the future might hold for you. I am a dismal failure, who cast aside the mantle of my life because I lacked the conviction. I am yesterday's man. You are the man of the moment. There is something I must tell you." He frowned, and brushed a tear away from his cheek. "It's very painful for me. My life has recently been turned upside down. An undesirable family recently moved into Lovington, and they're making my life hell." He grunted. "That's putting it mildly. They've already crossed your path."

My imagination was caught by this man. I was even prepared to forget that I was dreaming. "You're talking about the Grodams?"

He nodded. "The parents have twin sons, William, and Joseph. I've known of this family's existence for years and what they stand for. The past has finally caught up with me. I've always naively believed that in my role as a shepherd of the Lord's flock, religion and common sense would overcome the prejudice of the centuries. Neither God, nor the Grodams, are interested in my personal opinions."

"Some weeks ago I came across some graffiti on an old headstone in the churchyard. 'Dead, 10th December, 1993' was sprayed on it. I was horrified at the vandalism and asked my churchwarden to have it removed." The Reverend took a tissue from his pocket and wiped his brow. "Matters went from bad to worse. The rectory windows were smashed three times and we were burgled." Anger showed in his face. "'Burgled' is a polite term. The contents of every drawer were strewn over the floors. The three-piece suite was urinated on, and human faeces smeared over the walls. Nothing was taken.

The police were puzzled, but I knew what the burglars were after. This all happened within a four week period. The police carried out a thorough investigation, but made no inroads. I knew it was the Grodams."

I humoured my dream Reverend. "What were they after?"

He looked at me. "That's the first sensible thing you've said." He undid the buttons of his cassock, and nestled a pouch in the palm of his hand. "They want these stones. You know their significance. If your learning curve follows the same path as mine, then you saw Merlin with that dreadful Madrog. These images are Merlin's way of teaching the Milners about the stones." He poked me in the chest. "These are the same stones that Merlin gave to the traveller. We appear to be the kith and kin of that young man. You and I share the same stones. Mine are the stones of the present. Your stones come from the future, in your own time." My fingers moved to my neck. "The Merlin Stones hold the secret of life. You will witness that one day. If the Grodams ever get their hands on them, then God help us."

He sighed heavily. His voice grew in strength, and resonated through the church. "For goodness sake, Kit. You are blessed with gifts beyond your imagination. You can take control of people, and hypnotise them. You are capable of travelling through the pages of time. It was only recently that you fettered the feet of time." A worried smile creased his face. "I'm getting carried away. You are only a novice and have much to learn."

Julius Milner opened the neck of his pouch, and emptied four stones into his cupped hand. My dream had got things wrong. I only had three stones. "Look at them, Kit. Never undervalue what they can do for you. Remember. The pouch must never leave your person for any reason. Never."

The rector replaced his pouch. "I was telling you about the Grodams. Things got worse from their unhealthy interest." His hands came together in a gesture of prayer. He closed his eyes, and allowed his lips to move in soundless words. Tears trickled onto his cassock. "Something far more sinister was going to happen, that could only be the work of the devil."

Without warning, his whole body stiffened, his hands clutching at his throat. It looked as if he was trying to strangle himself. His face turned deep red, his lips moved, but he had trouble forming his words. He stared at me in desperation. His fingers dragged at the front of my shirt, as he managed to gasp a few words. "Walk…away…before…it's…too…late." His lips continued to move, but no more words came out.

Then, just as quickly, his whole body relaxed, and his face returned to its normal colour. He grasped me gently. "Forgive me, my boy. I've had several turns like this of late. Ignore what I said. I tend to talk a load of nonsense. I'm not in control of my faculties. I've seen my doctor. He says it's the pressure I've been under these past weeks." He braced himself, and took some deep breaths. "I spoke about things getting worse, and they did." Another tear dropped onto his cassock. "My wife Meg and I were blessed with a child fourteen years ago. We called her Carin. She was the most beautiful thing in our life."

"You talk as if your daughter is no longer with you?"

His hands clenched, and unclenched. "Carin is dead. She died on the date that was sprayed on that headstone. The 10th December, nineteen ninety three, will be etched in my mind until the day I die."

The emotional depth of my dream sent ripples of concern through me. I've never been subjected to such intense feelings in my sleeping mode. I was tempted to close the dream down.

A brief smile caressed his face. "My daughter attended the local grammar school. On the day that she died, Carin set out on the ten minute walk to school. She was always home by four thirty, unless she had some after school activity. It was gone half past five when Meg and I arrived home from Ely Cathedral. There was no sign of Carin. I telephoned the school, and managed to catch the head teacher. She said that my daughter had left school at the normal time."

He moved his backside around in the pew. "I knew something dreadful had happened to her. An image of the altar kept flashing through my mind. I asked Meg to ring the police, whilst I slipped across to the church. The poor woman thought that I'd gone to lock the church. The door was wide open. I called Carin's name, before tracing my steps along the nave aisle, and up the chancel steps, before pausing before the choir stalls. The blood in my veins turned to ice at what I saw on the altar."

Where I was dredging these dream thoughts from was beyond me. I had enough problems in my own life, without taking on someone else's dream grief. I stood up. "This has been an interesting dream, but I've got other things to worry about. I'm pulling the plug on this fantasy." I immediately regretted the words. What was I playing at, talking like this to someone who was a shadow of my thoughts?

"Please stay, Kit. I don't care whether you think this is a dream, or not. I've got to tell someone about what happened to my daughter." He eyeballed me. ""Will you stay?"

Don't ask me why I relented, but I did. "OK. But not for long."

He squeezed my arm, and raised a token smile. "Thank you. It's appreciated. The top of the altar was in disarray, the brass candlesticks scattered over the floor." Julius Milner licked at his lips, then blew onto the tips of his fingers. "My daughter's naked body lay there, her eyes staring at the stained glass window above the altar. I touched her to see if there was a spark of life. It was a waste of time. I'd known, from the outset, that she was dead. My child's throat was cut from ear to ear. I felt surprisingly clear of mind as my eyes fed on the carnage. The deeper shock would hit me later. My inner calmness was shattered by the ferocity with which she had been attacked. Cuts and bruises covered her body. It was the final act of indignity that sickened me. Her killer had shoved a candle up her backside."

He sighed. "I couldn't work out why my daughter was in the church. She must have been lured, or waylaid, on the way back from school. It's funny that it happened on the one day that Meg and I were late coming home."

He tapped me on the leg. "Surely you must have heard about her murder. The papers, and television, were full of it."

I'd been young at the time, but childhood memories stirred in my mind. I did recall something about a young girl being murdered in Lovington. This dream was nourishing itself on those early memories.

I allowed my dream to carry on. "I have this recurring image of myself in prayer, kneeling before a desecrated altar that stands beneath a beautiful stained glass window." Reverend Milner allowed himself a sad smile. "There's an irony in the picture that I paint. The stained glass window depicts Jesus. He is surrounded by happy, laughing children. Two of them are sitting on his knees, lying back in his arms. The mockery is in the inscription: 'Suffer little children to come unto me'. The words smacked me in the face."

He sat up, and pulled his shoulders back as far as his

deformity would allow. "For one who is grieving, you might feel that I have been over-explicit in the distasteful details of Carin's death. It's deliberate. You have to be aware of the kind of people you are dealing with. The Grodams are filth and vermin. I know for sure they murdered my Carin and won't hesitate to try and harm you." He tapped my pouch "That's why you must always wear the stones. They protect you."

He gripped my arm so hard that the pain shot down to my fingertips. "I know who murdered my daughter, and I can't do a thing about it. The only way to avenge her death would be to kill the Grodams myself." His obscene laugh filled the church. "Can you envisage the Rector of Lovington doing away with them? I don't think so. And it's no good telling the police. What specific evidence can I give them to incriminate the Grodams?"

He shook his head. "I'm protected by the stones. Yet my daughter wasn't. As I stood in front of the altar, I called on my Lord to bring the perpetrator of this crime to task. I regret uttering those words, and have asked for God's forgiveness." He thumped me on the shoulder. "People have this peculiar notion that a man of the cloth can handle death more easily. It's not true. I am flesh and blood, and subject to the same moods as everyone else.

"I broke the news to Meg, as gently as I could, then telephoned the police. The crime rocked the town. No one has been arrested. Carin is buried in the churchyard. Meg suffered a mental breakdown. The Bishop told us to take a holiday. For two weeks, we did nothing else but talk about Carin. It helped to convince us that our future lay in Lovington."

He looked at his watch. "At the first Sunday morning service on our return from holiday, the words of my sermon revolved around the text: 'Forgive our transgressors'. As the service progressed, I felt God's hand guiding me. Then it was time for me to mount the pulpit steps to deliver my pearls of wisdom." A beam of a smile lit his face. "Once in the pulpit, I composed myself and laid my notes on the lectern. The church looked beautiful, with bleak winter sunshine filtering through the stained glass windows. I let my eyes wander over the interior of this wonderful building.

"A sixth sense stopped me from launching into the sermon. Something had upset my concentration, jarring me into silence. The congregation began to whisper amongst themselves. I ignored them and allowed my eyes to roam along the walls of the church a second time. My senses told me that the unknown distraction was in the upper recesses of the building.

"I know every part of the church fabric, yet a subtle change had manifested itself. My eyes roamed slowly around the walls, and stopped at one particular spot. The abnormality was sitting on the wall, at the west end of the nave. The hairs at the back of my neck stood on end. The church had somehow procured another gargoyle. The original gargoyles have supported the wooden roof trusses for centuries, and the passage of time has worked their once sharp features into shapeless caricatures of their former glory. The new member of the gargoyle fold was crisp and smooth, as though it had been carved during the last few weeks." Julius Milner sucked at his teeth.

"The reason for my befuddled feelings became clear. The face of the new gargoyle was someone I knew. It may have been a trick of the light, but I swear that the gargoyle was crying."

The rector pointed above our heads. "Look for yourself, Kit. That gargoyle is the likeness of Joseph Grodam. What in heaven's name is his likeness doing up there? I was sickened to the pit of my stomach. I recalled the fervent manner in which I had pleaded with God to exact revenge on the murderer. Impossible I thought. My God doesn't work that way. If he hadn't, then who or what was responsible? Whatever the answer, the image of Joseph Grodam now decorates the upper church wall.

"My thoughts were broken by one of the churchwardens. The fellow had climbed into the pulpit. He asked in a quiet puzzled voice, if everything was alright. I assured the poor man that I was fine. I gave the best sermon I can ever recall, under the watchful eyes of Joseph Grodam." His face lit up. "I finished my sermon, and processed to the altar, to dispense the Eucharistic bread and wine. It was during the distribution of the elements that I received a second shock. I faced the stained glass window, and held a newly charged chalice above my head. My eyes chanced on one of the children, sitting on the lap of Jesus." A wistful smile flitted across his face. "The child smiling down was my daughter. She winked, as her eyes met mine. To say I was bewildered is an understatement. Why would my God show his hand this way, in his house of worship? It was beyond me. I kept my thoughts and feelings under control and completed the service. I didn't let on to Meg about the gargoyle, or the stained glass window. She was under enough stress as it was.

"This strange saga isn't finished. Several days later, the police found a headless corpse in the wood opposite the church. The body was identified as Joseph Grodam. His head hasn't been found."

With another of those expansive sighs, he got up from the pew. "Let's go and have a look at the stained glass window." We stood in front of the altar. "That is the face of my daughter."

He hadn't overstated his description of her. She was a

beautiful child. Looking at her jolted me into thinking that something was wrong, even though this was only a dream. "Why haven't the congregation noticed the new gargoyle, and your daughter's face in the window?"

He smiled. "Regular churchgoers never look at the church fabric, once they're ensconced. Only newcomers look more closely."

The Reverend led me out of the church, to the far side of the graveyard. He pointed to a new headstone. I peered at the engraved wording:

> 'Kareem (Carin) Anne Milner, deceased
> 10 December, 1993, aged fourteen years.
> She fell to earth before she had the chance to
> become airborne.'

He smiled. "We christened her Kareem, but she couldn't get her tongue around it, when she started to talk. Her best effort was Carin." He raised his voice. "I wish I had the strength of character to go back and change things to how they were." He shuddered, as if a ghost had walked across his grave. "I'm sorry I said that. It's against my Christian Beliefs. Only my God has the right of resurrection."

I took a fleeting look at the grave next to Carin's. A small metal plaque was set in the ground. I pulled it out. The name 'Joseph Grodam' stared at me.

The rector shrugged his shoulders. "His killer hasn't been caught. I couldn't bring myself to conduct the boy's funeral service. Since Carin's death, I've had no contact with the family." He grunted. "That's not to say things won't change in the future." His green eyes bored into mine. "You must be off now. Think about what I've said. We will meet again."

I was more than happy to escape this manic dream. I urged

my mind to end the images. A breeze plucked at my hair. I caught a last glimpse of the Reverend Milner. He waved to me, before fading from view. I woke up on Anne's settee. She lay asleep beside me. I stroked her hair. She moved, and muttered my name.

I briefly flirted with the dream journey that I'd just vacated. I felt guilty at becoming emotionally involved in an unreality caper, and gave up thinking about it. Dreams don't matter any more. Anne is more important. I don't need anyone to tell me that I've fallen in love. I can't make her feel the same way about me. So long as she's prepared to throw a few crumbs of comfort in my direction, that's fine by me. I won't expect more. With these pleasant thoughts drifting through my mind, I fell into dreamless, unbroken slumber.

CHAPTER TWELVE

Monday 8th October 2007.

ANNE'S CRYING WOKE ME. I reached out for her. She wasn't there. I rubbed the sleep from my eyes. The sounds led me to the bathroom. She was stretched out on the floor. I grabbed a towel and wiped away the beads of sweat running down her face. "What's the matter?"

Her eyelids fluttered open. Those breathtaking eyes which had disturbed my metabolism were dulled to the point of apathy. She clawed at my arm. "I feel dreadful. My body hurts like hell." A pleading look replaced the mask of pain on her face. "Please call an ambulance."

I felt angry. She should have gone to hospital last night. I swept her up in my arms, and carried her into the bedroom. The ambulance turned up within minutes of my call. Five minutes later, Anne was on the way to Bishop's Lynn Hospital. I followed behind in my car. Ignoring the beckoning car park ticket machine, I ran into the Accident and Emergency entrance. The woman at the enquiry desk pointed to the examination room, where a weary looking nurse intercepted me. Anne was lying on a bed, where a doctor was prodding her.

Sister Nightingale asked if I was her husband, boyfriend or other relative. I told her that I wasn't any of them.

We were joined by the young doctor. He was more persuasive in his line of questioning. "Are you her partner?" He wasn't prepared to take no for an answer. "What is your relationship, then? I can see you are not her father." I explained to him that I hadn't known her for long, but felt responsible for her.

Sister Nightingale sniggered under her breath.

The doctor hadn't got time for me. It must have been a long night for him. He threw his clipboard onto the desk. "There's no point in your hanging about. Telephone later this afternoon to see how she is." I gave Anne a peck on the cheek, and promised I'd be back. She managed a wan smile. Her fingers moved weakly, mimicking a wave, before she closed her eyes.

I pushed her to the back of my mind. It wasn't callousness, just a fact of life. There were things to be done. I drove to Lovington church, and walked through the lych-gate to the church door. It was unlocked. I made my way inside, and couldn't provide a sensible reason why the church interior was the same as I had seen in my dream.

The Reverend Milner had insisted that I'd travelled through time. That didn't wash with me. Seeing the table by the door reminded me that the Reverend had given me a service sheet. I rummaged through my pockets. The search revealed nothing. Even so, I breathed a sigh of relief. Some peculiar things have happened these past days, but time travel isn't going to be one of them.

I looked at the spot where the Joseph Grodam gargoyle resided. An empty space greeted me. A further feeling of relief flirted with my emotions. I walked down to the altar rail and feasted my eyes on the stained glass window. It was a representation of Jesus with the little children. Carin wasn't one of the children sitting on the Saviour's knees.

I touched the altar. I've never been a regular churchgoer, but I was compelled to sink to my knees and hold my hands in the sign of prayer. I found myself asking the Christian God to help me in the days ahead. A feeling of hope radiated through my body as if the deity was answering my prayer. The emotion went, as quickly as it had appeared. I made my way to the graveyard. I already knew what I wouldn't find. Joseph Grodam and Kareem Milner were not in residence. I'd had enough. The dream had been a detailed fabrication of my subconscious, and nothing more.

I made my way back to the car with a spring in my step. After parking in the marketplace, it was a short walk to the teashop that I'd found yesterday. The same friendly old dear welcomed me. A steaming cup of coffee and buttered toast went down well. I ferreted in my pocket for some loose change to pay her. The motley collection of coins in my hand wouldn't have bought a postage stamp. I delved in my wallet for a bank note. A blue piece of paper fell onto the table. With a feeling of unease, I unfolded it. The black print spelt out the arrangements for the February services at All Saints' church. The date burned into my brain – nineteen ninety four.

Fright, confusion and bewilderment all laid siege to my senses. The coins fell to the floor and rolled in all directions. I was sweating like a pig, as I scrabbled on my hands and knees. My shaking fingers located the last coin. I sat down, and ordered another coffee.

I demanded a rational reason of my brain for the existence of this thirteen year old piece of paper. And I mean rational. There is a logical reason for everything, no matter how inexplicable it may seem. I found the answer, as a fifty-pence piece dropped, with a noisy clang, in my head. I let out a generous sigh of relief, and ignored the puzzled looks of the other customers. I'd found a commonsense explanation for the piece of paper, even though my words will prove me a liar. I haven't been completely honest with you. You will remember my telling you that I wasn't able to bring bits and pieces back from my dreams. I lied, but you won't get an apology. Would you honestly have believed me if I'd told you that I had managed to bring something back to the real world from my dream forays? Of course you wouldn't.

You deserve an explanation. In one of my childhood dreams, I was in a castle, dining with an old man. He wasn't unlike Father Christmas - all beard and bonhomie.

A giant Christmas tree decorated the hall, lit up by the huge fire that crackled in the grate. This colossus of a man pulled a wrapped present from the tree, and thrust it into my hands. His voice boomed with affection. "This is for you. I am very proud of you. Take this gift back to your own time."

I woke up, and looked for the present. There was no sign of it. Later in the day, I went to the chest of drawers for a clean pair of socks. Lying in the drawer was the wrapped package that the dream man had given me. With trembling fingers, I tore it open. Lying inside was a 'Rolex' wrist watch. I hid it away so that my mother and Mister Grodam wouldn't find it. I still wear it today. At the time I glossed over this minor miracle. My childish mind accepted that it was an addition to my dream techniques. That was the only time it happened, until I found the service sheet in my wallet.

As I sipped my coffee, I thought about Julius Milner's assertion that I was time travelling. His words didn't stand up in the light of day. They flew in the face of what I hadn't found in the church this morning. Where was the likeness of the murdered girl in the stained glass window, and the two graves? And what about the gargoyle that looked like Joseph Grodam?

I put the service sheet in my wallet, paid the bill, and strolled up the busy High Street to the Standard Bank. I joined the queue. A friendly young female smiled at me when I reached the counter. "Good morning sir. What can I do for you?"

She reminded me of the girl that I'd taken to the cinema. Looking at her blonde hair and blue eyes, I thought of several ways in which she could have been of assistance. Unfortunately they weren't part of her job description. I passed her the slip of paper that I'd found in the Reverend Milner's envelope. She read it, and input some details into her computer.

She passed the paper back to me. "Would you mind sitting outside the manager's office, over there?" Within seconds, the door opened. A man fitting my mental image of what a bank manager should look like invited me into his office. He was tall and thin, with a shiny, bald dome of a head. He peered at me through thick, black framed glasses. A smile creased his face as he shook my hand. He couldn't hide his delight. "Mister Milner? Good morning. I'm David Harcourt. It's a pleasure to meet you, at long last. Please take a seat."

I accepted his offer. The profuseness of his welcome intrigued me. "You're acting as if you expected me."

He smirked. "Indeed, I am. Indeed, I am." He squirmed in his chair. "I meant what I said. I am delighted to make your acquaintance. Your particular case has filled me with a feeling of expectancy, ever since I first heard of you, twelve months ago."

Where, oh where, had my cosy, organised life gone? This smug looking person had welcomed me like a long lost friend, acting as if something spectacular was about to happen. He'd better have a good explanation. If he had, it would be the first one, in many days.

He scratched at his bald dome and shrugged his thin shoulders. "In all honesty, Mister Milner, my feelings are completely confused."

At least we agreed on one thing. "Join the club. I'm here

because of the whim of a dead man. I'm hoping you can throw some light on what's going on?"

He rubbed his hands together. Composing himself, he opened a desk drawer. With all the aplomb of a magician, he produced a red folder. "Don't worry. All will be revealed. But, first things first. Have you some means of identification?" That annoying smirk appeared again. "A driving licence perhaps." He took his glasses off, then balanced them on the end of a bulbous nose. "I have to ensure that you are…" he studied the file… "Kitchener Milner."

I rummaged in my wallet, and handed him my driving licence.

"Thank you. I'll just check this with your specimen signature in my file."

"You've got my signature? That's impossible. Where did you get it from?" I got to my feet, and thumped on his desk. "I thought you said you were going to clarify things."

The fierce look on my face alarmed him. He got up, and edged towards the door. One change of heart later, he moved back, towards me. His hands placated me. "Please sit down, Mister Milner. I'm sorry to disagree with you, but I do have your signature in my file." He pulled a piece of paper from the folder, compared it with my driving licence, and snorted in a knowing manner. "It matches the signature on your driving licence. Mind you, it should do. It's a copy of your driving licence."

This was too much for me. "I don't believe you." My voice increased by several notches. "Let me see that piece of paper." The manager's body language shouted that I should calm down. He passed the paper to me. It *was* a copy of my driving licence. This latest twist in my life consigned me to a state of resigned silence. I passed the paper back to the manager, and slumped in my chair,

His face showed relief. "May I suggest that we start at the beginning?" He pushed his spectacles more securely onto his generous nose. "Twelve months ago, I was contacted by a firm of solicitors. They are acting on behalf of a Reverend Julius Milner. Does the name mean anything to you?" I nodded. His fingers drummed a rapid tattoo on the top of the desk. His ill-disguised excitement was getting the better of him. "The solicitors told us that Julius Milner had asked the bank to act as an intermediary between them and yourself. We were delighted to accommodate them. I received this file, which includes a copy of your signature…" He gave me an old-fashioned look … "no matter where that signature might have come from." He was growing bolder by the minute. "After all we have to ensure that you are who you say you are, do we not? The solicitors knew nothing about you, and what relationship, if any, you had to the deceased gentleman. Their client furnished none of this information. His solicitors were under strict instruction not to make direct contact with you. This would have presented them with a problem, because they have no idea where you live."

Mister Harcourt was getting into his stride. His dome sparkled with beads of sweat. "The Reverend assured them that he had no doubts that you would find me. Julius Milner even provided them with the exact time and date when you would call on me. We all hoped that the old boy wasn't off his rocker." He glanced at his watch. "He was of sound mind, because he got the timing of your visit spot on." He swelled with happiness. "You haven't let him down."

I wasn't stunned by what he said. Bizarre events were becoming commonplace. I'd given up the guessing game long ago. I somehow know that everything will be revealed one day. The manager glanced through the solicitor's letter. He put it down on the desk and rubbed his hands together.

"The letter reminds me that you should have a key. May I see it, please?"

I passed it to him. He referred to a document in the file. "The number on the key matches with the detail in the solicitor's letter. It fits one of our security boxes." He looked at another piece of paper. "The box has been registered in your name." He pushed his chair away, and stood up. "I am fully satisfied that you have a genuine claim on the estate of the late Julius Milner."

In an overstated movement he pressed a button nestling on the corner of his desk. The door opened, and a young man entered the room. "Mister Smith-Adams will take you to the security room." He handed the key to the young fellow, and shook my hand. "It's been a pleasure meeting you. If I can be of further assistance, let me know. I hope you find the answer to your dreams in the box."

Mister Smith-Adams took me in tow. Several passage ways later he halted in front of a metal door. With light-fingered precision, young Smith-Adams punched a number into the security pad. The door swung open, under his touch, and I was led into the room. The four walls were covered in banks of drawers.

He re-checked the number on my key, and strode across to one of the drawers. With a deft flourish of his wrist, he unlocked it. The metal drawer was withdrawn from its slot, and handed to me. The young man had the hallmarks of a future manager. "This is your box." He returned the key, and waved me towards a table and chair. "This key will open the box. What you do with the contents is up to you. All we ask is that you sign the security register, before you leave, as a record of your visit today. Take as long as you want. When you're ready to go, push the button at the side of the door. Someone will let you out."

The key fitted easily into the lock. I turned it, and gritted my teeth. The lid sprang back on its hinge, quivering in the air as if it was bowing to me. I looked inside. Two brown envelopes lay in the bottom. I took them out. Both were addressed to me in that spidery handwriting that I'd come to know. One envelope was bulky in size, the other a standard sized one. I opted to open the smaller one, if for no other reason than it was marked 'read this first'. It was sealed with wax. I broke the seal, and found two letters inside. They were marked 'read first', and 'read second'. I did as I was told, and opened the first letter:

> *'Dear Kit,*
>
> *I have instructed my solicitor to rent a security box at the Standard Bank, Lovington, knowing that you will be calling today. The rent has been paid for six more months.*
>
> *You still don't believe in time travel, do you? For goodness sake, wake up to reality. How did I know that you'd be here today, at this particular time? It wasn't guesswork! It's simple, man. I travelled through time to today. I saw you go into the bank, years before you knew you were coming.*
>
> *I'm not sure why I should be trying to convince you. When we met in February 1994, in what you think was your dream, I gave you a service sheet. You found that same sheet today. I saw it drop out of your wallet, in the tea shop, before you called at the bank. Today's date, in your time, is Monday 8th October 2007. Doesn't this reinforce my point?'*

The letter dropped from my fingers. A cold sweat covered my body, even though the room was as warm as toast. My self-assessed thought processes were totally destroyed. Did I really hold the key to travelling through time?

A shiver of excitement passed through me. I convinced myself to keep these thoughts on hold, until my brain was in a more receptive mode. I picked the letter up and read through the rest of its contents:

'You have that gift of moving through time, mark my words. Use it, for heaven's sake. It is vital to your quest. There is no difficulty involved. Concentrate on the date in time, and where you want to travel to. Forget about your dream spinning. Many of your so-called dreams were exercises in time travel. You've travelled through time so often without realizing it. Our Master used to be amused by your desire to bring things back from your journeys. He couldn't allow this, although he did relent once, and gave you a watch.

I can provide further proof to show that I am not lying. Take a look at the date of this letter. My solicitor has authenticated in my second letter, that what you are reading was handed to him on the 4th of April, two thousand and six. Both letters were sealed in the envelope in the presence of my solicitor. This will prove beyond doubt that no skulduggery is involved.'

I looked at the top of the letter. It *was* dated the 4th of April, two thousand and six. I tore the second envelope open. A letter, from his solicitor, of the same date, verified that he had watched the Reverend place both letters into an envelope, which had been sealed, and handed to the solicitor for safe keeping. I carried on reading his first letter:

'You've got to pay a price for these gifts. Power and wealth don't come for nothing. You must know that the mission involves an ancient wizard named Merlin. I found it impossible to help him. My conscience, and religious beliefs, were uppermost in coming to this decision. I'm not sure if you read your bible, but there is a passage in the book of Matthew which made my mind up for me. It goes like this: "No man can serve two masters for either he will hate the one, and love the other. Or else, he will hold to the one, and despise the other. Ye cannot serve God and mammon." I am a Christian clergyman, Kit, who serves only one master, my God.

I have to surrender the stones to you. You have the spirit, and you have the abilities. All you need is the personal resolve, and the will to get off your butt.

You will need to learn more of Merlin, and his hereafter. Only one person can help you – my daughter, Carin. I've never mentioned your name to her, so as far as she's concerned, you don't exist. Carin is essential to your mission. Find her. You can't make it without her.

We love each other as only a father and daughter can. I lost her for one moment in time but we were re-united.

There is another envelope in the box. There's enough money in it to pay for my davenport desk that you bought at auction. I never dreamed it would fetch two thousand two hundred pounds! It certainly wasn't worth that much! I'm glad you put one over that dreadful man Grodam.

There is enough money to cover the commission that you have to cough up to your late employer, with a bit left over.

All good wishes, Kit. We will bump into each other again even though I lie in my grave as you read this letter.

Your sincere friend, Julius Milner.

P S You were puzzled as to how the bank had your signature. It's quite simple, my boy. I visited you by the medium of time travel whilst you were at work one day. I borrowed your driving licence and made a copy. I'm sorry this caused you concern. The bank manager got quite worried at your behaviour today, didn't he?'

I read through the Reverend's letter three times. It was full of inexplicability. Julius Milner was dead and buried but he'd known that I'd found the service sheet in the teashop as well as about my visit to the bank. Either the reverend gentleman had the services of a good soothsayer, or he had harnessed time travel. It had taken a long time to sink in, but I was no longer prepared to allow coincidence and figments of my subliminal to be hung out as excuses for the unfathomable things. Even so, one factor refused to gel with me. Why hadn't today's visit to Lovington church conformed to my previous meeting with the Reverend Milner? And what about his dead daughter? According to his letter, she was alive; my brain-box soon came up with a plausible answer, but it would need checking out. The only way to solve this teaser didn't fill me with joy. It would entail visiting All Saints' church, on the day that his daughter had died.

The bulky envelope sat staring at me. I tore it open and

stifled a gasp. A profusion of fifty pound notes slid onto the table. Within minutes, three thousand pounds were stacked in a neat pile.

I locked the box, and stuffed the letters and cash into my coat pocket. The manager let me out when I rang the bell. With a self-satisfied look, he guided me back to the banking chamber, where I signed the security register. I shook his hand, and bade him goodbye.

I drove back to Brine and Cherry and made a bee-line for my flat. I rang the hospital. A pleasant lady told me that Anne was making good progress. I asked her to tell Anne that I would visit her later in the day.

Plumping up the cushions, I made myself comfortable on the settee, before testing the Reverend's premise on time travel. My icy calmness surprised me. I was on the verge of achieving the impossible, yet I felt as cool as a cucumber. Closing my eyes, I mentally repeated "All Saints' church", and the date of Carin Milner's death: "Tenth of December, nineteen ninety three. Tenth of December, nineteen ninety three."

I ceased the monotonous mantra. Something was happening. A current of air ruffled my hair. It caressed my face, and teased my moustache and beard. A breath of icy air blew gently into my ear. It kissed my cheek, and then it was gone. The wholesome sensation ended as quickly as it had begun. My nostrils twitched at the smell of wood smoke. I allowed my eyelids to open. I was standing in the churchyard, outside Lovington church. A light layer of snow covered the ground. I pulled my overcoat more tightly around me to shield me from the icy wind that moaned through the bare tree branches. On a cold day, a warm, comfortable feeling filtered through me. I had achieved the downright impossible. The Reverend

Milner had told the truth. What else should I have expected from a man of God?

I tucked my hands into my pockets, and ambled down the road towards the shops. I came across the Standard Bank, and walked in. Only a few hours ago, I'd passed through these doors, in another time warp. Behind the counter, where I had spoken to the girl who only provided banking services, and nothing else, stood a middle-aged man with a mass of curly hair. He wore thick, black rimmed glasses. The name plaque told me that he was David Harcourt. I smiled to myself. It was hard to repress the urge to arrange a meeting with him in thirteen years' time, when he was the manager.

A calendar, standing on the counter, brought me down to earth. The tenth of December, nineteen ninety three, stared at me. It jolted me into the unpleasant prospect that the Reverend's daughter was going to be murdered today. Time was on my side. The clock on the wall showed it was ten past two. I adjusted my watch. Carin wouldn't be at the church until half past four.

I wandered out of the bank. The High Street was bustling with shoppers. I checked out whether my favourite tea shop was in business. I shouldn't have worried. Tea and toast were served by a younger version of the lady who had so readily looked after my needs on previous visits.

She was charming, and considerate as ever. I asked if my friend Julius Milner was still the Rector of All Saints'. She carried on with the habit of patting her hair whenever his name was mentioned. "You're a fortunate young man to count him as a friend. Yes. He's still there, looking after his flock." She touched her locks again and walked away to serve another customer.

I relaxed with my tea and toast. Time trekking, not surprisingly, was foremost in my thoughts. The idea of

143

moving through time opened up a glut of ideas. Personal gain, for a start. A journey back in time, armed with details of the winning lottery numbers, on a roll-over week, would scoop the jackpot for me. In the wrong hands, it could spell disaster for the human race if past events were meddled with. With time travel as a weapon in your armoury, every murder, and every outrageous act that has ever taken place, could be changed. If one small detail was altered, for the wrong reason, the effect on future generations could be devastating. It didn't bear thinking about. On the other hand, time travel would resolve the most contentious issues in history. Imagine going back to the time of Moses, Abraham, Noah and Jesus.

Unwittingly, I'd meddled with history in the auction house car park. No serious harm had been done. That saga had thrown up one interesting factor. I was the only person who remembered how things were, before they changed. My feet were set in the fabled parallel worlds of time.

I took a sip of tea, and checked my watch. It was time to go. I needed to be in the church by four at the latest. The shop owner, an old, grey haired lady, took my money. I tipped the waitress, and wished her well. She was destined to enjoy the good life as the future owner of this desirable tea shop.

Ten minutes later, I was at the church. The lights were on inside. With an air of furtiveness, I opened the door, and slid inside. I looked around the church in a vain attempt to satisfy myself that no one was lurking in the shadows. I couldn't control my shivering. The temperature was nudging the bottom end of the thermometer. I had to hide somewhere. Behind the pulpit, to the left of the chancel steps, looked a likely place. I made myself as comfortable as the chilled stone floor would allow. Pulling the collar of my coat around my ears made no difference. A numbing cold crept into my bones.

Ten minutes passed. It seemed like an hour. The only noises breaking the wall of silence were the fluttering of bats, and the solitary vehicle passing by. The church door creaked in objection, as it was slowly opened. I craned my head, but couldn't see who'd come in. The door closed, declaring its ominous protest. Was it the killer, preparing himself for the girl's arrival?

The unknown person came into view. I wasn't surprised to see him. His presence supported my theory of what had happened since I'd last seen him in this church. He'd broken his God given promise. The Reverend Milner had already travelled through the pages of time to save his daughter's life. That's why I hadn't come across the 'Grodam' gargoyle, or the subtle change in the stained glass window, and why Carin Milner wasn't buried in the churchyard.

He didn't need my help. This was a re-run of something that had already happened. For a fleeting moment, I was tempted to stay and see what happened. I opted out, and closed my eyes to return to my own time. Sod's law came into play. I sneezed. Julius Milner came as near as possible to jumping out of his skin. "Who's there?"

I stood up. "Sorry to startle you, Reverend. It's me, Kit Milner."

He walked across. "What do you think you're doing? It puzzled me why I had been called back to the church this afternoon. I'm not pleased to see you. I've already saved my daughter. I wish you'd stayed at home." He tut-tutted. "You'd better not get in my way."

"Don't worry, I won't. I only came back to see why everything had changed since I was last here. I guessed you'd broken your pledge not to go back and save your daughter. Now I know the answer, I'll be on my way."

He put a hand over my mouth. "It's too late. My daughter's

here. Get your head down. You're the last person I want her to see." To say I was surprised, was an understatement. What was she doing here?

The church door creaked open, then closed with a firm push. A girl's voice rang out, "Are you there, Daddy?"

The Reverend Milner poked me in the chest and whispered. "Not a word from you." He called out to her. "I'm here, darling." He made his way to the main door. I caught sight of them, as they walked, arm in arm up the aisle. Her beauty hadn't been exaggerated. The structured loveliness of her young porcelain white face was outlined by a mass of auburn coloured hair. I couldn't see, but I would have bet my soul, with the devil, that she had green eyes. It wasn't a reckless bet. I'd already met this young lady. I lost my heart for a second time in as many days. The girl was a younger version of the lovely Anne Wood. Why had she changed her name? The two of them chatted happily, before they disappeared up the chancel steps. I heard a door slam shut. The rector hurried round the pulpit, and knelt down beside me.

"What was all that about?" I asked him.

The church door opened. "There's no time for explanations. This is Joseph Grodam coming in. Don't worry about the knife that he's carrying!"

Footsteps sounded down the south aisle. Joseph Grodam was the spitting image of a young Billy Grodam. His sallow features sported small piggy eyes. The weak chin was not helped by a wide gash of a mouth. Long greasy, black hair hung to his shoulders. His looks weren't helped by a bad case of acne. The youth suffered from spots sprouting on spots. He disappeared from sight, as he walked up the chancel steps. I peered around the pulpit. The young man made his way to the altar, and ducked down behind it. With Carin presumably sitting back home, in the rectory, I wondered how long he was prepared to wait. Not too long, I hoped. It was freezing cold, and we could all go home.

Julius Milner put his fist against my chin. "Wait here, and don't get in the way. I know what I have to do. He's going to get everything he deserves."

His frantic whispers scared the wits out of me. "What are you on about? You're letting him go home, aren't you? Your daughter's safe. That's what you wanted, isn't it?"

The look on his face concerned me. "The buck doesn't stop here. The Grodams won't give up, if I let him go. There will always be another day. I'm going to put a stop to the young man's antics. It will earn me some breathing space." He swallowed noisily. "I'm about to kill him. It's the only chance I'll have of freeing my family from a living hell."

I spluttered in disbelief. How could this mild-mannered man, servant of God, contemplate murdering a fellow human-being? What had happened to 'Thou shalt not kill'? I put my mouth to his ear, to remonstrate with him. He pushed me away. "Shut up. I killed him, the first time, and he didn't feel a thing."

I should have put my foot down. He didn't give me the chance. Julius Milner got to his feet, and strode up the chancel steps. "Come out from behind the altar, Joseph." He was coolness personified. "Carin won't be joining us, this time." Sarcasm took over. "What a shame. She has a prior engagement." He raised his voice. "Don't do anything silly with that knife. I have a gun, and I'm going to use it."

Priests are supposed to save souls, not create them. I took a quick look around the pulpit. He wasn't bluffing. The rector was holding a pistol. "Put the knife on top of the altar, Joseph. You won't be using it, unlike the last time you were here with my daughter."

The youth did as he was told. With structured fascination

I watched the scene unfolding before me. The boy was in no position to argue, with a gun pointing at him. His spotty face took on a look of total disbelief. It didn't take long for his composure to return. He cocked two fingers at the rector. His profound confidence showed in his cocky bravado. "You don't scare me, vicar." He laid his head back, and laughed. "Are you going to shoot me because I've come into your bleeding church? I thought you were supposed to get people to come here. Well here I am. Going to preach me a sermon, vicar?"

The rector was unimpressed. "Cut out the back-chat. Get over there in that corner. You're going to taste the same medicine that you handed out to my daughter."

A perplexed look crossed the youth's face. "What are you talking about, you wanker? I've done no stuff to your daughter. I might have shouted a few things at her in the street. But I never touched her."

The Reverend's voice carried a malicious edge. "Shut your rotten mouth. I've had more than my fill of you and your family. You don't deserve to live."

Joseph Grodam realised the threat he was facing. He dredged up a fleeting moment of courage. "You'd better let me go, or my dad will sort you out." He retreated from his cocksure stance, and whined. "Look Mister Milner. I'll be honest with you. I followed your daughter from school, and saw her go in the church. So what. It's no big deal. Nothing's happened, because she's not here."

Julius Milner was not impressed. The gun pointed unswervingly at the boy. "You wouldn't know honesty if it kicked you up the backside." He waved the gun in the air. "I will do anything that I have to, if it means putting an end to your capers."

I was affronted by the Reverend's behaviour. His daughter

148

was at home, completely unaware of what had happened in a previous time-span. This nonsense needed stopping before somebody got hurt. I got up, and stood at the chancel steps. "Hold on, Reverend. This isn't necessary. Put the gun down. Let's discuss things in a calm and rational way."

My words were a waste of time. He yelled at me, in a high pitched voice. "I told you not to interfere." He shook his head aggressively. "Did this scum allow my daughter to discuss things rationally? Stay where you are, and keep your nose out of my affairs. You shouldn't be here. I didn't ask you to come. If you feel upset, go back to where you belong." His face reddened, eyes protruding from their sockets. "He doesn't deserve to live. Any person who could inflict those indignities on my daughter deserves a bullet in the brain. I'm letting him off lightly. I don't intend to torture him, and I certainly won't bugger him."

Young Grodam was gob-smacked. "I never hurt your daughter." His voice took on a threatening tone. "If you don't let me go, I'm going to tell the police."

The rector shook his head. "You wouldn't understand, Joseph, even if I tried to explain things to you."

Julius nodded towards a marble memorial slab set in the chancel floor. "Move over to that slab, Joseph."

Grodam did as he was told. The rector swiped him across the head with the gun. The young man slumped to the floor. I was furious. "What are you doing? Let's put a stop to this."

He looked at me. It wasn't a pleasant sight. "I've made my position clear. I won't tell you again. Back off."

I pleaded with him. "But there's no need to kill him. You're a man of the cloth. It's against your beliefs," I blustered. "If you kill him, what are you going to do with the body? The police will track you down, and put you away for the rest of your life. You can forget spending quality time with your family."

He snapped at me. "It's me that's got to live with my actions. Nobody will find his body. I'm going to shoot him, and hide his body under that stone slab."

"And how are you going to lift it? Don't ask me to help you."

His words were scathing. "You're not the only one with powers. Watch carefully, while the master gets to work." He extended his arms toward the slab and muttered some words under his breath. The effect was staggering. The marble slab raised itself off the floor, and pivoted open, until it stood on its end at a ninety degree angle. The rector leered at me, and Joseph couldn't believe his eyes. "That's how it is done. Joseph is now going to climb into the hole, before I shoot him. Nobody will smell his decomposing body. There's an airtight seal, once the stone is in place." He kicked the youth. "I didn't hit you that hard. Get up."

Grodam panicked, and shook his head. "I'm not going in there. You can get stuffed."

In situations of grave danger, cowards as well as brave men have been known to take on the cloak of courage. Joseph was no exception. The young man was about to display some form of singular valour, at a time when his chips were well and truly down. With malicious calmness, he kicked the rector in the shin. Julius let out a cry, and slumped to the ground. The gun slipped from his fingers. The young man's reaction was quicker than the older man's response. He swooped on the weapon, and snuggled it into his right hand. The look on his face reminded me of Billy Grodam. They shared the same knack of showing the unspoken look of cruelty, before inflicting misery on people. We were going to suffer the ultimate price for daring to threaten the bully with his own brand of intimidation. I hoped the Merlin stones were as good as they were made out to be.

"Stay where you are, you silly old sod. I don't know what you're going on about, but you can spin on my finger. You're right, though. I would have given your daughter a good going over, if she'd turned up. I might even have got rid of her. It'll be your missus next." He chuckled. "Lucky old me. I didn't expect to find you here. You've got a bag of stones that my dad wants." He pulled his shoulders back, and poked Julius in the groin with his foot. He grinned at the Reverend's agonising cries. "Where are the stones, you twat?" The little sod swiped Julius across the head with the gun. The rector grunted. A trickle of blood ran down his face. "What's it going to be then, vicar? The stones or a bullet?" The youth turned to me. "Come up here, where I can keep my eyes on you." The lad spoke in an assured manner, well beyond his tender years. His fine-tuned cruel streak was working to our disadvantage. I stood by the rector. The little sod stuffed his foot into the rector's midriff. "For the last time, where are the bloody stones?"

The rector's words entwined with the pain he was feeling. "I have to disappoint you. I don't have the stones with me. They're in my desk, back at the rectory. Search me, if you want to. You won't find them."

I couldn't believe my ears. The number of times he'd impressed on me the need to wear the stones. Yet he was slumped on the church floor, with a gun pointed at his head, and the stones were lying in state at the rectory.

Young Grodam wasn't amused. "I don't believe you." He pressed the gun into my stomach. "Move over there, while I search him. Don't try anything. The gun will be aimed at his heart." I did as I was told. Grodam made a frantic, fruitless search of the rector's clothing. He went spare. "I've had enough of this. You're both dead men." His tongue licked his lips. A grin covered the spotty face. He looked as if he'd thought of something particularly nauseating. "After I shoot you, I'll call in at the rectory." The grin vanished. "I'll kill your wife and daughter nice and slowly…" The stupid look came back "…but only after they've enjoyed a shafting. I'll make them take their clothes off, then tie them up. It's not much fun when they struggle. I've never shagged an older woman. Thanks for telling me where the stones are, vicar."

The rector wiped blood from his mouth. "Wait a minute, Joseph. There's no need to harm my family. Let me go and get the stones for you. My friend will stay here as a hostage." He gave me a knowing look. "I'm sorry Kit. I didn't bring my stones with me. At least yours will protect you."

Joseph cocked his ears. I shook my head in disbelief at what the Reverend had said. Perhaps the pain had addled his brains. Otherwise, I would have sworn that he had deliberately dropped me in it. My words were laced with lashings of derision. "I appreciate your thought of leaving me as a hostage. That's a first class idea. Your timing is impeccable. Thanks for letting him know about my stones. I was on the point of telling him myself."

That humourless grin covered the boy's face. "That's interesting, vicar. So your mate has got some stones, has he?" His insolent attitude resurfaced. He kicked Julius in the stomach, and stuffed the gun in my face. "Give them to me, or you're a dead man."

The poor bugger had no idea what he was about to spark off. In the next few minutes, I became a convert to the firm belief that the power to control and change life lay within me. A sense of latent perception seeped into my brain. It willed me to counter my innate feelings of frustration. A candlestick standing on the altar came into focus. My mind slipped into gear. A single, consuming thought converged on the candlestick. The outcome was terrifying. It took on a life of its own, as it stirred from the altar's surface. The candlestick hovered with purposeful meaning, before turning in the air to a horizontal position. The base was pointed at the youth. I barely saw the candlestick as it hurtled towards him. It caught him a sickening blow on the side of his head. He staggered across the floor, the gun still clutched in his hand.

I wasn't finished with him. Whatever was working me pointed my hand at the gun. A vivid flash of white light spewed from the tip of my forefinger. It struck Grodam's wrist. The youth's hand dropped to the floor. The fingers of the dismembered hand slowly unfolded and let go of the weapon. I stared at my finger, trying to come to terms with the devastating power that had been fashioned from my flesh and blood.

Joseph Grodam sank to his knees He stared in disbelief at the hand, which lay twitching on the floor. The ray had created a temperature of such intensity that the stump was cauterised. There was no trace of blood, only a lingering smell of scorched flesh. He raised his useless stump, and stared at it. He eyeballed me and shouted profane words. "What the… You're going to pay for this, you bastard." Courage streamed back to him. He reached for the gun with his good hand, and pointed it at me.

Lightning isn't supposed to strike in the same place twice. Take my word for it, it does. My hand moved. The same finger lined up Grodam's body. A violent bolt of blue light leapt from my digit, totally engulfing his body. I could feel the heat from where I stood. From the screams of agony which forced their way out of his throat, the pain was excruciating. His clothes burned and the ashes dropped to the ground. He dashed past me and ran down the south aisle.

The outline of his burning, naked body diminished in size. His head vanished, then his torso. The only part remaining, as he reached the south door, was his legs. They evaporated in one final flash of bright blue light. Then there was nothing. The only testimony that Joseph Grodam had ever been in the church was the nauseating stench of burned flesh.

I hurried to the church door, expecting to find scorched body parts littering the medieval tiles. There was nothing. No scraps of flesh. No blood, no clothing, No gun. No mess. No nothing. The flash of light had vaporised him into oblivion. Joseph was dead for the third time in his life.

I made my way back to the altar. Julius Milner was on his knees wiping blood from his head. "Are you alright, Reverend?"

He waved a hand and managed a smile. "Don't worry about me. Grodam got what he deserved, seeing what he did to Carin, the first time round." There was no compassion in his words.

The full impact of the youth's death came home to roost. I'd killed a fellow human being. Correction. A mysterious, unknown force had used me to kill a fellow human being. Whether or not the youth deserved to die was beside the point. It was me who had killed him. Not the rector, nor an act of God. It made me feel only slightly better to think that I'd saved Julius, and his wife, as well as Carin. If the rector had handled things differently none of this would have been necessary.

I led Julius to one of the pews. He shook my hand. "You saved my life. I'm not sure what else I can say in the circumstances. Just forget that it happened."

I was flabbergasted. "For someone whose job description is man of God, you're taking this very calmly. Don't thank

154

me. I didn't consciously save your life. How was I to know that I've acquired the knack of dispensing death from my fingertips? I get the feeling that you've been controlling everything I do, ever since that evening in the car park. What about that light that sent Grodam to kingdom-come? You showed no surprise; did you control that, as well?"

He pulled a face. "No, I wish I could. That was down to you. That bolt of lightning is another of your latent talents, so that you know what you're capable of. No, I'm not controlling you, only guiding you. You're in command of yourself. There are many more powers yet to be revealed." He shook his head in admiration. "You are singular, Kit. You have something that no other human being shares. Don't worry about it. You'll learn."

His cool indifference flummoxed me. "So. Can I throw the stones away, and forget about this mission?"

"You can't opt out. You're the end of the line. Merlin has need of you. A word of warning, though. You must accept the beliefs and creed that will be demanded of you. If you refuse, then even the stones won't save you." He flapped his hand, and spoke in a matter of fact way. "Don't concern yourself about your powers. You began to find your natural abilities when that car tried to run you down. That incident introduced you to time travel." He laughed. "You shouldn't have worried about your injuries. Even if you had not time-travelled that evening, your injuries would have healed themselves, including a new set of teeth. Don't feel badly about the young man. Just forget him. One of your natural talents came to our rescue. End of story"

A surge of anger swept through me at his offhand attitude. "How can you talk in such a detached manner, and glibly tell me not to worry about killing a human being? Am I missing something? I nearly soiled my underpants when that light ripped from my fingers. You're acting as if that boy's murder is an everyday event. I couldn't believe it when you told him that I'd got a set of stones. I thought you'd dropped me in the mire on purpose. I'll give you the benefit of the doubt. I'm really happy for your daughter, but I've had enough of this. I'm off."

He grabbed me by the arm. "Just a minute. I have something to tell you, which will change your mind about me. Sit down Kit. Hear me out." He looked at me, pangs of uncertainty etched across his face.

I relented. "Your words had better be good. I'm going to need a lot of convincing."

His voice became hard. "It's all your fault. You shouldn't be here. I saved Carin, the first time, by shooting him and hiding his body under that slab. It was clean and clinical. Today's nonsense happened because you decided to stick your nose in. Don't you dare blame me for what happened. It's down to you that the youth was obliterated by your killing ray." The Reverend wasn't happy. "And stop going on about how cool and calm I am. There's a reason for everything. You'll learn." Then, as quickly as he had blown his fuse, he calmed down. He smiled at me. "I'm puzzled, Kit. I've kept meticulous notes of everything that happened to me and my family since the stones came into my life. I left instructions with my solicitor that those notes should pass to you on my death. Didn't you get them, when you called in at the bank? My notes included an account of how I resurrected Carin. You needn't have turned up, if you'd bothered to read them."

The rector had clothed me in a garment of guilt. My apology was grudging. "I'm sorry for gumming up the works, but I've never seen your so-called notes. How was I to know what you'd done?"

An irascible noise passed his lips. "Your apologies aren't

necessary. I've been a bit hard on you. It took courage to come here. You were only trying to put a dreadful matter right. For some reason, my solicitor didn't pass my papers to you. Never mind. You asked the question, so I'll tell you why I seem so calm about the youth's death."

He crossed his legs and settled back. "A few weeks ago, I went back in time, and witnessed what happened to my daughter in this church. I don't know why Carin went into the church, but I saw Grodam follow her in. What he did to my daughter brought on a manic hatred for that young man. It doesn't come easy to break my vows, in planning to kill someone. I'm not endowed with natural courage, neither am I easily filled with hatred for my fellow man. That's why I went back to the church. I had to hate him enough to kill him."

"Am I hearing you right? All you managed to achieve was self-inflicted torture."

The Reverend gentleman flew at me. "It's all very well for you. You've been handed the cloak of courage, with the added advantage of a mentor who is prepared to throw a lifeline to you every time you get into a scrape. Don't you dare judge my motives. You weren't in the church to see what that low-life did to my daughter." He laughed, in a demented way. "There is a way of showing you what she went through. You can see for yourself what Grodam did to her. It will mean tapping into another of your talents." I must have looked startled.

"Don't worry. It's simple, and it won't hurt. You're going to bond with my memory cells. Put your hands around the top of my head, and concentrate on my mind. Close your eyes and you will see the images that are stored there. Think about what happened in this church, on the day that Grodam murdered my daughter."

157

I did as he asked. It was so simple to key into what I was looking for. A sequence of moving pictures paraded themselves in my mind's eye. I was repulsed at the image of Joseph Grodam staring at Carin Milner's naked body. She lay on the altar, her life blood flowing into the altar cloth and dripping onto the floor. He moved across to her, and slobbered at the blood flowing from the gaping wound in her neck. Then he walked across to the choir stalls, and carried a chair back to the altar in his gloved hands. He used it to clamber onto the altar. Without a care in the world, he took his gloves off, dropped his trousers, and wrapped a condom onto his stiff manhood. He straddled Carin's body and moaned as he satisfied himself. He hummed a tune while he wiped himself on one of Carin's discarded socks, before pulling his trousers up. He slid the sock into his trouser pocket, and put his gloves back on. As if he hadn't degraded her body enough, he picked up a candle, and rammed it up her backside. Still humming that inane tune, he made his way out of the church.

I couldn't find the right words to describe my feelings. One thing I was sure of, I was bloody glad that the toe-rag was dead. I removed my hands from the rector's head. "I've seen enough. I'm sorry for the doubts that I had. I'm glad we killed the little sod."

He patted me on the shoulder. "It's a pity things turned out this way, Kit. It wasn't pretty was it? All you've accomplished by being here is to rework what I had already done, albeit in a different way." He cocked his head on one side and pulled a face at me. "That aside, thank God you were here."

He let out a sigh of relief. "My daughter lives on to enjoy her life. She and Meg have no recollection of the cards that life originally dealt them." He allowed himself a smile. "The Grodams will suspect it was me who killed their son. They've moved away from Lovington. I'm not naïve enough to think that I've seen the last of them." He wiped at his eyes. "What happened to that young man is only a part of a larger canvas. You're only a smudge of the artist's brush. Don't condemn yourself. Blame the divinity of Merlin. Before we leave, I can reveal another gift that you possess. You are going to have need of it, soon. You can live in a person's body and take command of their brain. The knack is simplicity itself. Focus your thoughts on entering their body. The stones will do the rest."

"You're way ahead of me. What do you know, that I don't?"

"You'll find out. Leave it at that."

"How do I get out of the body?"

"Concentrate on leaving. Most of your gifts only require a thought wave to enact them!"

"What was that business about earlier on, with your daughter? When she gets home, won't she meet the present day rector?"

"I was forced to meet my younger self, a few days before Carin was killed, to tell him what was going to happen today. We agreed that I would be in church to get her out of Grodam's way. I let her out of the altar door, on the pretext that I wanted something from the local shop, which happens to be on that side of the churchyard. The younger me cancelled his trip to Ely cathedral today, and met her when she came out of the shop, and took her home."

"Things aren't making sense. You saw your younger self, in the past, so why didn't I meet myself in the auction car park, when I went back in time?"

He scratched his head. "Because you're different. Whenever you travel to the future, or the past, you can never meet up with yourself." He looked perplexed. "I can't explain what I mean, in simple terms. Let's just say that, because of who you are, and what you represent, you only forge one path through life, that leaves no shadow of yourself behind. Leave it at that my boy. One day you will understand what I am putting so inadequately."

He checked his watch. "We've been here too long. I always lock up about this time of day. Let's go before Reverend Milner arrives. We'd better clear up what's left of Grodam." He sniffed at the air. "At least the smell has gone."

We hurried to the chancel. The Reverend bent down to retrieve the hand, but had a hasty change of heart. "Would you do the honours, whilst I sweep up the charred clothing?"

I picked the limb up. It felt warm to the touch. I threw the hand into the recess. The slab closed of its own accord. We left the church, only pausing inside the porch whilst he checked that the coast was clear. We skirted through the graveyard, and made our way to the back gate.

I had one last question to ask of him. "Does the name Anne Wood mean anything to you?"

His shoulders moved in silent mirth. "It should do. It's my wife's maiden name. She was born Anne, but I call her Meg. I have this inclination to change people's names. Why do you ask?"

"No particular reason." I sidetracked him. "When I meet up with your daughter, does she know about the stones, and their special powers?"

The digression worked. "She's wearing one of the stones now. I wasn't having a recurrence of what happened to her." That explained why there were only three stones in my bag. "She doesn't realize what the stones are all about, and she knows nothing of you. I'll tell her about the stones when she's older. Goodbye, Kit. Our paths will cross again. In the meantime, I intend to enjoy my life with Meg, and take pleasure in seeing my daughter grow into adulthood. Watch your back for the Grodams."

With one last smile, he vanished. I took a last look at the church, before returning to my own time. The wind blew around my face for a few moments, and I travelled down a tunnel of light, to find myself in my flat.

The realization that I commanded time prompted me to pursue another avenue in my life. I had lost my mother's love but it still hurt me to think of the way she had died. If the rector could resurrect his daughter, then why shouldn't I bring my mother back to life? I closed my eyes, and willed myself back in time. A feeling of frustration enveloped me. Nothing happened. I tried again, with the same result. I gave up the idea, in the belief that I needed to learn more about the technique of time travel.

A lot has happened in the last few hours. Most of it is double-dutch to me, but some of the wrinkles of the past few weeks have been ironed out. There is a plus factor. I don't need to take the trouble of tracking Carin Milner down.

When I look back to that day, I have to smile at how little I really knew. My initial revulsion at the death of the young man was premature, as was my lack of understanding of what I was capable of. Worse was to come. My learning curve was only just beginning.

CHAPTER THIRTEEN

Monday and Tuesday, 8th and 9th October 2007.

THERE'S NO PEACE FOR THE wicked. The phone rang. "Hello, Kit. How are you?" It was Billy Grodam. I registered no hint of surprise. I felt a little sorry for him. I'd just killed his twin brother. I humoured him. "What can I do for you, Billy?"

He tried to sound like a kid brother, but came over as an evil, odious slob. "You've got something that I want. I'm willing to pay for it."

"Didn't you find what you were looking for in the desk you stole? I've got to cough up the money for it. I want it back."

Grodam coughed. "No can do. We had to dismantle it slightly. Tell you what. Give me the stones, and you'll be richer by ten thousand pounds. That's enough to pay for the desk, with some spending money left over." His new-found familiarity annoyed me. Why was I holding a conversation with this scumbag? The vision of the smashed davenport desk didn't fill me with any geniality towards him. "Get stuffed, fat man."

There was a splutter at the other end of the line. "You've just made the biggest mistake of your life, Milner. You're dead meat. There is a way of getting those stones from you. You'll be hearing from me, you bastard."

I lowered myself to his level. "Bollocks. These stones protect me from bullying little toe-rags like you." I spiced up the verbals. "Do you ever think of Joseph? Pity about what happened to him. Watch your own back, Grodam. Your

162

hoodlums won't always be around, unless they wipe your arse, and sleep in the same bed as you."

He had trouble finding the right words. "What do you know about my brother? That was years ago." He laughed. "We nearly got the girl, last night. If that prat hadn't tried to shaft her, I might have got her stone. Think about it Milner. There's more than one way of skinning a cat."

"You won't get near her, Grodam. I'm protecting her." The contemptuous side in me came to the fore. "Talking about skinning a cat, how's the wig? Next time I bump into you, I'll set fire to the bloody thing."

Grodam slammed the phone down. He left me a worried man. It was his thugs who had been after the girl's stone. How had he known that she'd got one? I put Grodam out of my mind. I had promised to visit Anne. Before doing so, I counted out two thousand two hundred pounds plus another two hundred and seventy five from the envelope to cover Martin's commission. I tucked the rest of the money into my wallet.

Martin's car was parked outside. I barged into his office. He was at his desk, dictating a letter to his secretary. He looked up and scowled at me. "Thanks for knocking. Didn't expect you until Saturday. What do you want?"

"My client has coughed up the money." I threw the notes onto his desk. "Put a receipt through my letterbox, when you're ready."

He counted the money twice. The cheeky sod even compared some of the numbers, to satisfy himself that they were real. With shaking hands he tidied them into a neat pile. Martin's whole body language changed. His enigmatic smile would have done credit to the 'Mona Lisa'. He waved his secretary out of the office. "Look Kit, I acted in haste." It

163

came out as a grudging, patronising attempt at an apology. "How about coming back?"

He extended his hand, believing he'd made me an offer I couldn't refuse. I shook the proffered hand. "Sorry. No way. I'll be vacating the flat, as arranged. Goodbye, Martin."

I left his office, with more important things on my mind. A beautiful woman was lying in a hospital bed. If I was to believe her father, she held some of the answers about Merlin. There was also Grodam. One slip on my part, and I could be joining the ranks of the deceased. Two slips on my part, and Anne would be lying in the same hole.

I parked the car in the hospital grounds and made my way to the enquiry desk. A nurse directed me to Anne's ward. I pushed the door open. Her eyes lit up when she saw me. "Kit. Thanks for coming." Her hands clutched at mine, and squeezed them. "I've missed you."

I allowed myself to wallow in the depths of her welcome. Was I being gullible, or did I detect tenderness in the way she stroked my hand? I planted a gentle kiss on her cheek. She didn't object. "What has the doctor got to say?"

She carried on stroking the back of my hand with her thumb. "There's no physical injury. I need a few days' rest. I'm feeling better, already. They want to keep me in for one more night." Her face lit up. "I can go home tomorrow. Will you pick me up?"

The look on my face telegraphed the answer. "Of course I will, someone's got to look after you. I'm even prepared to provide some tender, loving care."

My directness surprised me. She blushed, and lowered her eyes. "That's great, so long as you don't spoil me too much." It was a simple banal conversation, but I was happy to flounder in the intoxication of the moment. Our cosy chatting came to an abrupt end when a nurse reminded me that visiting time had ended twenty minutes ago.

I got up to leave. Anne pulled me towards her, and kissed me on the lips. "That's for being so caring."

I returned her kiss. "I'll give the hospital a ring tomorrow morning to see when I can pick you up." I floated away from her bed. She called me back. "Would you bring a change of clothing for me? Any trousers, a top, a pair of shoes and a warm coat. Everything's in my bedroom wardrobe. You'll need the security code to get into the building." I wrote the number down. She lowered her voice. "There's a key hidden under the mat by the front door of my flat."

I unlocked Anne's pad. The smell of her perfume lingered in the bedroom. I raided her bedroom for the things that she'd asked for. On an impulse, I thought she might need a change of underwear. I opened a chest of drawers, and struck lucky. Hardly daring to touch them, I removed a pair of flimsy panties. Something else caught my eye. Peeping out from beneath her underwear was a yellow folder. I couldn't resist picking it up, when I recognised Julius Milner's spidery writing. Something was written in the top right hand corner: 'Strictly Private and Confidential. Only to be opened by my solicitor, after my death.'

The folder answered two things. Anne and Carin were one and the same and I knew why Julius Milner's notes hadn't reached me. I opened the folder. It was empty. I put it back in the drawer.

I made my way to Linmere. It was just after nine when I drove into the auction house premises. Martin's car was parked outside his office. He was working late, even by his standards. After a nightcap I made myself comfortable on the settee. The feel of Anne's lips lingered on mine as I fell asleep.

There's no telling where my dreams might have taken me. I wasn't given the chance. One minute I was sleeping, the next moment my smarting eyes were forced open. Smoke filled the lounge, and I heard a sinister roaring sound coming from behind the closed lounge door. The staircase was burning. That presented a problem. It was the only way out. My one chance of escape was by jumping out of a window. The prospect of falling twenty feet didn't appeal to me. I made my way to the bedroom and opened the window. The fresh air ventilated my muddled brain. A long submerged thought emerged, asking why the need to jump? I scrambled onto the windowsill, and stepped out into the night air. It's impossible to put into words the feeling of elation that plucked at my senses as a latent power floated me gently down to the ground. I was just in time to see two figures running past Martin's office. A car started up, and squealed away. The building was well ablaze, if the roar of flames and the sound of splintering glass were anything to go by. The strident sounds of a fire engine clamoured in the distance.

It smacked of Grodam's doing. I didn't hang around. I went back in time to find out who had started the fire. I materialized, at a quarter past nine, on the far side of the car park. It was comforting to see that the flat wasn't on fire. It was wait and see time. I wondered how Grodam hoped to get his hands on the stones by starting a fire. He wasn't to know that the stones never left my body. Perhaps it was out of spite.

An hour passed, and nothing happened. Not only was I getting colder, but I wondered if my dishonourable thoughts of Grodam were a figment of an over-active mind. I muttered under my breath, out of sheer boredom: "Gentlemen. This year's Nobel Prize winner, for the most active imagination in the world, is…Kit Milner, from the Ministry of Dream

Spinning. The prize of fifty thousand pounds will be presented to him by Father Christmas, a figment of somebody else's imagination."

The imaginary applause rang in my ears, followed by a real life sound. It wasn't a figment of anyone's imagination. The sound of two voices carried through the air. Alfie and Reggie Grodam scurried toward the flat and sidled up to the front door. Reggie was carrying a can. He put a finger to his lips. Using his own version of sign language, he pointed to the can, opened the letter box, and started to pour petrol through it. I sneaked up on them. "Good evening, gents. Do you need my help, or can you manage to set fire to my flat on your own? I've got a box of matches, in case you've forgotten to bring some with you."

They gaped at me. Reggie came to life. "Well, well, look who it is. It's Milner, and he's on his own." Alfie sniggered. "It will save us firing his flat. Give him a dose of the gas."

They each pulled a canister from their pockets. I pointed a hand at them. A pink coloured light poured from my fingertips. It played over them, with a muted, crackling sound. They were unconscious before they hit the deck.

I picked the canisters up. It was CS gas. Grodam obviously had friends in the police force. I put them in my overcoat pockets. Reggie was unconscious, but he was going to spill the beans to me. I put my hands on his head and flipped through his memory files. The two of them had followed me from the hospital. I detected a phonecall from Grodam. He was telling Reggie to set my place on fire, after which he was to ring him back, so that Billy could alert his contact in the Fire Brigade. He hoped that his contact might find the stones. The next mind picture sickened me. I chased across to Martin's office. He was lying on the floor, in a pool of blood. I knew that he was dead. I'd seen Reggie cutting Martin's throat as I read his thoughts. What a silly bugger Martin was. Fancy choosing tonight, of all nights, to work late. How could I leave him in this state? I willed myself back to ten fifteen, and tiptoed across the gravel to Martin's office window. He was working at his desk. I hid in the shadows. It wasn't long before a car drove slowly down the road, and stopped. The car doors clicked shut, and the Grodam twosome sneaked towards me. They didn't know what hit them as I zapped them with the pink beam.

I put my hands on Alfie's head, and planted my orders in his mind. He would do whatever Reggie told him, and wouldn't recall visiting the auction house. I shut his thinking processes down. Dealing with Reggie was easier. I made myself comfortable in his body. It was an uncanny feeling, being a part of someone else. I touched the pouch around my neck, and felt the keys in my pocket. In my inert state, my personal effects and my clothing had also materialised inside Reggie's body.

His brain became my refuge. Every thought and all the secrets stored in his memory, were implanted in my grey matter. Whether Reggie liked it or not, he was reduced to the role of a robot, with me in the driving seat. He was incapable of thinking for himself. I was manipulating his brain and his limbs. The element of surprise at my array of abilities had long deserted me. I'd become prone to taking things in my stride.

The two goons didn't know, but they were about to satisfy my Grodam hate complex. He'd done his best to blight my life at the auction and it hadn't stopped since. Martin should have been a dead man, my flat burned out, and Anne raped. I'd had enough. Reggie's memory banks told me that Grodam lived an hour away. I ordered him to drive there. Three quarters of an hour later, we pulled into a lay-by. I got Reggie to ring

Grodam on his mobile phone.

Billy answered. He wasn't a happy bunny. "It's about time you rang. Have you fired Milner's place? I want to get the Fire Brigade down there."

I put my thoughts into Reggie's mouth. "No, boss. Things haven't worked out as planned. Milner must have seen us following him, and he's just pulled into a police station. What do you want us to do?"

"You bloody idiot. Can't I trust anyone to get things done? I don't want the police involved. Get back here, you twat. Make sure Milner doesn't follow you."

The line went dead. I put Reggie's phone away, and dialled Grodam's number on my own mobile. He sounded peeved. "Hello, who's that?"

"Evening William. Thought I'd give you a bell."

He swore at me. "Where did you get my number from? Listen to me…"

I interrupted him. "From the Fine Arts bidding records. Never mind about that. Listen, toe-rag. Your goons have been following me since I left the hospital. I called in at a police station, but your gorillas have buggered off. I don't know what your game is, but I've had enough of your antics. I know where you live. It's time I called on you."

Grodam laughed. "If you manage to get by my guards, come and join me for tea. I'll even provide biscuits." He paused. "You don't stand a chance. The stones might stop a bullet, but there are other ways of getting them." He sniggered. "Do you want to be buried, or do you prefer a cremation?"

He slammed the telephone down. It was the reaction that I'd expected. He felt safe and secure surrounded by his gorillas, lapping up to him in their asinine manner. His cocky attitude made me more determined to present my visiting card.

I ordered Reggie to finish the journey. We were soon driving down a tree-lined road, where the street lamps struggled to reveal the outline of the houses in their meagre light. The smell of wealth wafted through my nostrils. I counted six plush residences, each standing in acres of open space. Sandwiched between two of them was a small cemetery. I wondered how many of Grodam's victims had been laid to rest there, unbeknown to the vicar and the parochial church council.

Five of the houses stood in darkness. The other, next to the cemetery, was ablaze with light. We drew up outside. I made out the name plaque. Madrog House. Grodam lived here. We walked up the drive, where we were welcomed with grunts from the dozen or so minders standing in front of the house. The front door opened, and another gorilla walked out. He growled at us. "Listen you lot, the boss has had a phone call from Milner. We're going to surround the house, and catch him when he turns up. The wanker won't be here, just yet, but Billy's taking no chances. There's no telling what Milner's capable of. Billy doesn't want him hurt, too much. When you see him, spray him with this gas. There's a canister for everybody." He chuckled. "Billy borrowed them from a policeman friend." We all laughed. "The gas will put him out of action and stop him from yelling commands, or pointing his fingers at us. That's what Billy told me. I don't know what the hell he's on about, but that's the way he wants it done. Once you've gassed Milner, gag him, and tie his hands behind his back. Now, listen. This is important. There should be a pouch round Milner's neck." This puzzled me. How did Billy Grodam, and for that matter, Joseph Grodam, know that the stones were in a pouch? The gorilla carried on, "Cut it away, as soon as you've disabled him, and hang on to it.

Don't look inside, or you're for the chop. It sounds like a load of bollocks, but that's the way you are going to play it, or else. When you've got him, bring him to me, with the pouch, so I can take him to the boss. There's a thousand pounds for the man who catches the twat and gets his hands on the pouch."

The gorilla barked out more orders. "Out you go, then, boys. Cover the boundary and the grounds. Four of you position yourselves in the road. But stay out of sight. And no lights, or smoking. Remember what Billy said. It's important. You can hit him after you've gassed him but your first job is to get your hands on that poxy pouch. You stay in the porch, Wayne, and put that bloody cigarette out. Come on, the rest of you. Don't just stand there. Get out and find Milner."

Alfie and I started to move. The thug called us back. "Not you, Reggie. The boss wants a word with you." He disappeared into the darkness. I opened the front door and walked into a large hall. My shoes trod across a monstrous floral carpet. Reggie stopped in front of a door. A feeling of trepidation arced through his body. His heart was beating like mad. He knocked on the door. Grodam shouted at him to come in. Reggie swung the door open. A huge desk and swivel chair dominated the room.

Two of the walls were covered in bookshelves. The presence of the books didn't subsist happily with a low-life like Grodam. Billy lounged on a groaning double settee, his grotesque body bathed in the light of a standard lamp. His ill-judged attempt at casual clothing ran to a pair of baggy trousers and an oversized jumper, while a pair of slippers struggled to hide his huge feet. The black cat was asleep on his head. A foul smelling cigar hung from his lips.

Grodam looked up, piggy eyes set in that flat, ugly face. His words slurred through the hare-lip. "You're a waste of space. Have I got to start doing the dirty work, myself? At least things would get done. What have you got to say for yourself?" He waited for a response that didn't come. "Have you lost your bloody tongue?"

My loathing towards him spilled over. I put words in Reggie's mouth. "If you want Milner, and his stones, so badly, then sod off outside you fat bastard, and get them yourself."

The cigar shot out of Grodam's mouth. He spluttered in disbelief. He struggled to his feet. The settee let out a sigh of relief. "You little shit. Nobody speaks to me like that."

Grodam waddled across to Reggie and hit him in the stomach. He passed wind, from the exertion. Reggie grunted, but I willed him to stand his ground. I exploded Reggie's fist into Grodam's face. His body collided with the desk, pushing it against the wall. He slid to the floor in an untidy, bleeding heap, out for the count.

I told Reggie to get his gun out. I pointed it at Grodam, and fed Reggie an order. His finger tightened on the trigger. The bullet never left the gun. An intense gust of wind gushed through the air vent, in the outer wall. The gun was plucked from Reggie's hand. The wind hammered at his head, as if it was trying to punish, and chide him, at the same time. A melodic female voice whispered in Reggie's ear. "Azur. You mustn't kill him. What you are doing is wrong. Leave this place before you regret what you might do. Take my love with you."

"You're my mother, aren't you? Let me see you. Please."

The wind ebbed, and I thought she had gone. The voice spoke to me. "It is forbidden. I am a daughter of the wind. Although I have human form I should not show myself to anyone, including my son."

"You say that you love me, but you won't let me see you. That does not sound like a caring mother."

A petite female, in flowing white robes, took shape in front of me. It was the woman who had held me as a baby. She looked more beautiful than my memory had allowed. Long, blonde hair reached to her waist. Vivid cornflower blue eyes smiled from a face of intense beauty. "Release yourself from that man's body. Let me see you." I did as she asked. She hugged me. "Of course I love you." She kissed me on the lips. "I am a strange choice to be your mother, but I am she. It was me who christened you 'Azur'. It means 'prince of the heavens'." A worried look came into her eyes. "I shouldn't have shown myself. You must be gone."

I pulled away from her. "Before you go, tell me who my father is." My mother took me in her arms. "You will find out, when your father is ready to tell you. Listen to me. There are many dangers ahead of you. Whatever happens, always remember your true God. My love goes with you."

Then she was gone. My brain was stuck in limbo. This woman that I called my mother wasn't human. What did that make me? Certainly someone you can't stick a label on.

I looked at Grodam's unconscious mass, and booted him in the stomach. In a moment of sheer spite, I set fire to his wig, with one of his matches. It wasn't going to end there. I hurried into the hall. I pointed my fingers at the staircase. A multiple crop of fire poured over the stairs. Flames spread across the stair carpet, and the wallpaper began to smoulder. It was time to leave. I walked into the study. Grodam hadn't moved. I kicked him again. It made me feel better. Reggie had some explaining to do, but that was his problem. I wished myself back to Linmere.

CHAPTER FOURTEEN

Tuesday, October 9th 2007.

IT WAS COMFORTING TO SEE that the flat hadn't changed. No smoke. No fire damage. Just blessed silence. My brain asked no questions about what had happened at Grodam's house. I wasn't suffering from symptoms of shock, or bewilderment, even though my mother was probably blowing her wares outside the flat, at this very moment. It had all been taken on board, and filed away in my brain. I curled up on the settee, and slept pleasant slumbers.

After breakfast, I phoned the hospital. A friendly nurse said I could pick Anne up at half past eleven. She was waiting for me. I kissed her on the lips. She took her clothes, and dressed behind the bed curtains. When we got home I couldn't stop myself from fussing around her, competing with myself to attend to her every whim. She giggled as she enjoyed my attention. I sat her on the settee. "Now. We've got to get you better."

"Kit. As much as I love you waiting on me, we must talk." Anne pulled a face. "I'm going to be open with you. For a start, I'm not in the habit of picking up men friends." She became flustered. "I've never had a boyfriend." The girl bit at her lip. "I can't believe I'm telling you this. But, I don't care. You're different. You make me laugh, and I feel safe with you around." She started fiddling with her clothing. "I don't want to send out the wrong vibes. I've had no experience of men, but it's pretty obvious that you've got feelings for me. I'm sorry, Kit, but I don't know how to handle a one to one relationship."

My heart pounded with fright. Was she about to blow my feelings for her out of the window? Anne held my hands. "If you do fancy me, then I don't mind. But don't rush me. There. That's all off my chest." No woman has ever spoken to me like this. I started to speak. She put a hand on my lips. "Don't say anything. I've got no idea why I'm talking to you like this. It doesn't matter. You're a stranger who walked into my life when I needed you most." She slapped me playfully on the hand. "There're a few things you ought to know. You'll probably change your mind about me."

Tears welled up in those green eyes. I rubbed her cheek with my fingers. "It won't make any difference to me. I've got secrets as well. You're not the stranger you think you are. Some weird things have happened to me these last few weeks. Try and believe what I'm going to tell you, no matter how ridiculous it might seem."

I peddled my words. "Anne isn't your real name. It's Kareem, better known as Carin. You're the daughter of Julius Milner, late rector of Lovington."

Her face took on an incredulous look. "How did you know? There's…."

It was my turn to butt in. "This isn't easy to explain." I was economical with the truth. This was unknown territory, and I was walking on eggshells. "I saw you, with your father, in a dream vision. Yesterday I read about you in a letter that your father sent me. He told me…"

She shoved her hand over my mouth. "That's impossible. He's dead, for God's sake…" She stopped and rubbed her hands together. The girl was showing all the signs of a rattled lady. The withering look on her face stopped me in my tracks. "You seem to know all about me, yet I know nothing of you. My father never mentioned you." She laughed coarsely. "That's a bloody stupid thing to say. I don't even know your full name."

"I'm sorry. You're right. I'm Kit Milner. I've apparently been chosen to carry through some mission. Your father told me, in one of his letters, that you can help me."

Her coldness vanished. "You're mixed up with the Merlin stones, aren't you?" She smiled in a knowing way. "Things are beginning to make sense, Kit Milner. We share the same name, and have a common bond, if we're talking about the stones."

I sighed with relief. We were on the same wavelength again. "This all started when I bought your father's davenport desk at an auction. The stones were hidden inside. He also left me several letters that told me a lot about myself and this mission. If you promise to believe me, I'll tell you what's happened to me these past weeks." The woman listened patiently as I told her everything that I'd been through since the Fine Arts sale, including the vivid vision of Merlin, and Madrog, and the first vision with her father. I didn't tell her that she'd once died, or about my church meetings with her father. I certainly didn't mention the killing of young Grodam.

She didn't blink an eyelid. "Did you ever meet up with my father?"

A sixth sense warned me to play safe. "No, I got to know him through the dream vision, and the letters he left for me. Can you fill in some of the missing pieces?"

"First things first, Kit. Let me tell you about my life. My father was a lovely, happy man. He spoiled me rotten. When I was about fourteen, he changed. I found out, later, that his misery was caused by this hateful Grodam family."

Her face melted into a mask of sadness. "Daddy's unhappiness affected me and my mother. We went through hell." She managed a smile. "Then, one day, his passion for life returned. His old sparkle came back. We became a complete, loving family again. That was until my mother died. She was killed by a hit and run driver. We were devastated. But life had to go on, as everyone was eager to remind me. I left school and was fortunate enough to get a brilliant job at the British Library in London. The one thing missing from my life has always been boyfriends." She let out a loud laugh. "My closest friends used to kid me that I was a female gender-bender."

I stifled a laugh. She punched me in a playful way. "It gets worse. This woman that you care for has never felt the need for an emotional bond with the opposite sex. I've got used to the idea that I'm destined to become a shrivelled, old spinster." She clasped my hand. "That was until I met you." Her face coloured up. "I'm getting on for thirty, and I'm still a virgin."

I kissed her on the forehead. "We come from the same mould. I've never had a girlfriend. The thought scares me stiff. So what are you worried about? I'm one of the longest serving members of the society of the over-twenty male virgins. There aren't many of us around." She looked at me, with doubt written in her eyes. "It's true, Carin. I've never kissed a girl, or anything else for that matter." She went quiet. I pushed the conversation in another direction. "What do you know about Merlin?"

"Everyone's heard of Merlin. I came across his name eighteen months ago, when Daddy went down with a bad bout of flu. I took some holiday to nurse him. That's when my life turned upside down. One morning, Daddy asked me to fetch his diary from the study. He wasn't sure where he had left it." She shook her head. "He was always forgetting things. I ended up looking in his desk. The drawers were stuffed with papers. I didn't find the diary, but I came across something else. In the bottom drawer was a folder. My father had written on it that the contents were strictly confidential, and the folder was to be passed unopened to his solicitor after his death. It was sealed with sticky tape. The fact that it was marked 'confidential' made me open it. I wish that I hadn't."

She tossed her mane of red hair. "The folder was full of my father's handwritten notes. I put it back in the drawer. That night, I bedded my father down and went to bed. I tried to sleep, but it was wasted time. My mind was too full of that folder. I gave into temptation, and crept downstairs. Before I knew it, I was sitting in the study, with the papers spread out on a table. Daddy had written about the Merlin stones and the powers they possessed. His notes were utterly surreal, more like a work of science fiction. Daddy revealed a strong conflict between the abilities of the stones and his own powerful religious beliefs. It was when I read that he had journeyed through time that I lost patience. I have never read so much rubbish in all my life. For a moment, I thought he was writing a fantasy book. I couldn't understand why he'd want the notes to go to his solicitor."

"I started to put the papers away, when I came across a brown envelope, in the bottom of the folder. My father's words, on the envelope, were forbidding: '*To be passed to my solicitor. Not to be opened by anyone else, under any circumstances.*' The words presented me with a challenge. I ripped the envelope open, and read the two sheets of paper inside."

Tears trickled down her face. "My father had written an account of something that happened in All Saints' church in 1994. He had broken his religious beliefs, and made use of the Merlin stones."

A feeling of guilt gnawed at my mind. I knew what she was on about. What I couldn't understand was why Julius

Milner had felt it necessary to put it in writing. It served no purpose. I'd been there the second time. She wiped the tears away. "It was my fault. I shouldn't have been nosey. It was marked clearly enough. My father's words didn't make pleasant reading. It did explain why I am saddled with an inbuilt fear of men."

My stomach tied up in knots, with a sense of foreboding. I made a vain attempt to change the subject. "Forget it Carin. Don't upset yourself. Tell me about Merlin."

She snapped at me. "Shut up. This is the first time I've had the chance of telling someone. I've got to get it out into the open. I don't care if you think I'm a hardened bitch, but I'm not going to break down in a flood of tears. I have to accept that it really happened." Her fingers scrubbed at her lips. "It's because my father travelled back in time that I'm sitting here. It's as simple as that."

I was in a quandary. I took her bait. "What did your father have to say?"

She waved an agitated hand at me. "You'll have to wait. I want a drink." She vanished into the kitchen. I didn't expect to see her return with a bottle of gin and a glass. She sat down and poured a generous measure. She downed it, poured another glass, and swallowed it. "Don't get the wrong impression. I'm not an alcoholic. I need this, if I'm going to tell you." Carin helped herself to another gin. "Daddy's writings horrified me. In the full bloom of life, I'd been raped, and then murdered, by Joseph Grodam in a former lifetime." She poured another glass of mother's ruin down her throat. "My father snatched my violated body from the grave, by changing the past. He recorded every last detail in his writings. How my body was desecrated and buried in the churchyard, only to be born again by a trick of time." Her speech was beginning to slur. "I know his words are true.

He's never told a lie in his life. Daddy mentions that someone helped him. The bastard isn't named, but I assume it was a man. Just think about it. Some arsehole has to live with his conscience. Not only did he kill the boy, but he knows what happened to me. I hope he rots in hell. He's condemned me to a life which is an everlasting lie."

I felt as guilty as sin. But the rector was just as bad. He'd killed Grodam, but for some reason hadn't made mention of that in his notes. "Did you tell your father that you'd found his papers?"

"No, I didn't. I had to move out of the rectory. How could I live with him, knowing what he and his mate had done? I needed space to get my head around things. I didn't tell him the real reason for going. I took his notes with me when I bought this flat."

I tried to steer her away from the subject. "You must be earning a good salary at the British Library to afford a pad like this. You should see the pig-sty that I live in."

She slapped me down, as if my words had offended her. "So what if I have got a nice flat! There's nothing wrong with that, is there? I hadn't got two pennies to rub together when I left Daddy. He offered me some financial help, but I turned him down." She pouted. "I bought and furnished this flat with money that I raised by using the Merlin stones." I pulled a face. "So what? Why shouldn't I?"

I didn't pursue her on that subject "Did you cut your ties with your father?"

"No. But I never looked on him in the same way. Something in me had died. The Milner moniker was dirty. I changed my name. When Daddy passed away, I couldn't bring myself to keep all of his possessions. Other than a few bits and pieces, I let his solicitor dispose of the rest."

Carin put her head on my shoulder. She was shaking, but

I knew she wasn't crying. I began to doubt whether Julius and I had been right in tearing up the pages of history. If we were to have any chance of a life together, I had to be truthful with the girl. I stood a good chance of losing her, but if I didn't tell her, I could never forgive myself, knowing that we were both living a lie. They were easy thoughts, but I found myself at odds with how to tell her.

Carin sat up. She thumped the arm of the settee. "I've gone through years of hell. I shouldn't be sitting here. By rights, I ought to be lying at peace, in my grave. I'm dead, really. This woman, that you profess to like, is some kind of living-dead freak." She stared into my face. "Don't you understand? I'm dead, dead, dead!" As hard as I tried, I couldn't and didn't register any kind of emotion. I was floundering in a sea of uncertainty. Her forehead furrowed, questioningly. "Why don't you say something?"

She was looking for the right signs in my face, and some appropriate words of comfort. My face was speaking volumes, but it wasn't on her wavelength. My looks gave me away. She shook her head. Her eyes stared in disbelief, a look of revulsion straining at her features. Without warning, she slapped me across the face; I rubbed the stinging pain. Her eyes showed the anger that was raging inside her. "You bloody bastard. You know who the accomplice is, don't you? Did my father tell you?" The last piece of the puzzle dropped into place in her mind. She slapped my face again. "You little shit. I can tell from your face. You were in the church when it happened. You travelled back in time, and got my father to break his religious vows."

The woman realised the enormity of what she had said. She pulled away from me, a withering look on her face. "It's you that I've got to thank for the rift between me and my father. *You* killed Joseph Grodam. You're a murderer. They

181

should lock you up and throw away the key. You didn't even have the guts to tell me." Her glass smashed against the wall as she threw it across the room.

"What's this all about then? Are you getting some weird kind of thrill, touching someone who has been raped and murdered, and then been brought back to life? Is that why you let me put myself through the torture of telling you something that you already know? You were enjoying it, weren't you? I thought I'd met someone who wanted me." She shoved her face into mine. "Did you want to bed a dead woman, to give you that extra thrill? You're a sick man, Milner, and I hate you!"

Our relationship collapsed. Gone, before it had even started. I tried to redeem myself. "Listen to me, Try and understand my position. I admit I was there, with your father. We used the stones to put right what we thought was a tragic wrong. You deserved to live." I couldn't tell her that it was her father who had first killed Grodam, and brought her back from the dead. She wouldn't have believed me. "We did it for you. Your father was thinking about your mother. She'd have done herself some serious harm. Reverend Milner was caring for the people he loved. We did it for you." She was unmoved. I threw my last card onto the table. "I meant it, when I said that I've got feelings for you. They're real. I'd never hurt you."

My words fell on barren ground. They withered and died. My trump card curled up at the edges. She got up and looked down at me. Her mouth took on a twisted derisive look. She loathed me. It was written all over her face. "Don't you dare bring my mother into this, because you didn't have the courage to tell me. I thought you were someone special. You're a nobody that I want to forget." She walked across to the front door and opened it. "Get out of my life. Don't

182

bother to come back and don't you dare ring me. Goodbye, and good riddance."

I wasn't surprised by her behaviour, knowing what she knew. Things hadn't been helped by the attempted rape the other night. Her sanity had failed to suppress the seething mass of nightmares stewing in a psychotic cauldron. Sooner or later, someone was destined to bear the brunt of her pent up feeling. I'd managed to unlock Pandora's Box and lose the girl in the process.

CHAPTER FIFTEEN

Tuesday, October 9th 2007.

S HE TRIED TO MANHANDLE ME out of the flat. I shoved my foot in the door. The girl's unseeing eyes stared at me as I waved my hand in front of her face. She was under my control. "Forget what has just happened. Go and sit on the settee. You're incapable of moving, or thinking, until I get back." She did as I asked.

My chances of retrieving Carin's affection were as likely as the Pope taking a wife. I couldn't accept the inevitable. She might do something silly. It was no good hypnotising her, and telling her to forget what she had read. That wasn't a permanent solution. I time travelled back to nineteen ninety five. The Lovington Rectory hadn't changed. I walked up the path and knocked on the front door.

Julius Milner answered my knock. He gave me a bear hug. "Kit, this is a surprise."

There was no time for socialising. "There's something that needs sorting, and quickly."

"You'd better come in." We passed through the hall, and into the room that I had seen in my dream. Everything was in its rightful place, including the davenport desk. I stared at it. Julius Milner gave a knowing smile. "Don't worry. I'll be making arrangements for the desk to come into your possession when the time is right. The envelope is already in the desk. What are you doing here?"

His words made me smile. If someone had bothered to tell me, a few days ago, that I could time travel, I could have collected the envelope today. It would have saved a lot of

184

trouble. "The good news is, I've met your daughter. The bad news is, she threw me out, less than five minutes ago. It's your fault. She found the notes that you wrote about finding her dead in the church and our doing away with Joseph Grodam. Carin knows that I killed him second time round. She took your notes when she left home. Why the hell did you need to write about everything? I was there, remember? I'm beginning to think you did it deliberately, so that I could be tested, as you keep telling me. All you've done is queer my pitch. You've got to destroy any reference to what happened in the church. If you don't, then you can forget this mission."

He gripped me by the arm. "I'm sorry that I dropped you in it. The fact of the matter is, I'm in the habit of writing about all my experiences with the stone. I didn't think things through. My strict routine is my only excuse. I had no idea she knew about our bringing her back to life. I'll burn those notes today, and that's a promise."

His total lack of concern worried me. "Didn't you miss the papers when you contacted your solicitor? You managed to pass everything else to me. You must have realised they were missing. Didn't you ever wonder why Carin left home, and virtually cut off her ties with you?"

He tried to disarm me with a smile. "I must have overlooked the fact that they were missing. There was a lot happening at the time. As for Carin leaving home, I thought she had grown up, and wanted to get out into the wide world. At least, I can put things right."

There was no trace of a real apology. He must have known that the papers had gone missing. His reasoning for Carin leaving home sounded pathetic. It was a load of old tosh.

"I'd better be on my way back. Goodbye."

He grabbed me by the arm. "Before you go. Have you

discussed the mission with my daughter?"

"No, I haven't. Your notes destroyed that train of thought. I've got to get back."

I didn't get the chance. The Reverend began to sweat. It became an effort for him to speak. He spat his words out with great deliberation. "Before…you…go…something… for you."

He stumbled across to the hall table, fumbled the drawer open, and took out two small brown bottles and a crucifix. "Take…with…you." He took a deep breath, in an effort to control himself. His words became garbled. "Stones… don't…believe.."

I grabbed hold of him. "Sit down. You don't look well."

The Reverend shrugged me away. He pointed at the bottles. "Holy…water." He clutched at his chest. "Go…quickly. He's …coming." His face turned red, and he coughed. "Trust.. in…God…"

The Reverend's behaviour concerned me. I wasn't happy at leaving him, but I did as he asked. Seconds later, I was sitting on the settee with Carin. I sighed with relief. It wasn't the same room that I'd left ten minutes ago. I recognised the furnishings, including the what-not, and the Canterbury, as well as four splendid water colours hanging on the walls. I'd last seen them at Martin's auction. They had once belonged to Julius Milner. I felt a tinge of conscience. It was the second time I'd manipulated her life.

I snapped my fingers in Carin's face. She came to life. I was rewarded with a full blooded kiss, and no smell of drink on her breath. "I'm glad that we've got our lack of male and female relationships out into the open."

I played along. "So am I. I meant to ask you. How long have you lived here?"

"I bought this place after Daddy died. I've always wanted to live in an old cottage. This place wasn't big enough to take all of Daddy's furniture. I put some of it into auction."

Another sense of guilt passed through me; I hoped she had chosen Martin to sell her stuff. She was straining at the leash. "I enjoyed listening to your recent encounters. I believe every word. I was telling you about Daddy's papers that I read when he was ill. I told him what I had done a few days later. He wasn't angry. If anything, he showed relief. He'd wanted to talk about them, but hadn't managed to find the right opportunity. Daddy told me about the stones, and what they were capable of."

I couldn't help laughing at the serious look on her face. "Did you believe him, when he said the stones could carry you through time?"

"No, I didn't. I thought he'd been supping the communion wine. He offered to give me a demonstration. I turned him down."

"Did your father show you the stones?"

"He did better than that. When I was fourteen he gave me a bracelet." She showed me a small rounded piece of stone, set amongst the other gems. "Daddy told me to wear it all the time as a lucky charm. I had no idea then what the stone was all about."

"Why didn't your stone protect you from those thugs? And something else puzzles me. If you've got this fantastic job at the British Library, what are you doing working in a pub?"

She shrugged her shoulders. "I wasn't wearing the bracelet last Sunday evening. I forgot to put it on before going to work. The pub job has nothing to do with money. I thought it might be a way of finding a boyfriend." A smile played at the corner of her mouth. "I wasn't wrong, was I?

I found you, and I'd only been there a week. I told you my car broke down that day. The landlord asked me if I wanted a lift home. I turned him down. I'll never know why I walked home." Her green eyes bored into mine. "Do you have any answers?"

I scratched at my head. "I'm not sure. I used to be a simple, working lad. That all changed when I got these stones. I've been putting two and two together. Most of it's making five, but I can see a chink of light. We know this is all about rescuing Merlin from that bloody great rock. How it's going to pan out, is another matter. You asked me if I had an answer for the other night. I have. Merlin arranged it."

Carin squeezed my arm. "Now you're being stupid. How do you make that out?"

I thought about the twisted paths we'd both trod, with no conspicuous signposts to direct us. Our meeting, the other evening, was too coincidental, and too good to be true. "I'm certain that Merlin set the whole thing up, to test me, and to make sure that we found each other. It was an over-contrived way of ensuring our paths crossed. What annoys me is that you suffered in the process." I snorted. "It's not his first long-winded method seeing that it's taken him fourteen hundred years to get us together. I said that Merlin is arranging things, but, I could be wrong, seeing that he must be dead by now."

She didn't comment, so I changed the subject. "What happened to your father? Was it to do with the Grodams? It was his yobs that attacked you, the other evening."

"I know all about them, I remember William Grodam, as a boy. He wasn't exactly a charmer. He had a twin brother, Joseph." She shivered. "He used to shout crude things at me. He disappeared one day. People reckon he ran away. His family made Daddy's life a misery. He didn't enjoy the safety net of the stones once he'd let go of them. That's not your fault. It was his decision."

"Correction, Carin. I think it was Merlin's choice."

"Whatever. The coroner concluded that Daddy had taken his own life in a moment of depression. He once told me that when he died, it wouldn't be forever. Don't ask me what he meant. One thing for sure. He didn't commit suicide. That's the one and only time I had a shot at time travel. I had this quaint notion of saving his life, by travelling back in time. Nothing happened. I don't seem to have the knack."

"Merlin probably made sure of that. Have you got any idea what this so-called mission is all about?"

She shrugged her shoulders. "No, I haven't. I'm sure that we'll learn more in time."

"Do you really think that Merlin's alive, after fourteen hundred years?"

She looked a trifle pissed off. In a split second, her mood changed. "He needn't necessarily be dead. Perhaps his influence still lives within the stones. Does it matter?"

"Are you feeling alright, Carin?" She said she was fine. I knew she was lying. She didn't seem anxious to continue chatting. I changed the subject. "Do you fancy going out for a meal?"

Her face lit up. "Why not? It will get us away from this endless chit-chat."

We didn't paint the town red. To other people we would have looked like two young people enjoying each other's company.

Her earlier moodiness was gone by the time we got home. "It's pretty late, Kit. Why not stay the night? There's no point in driving all that way home."

I didn't need convincing. "Great. It'll give us more time to talk about Merlin."

She let out a loud yawn. "Let's save Merlin for tomorrow.

I feel whacked. We'll have a night-cap, then I'll make some sleeping arrangements." She moved towards the drinks cabinet, and came back with two glasses and a bottle of vodka. She poured two generous measures. "Here's to us, Kit, and the future."

I raised my glass. "I'll drink to that."

"It's time for shuteye. You'll have to make yourself comfortable on the settee. Sorry, I can't offer you any pyjamas."

She found me a blanket, kissed me goodnight, and disappeared into her bedroom. I stripped down to my underpants and turned the light off. No sooner had my eyes closed, than the lights were switched on. Carin stood in her bedroom door, dressed in a flimsy outfit. "I feel lonely without you. Will you come and keep me company? Let's get one thing straight. That's not an invitation for any funny business. Do you understand?"

"You have my word." We settled down in her bed. She let me kiss her. There was no passion in her kissing, only tenderness. She'd laid the ground rules, and I wasn't going to let her down. In any case, where would two totally inexperienced virgins begin?

I drifted into sleep. It was rudely shattered. I woke to find Carin stroking the hairs on my chest. "What's the matter, Carin? Can't you sleep?" No other words came to mind. I hadn't expected to be awakened by a beautiful woman, caressing my chest. Particularly by someone who'd made the ground-rules for sleeping in her bed. My manhood stiffened.

"Sorry to wake you, but I can't sleep. I must be over-tired." She giggled, and rolled her tongue across my lips. "I was thinking about that young handmaiden you told me about who came across Merlin in the woodland clearing. You said it was Lady Emuline in disguise. I found an explicit account of what went on between them, that was written by Merlin himself." She let out a throaty chuckle. "She was a bit of a girl, and must have bedded hundreds of men."

I sat up. "You didn't tell me that you'd come across something written by Merlin. When was that?"

She pulled me down into the bed. "Don't worry about that now, I'm saving it for another day." She gave me a lingering kiss. I thought of what Confucius had once said: 'Lingering kisses like spider's web. Leads to flies undoing.'

Carin sighed. "Emuline pretended to faint, and Merlin came to help her. He hadn't seen a woman, since his wife died. Merlin knelt down by the maiden, and loosened her clothing, at the neck. It was meant to help her breathe. It did more than that. The young woman's breasts flopped out. They were marble white, with erect dark brown nipples."

Carin slid her hand into my underpants, and gently stroked my manhood. I was jolted into disbelief. It had been her choice not to rush things. So why the change of heart? I didn't ponder the point for very long. The deep lust welling up inside me drove these things from my mind.

She whispered in my ear, "Merlin couldn't resist the temptation of her breasts. He stroked them, and teased her nipples with his fingers."

Carin guided my hand underneath her night-dress. Her breasts grew hard, under my touch. Her nipples swelled as I rubbed them. My mouth found hers. Her tongue burst through my lips. Our tongues met, and danced together. She pulled her mouth away. "It's time for us to lose our virginity. Take your underpants off."

I did as she asked. In the heat of the moment, one thought niggled me. "What's going on, Carin? I thought you wanted to wait."

She laughed, shrilly. "You want my body, don't you?"

The nagging thought faded away. I took hold of her nightdress and pulled it over her head. Carin moaned. "Give me your hand." I lay beside her. She guided my hand between her legs. The unsuspected depth of Carin's sexual expertise was brushed aside by the pleasurable sensations developing in my groin. She let out a soft painful cry. "Don't worry, Kit. I'm not a virgin anymore." Carin took hold of my manhood. Then, I spoiled the moment. A sticky mess burst from me.

I cursed. "Sod it. I'm sorry. I couldn't stop myself."

"Don't worry. You can pleasure me as many times as you want. Touch your stones." I grasped the stones in my hand. Her fingers caressed my limp manhood. It bulged under her touch. The temptress whispered in my ear. "Make love to me. And this time, do it for real." I covered her body with mine. "Kiss my breasts, Kit, and tease my nipples with your teeth." I did as she asked. Her nipples bulged like grapes in my mouth. I moved my rear-end up and down. She let out a shriek. Her sweat mingled with mine. It didn't matter. We were as one. We kissed a long kiss. Carin sighed with satisfaction. "That was wonderful."

I rolled off her. I hadn't a care in the world. "Where did you learn to make love like that? And how did you know that the stones could revive me?"

She hit me around the head with a pillow, and skirted my questions. "It's not important. Come on Romeo. I think we ought to clean up, in the bathroom."

We cavorted under the shower, washing each other's bodies. This wasn't the girl that I'd known an hour ago. This woman was outrageous in her behaviour. She was awash with confidence. Her libido knew no bounds. We dried ourselves and returned to bed, where we lay, side by side, in our nakedness. Carin asked me to cuddle her. I shouldn't have. My manhood swelled, and we indulged ourselves in each other's bodies. We finally fell into exhausted sleep.

When I awoke, the girl was still asleep. I couldn't resist kissing her. She stirred, and stretched her arms. "Good morning, Kit." She looked under the duvet cover, and pulled a face. "I'm afraid we won't be doing any more cavorting, for some time. The monthly curse is upon me." She chuckled at the puzzled look on my face, and ruffled my hair. "You have led a shallow life. A woman's hormones change every month, when sex becomes impracticable. It shows that a woman isn't pregnant." She gave me a kiss. "So, that's good news." She playfully slapped my behind. "I'm going to the bathroom."

I was the happiest, if most puzzled man in the world. Nothing else mattered. It's naïve to think this way, because something always tends to intrude on a happy moment. This time, it was the bedroom wall. It flickered in shades of grey and white. It didn't panic me. I called out to Carin. "You'd better come in here. There's something you should see, and I'm not talking about my body."

She ran into the bedroom. "What are you going on about?"

"Look at the wall. Don't worry. I've been through this routine before. It's like watching television, except it's far more entertaining. And you don't need a licence."

"You're being frivolous, Kit. It's probably Merlin contacting us."

I got a warning signal. She seemed pretty sure of herself. I played her along. "Just sit back, and watch the pictures on the wall. You won't be disappointed, if my previous experiences are anything to go by."

My words were bolder than my feelings. I hoped there wasn't going to be any blood and guts.

CHAPTER SIXTEEN

Wednesday, October 10th 2007.

A PICTURE GLIMMERED UNSTEADILY ON the wall. It kept fading away, leaving muzzy images. I made light of it.

"Reception isn't very good tonight. I'd better go up on the roof, and move the aerial around."

She thumped me in the ribs. "Stop arsing about. This is serious. Let's see what's going to happen."

The images finally sorted themselves out. I recognised the outline of a rock. Merlin's face was superimposed on the rock face. He stared at us, his hooked nose, and white beard, looking resplendent within a patchwork of wrinkles and warts. "Welcome, my children, from myself and your deity. It pleases us that you have sealed your bodies together, harmonising the desire that you feel for each other. I prophesied this union, many years ago. We can now complete the plans for your mission."

I took a fleeting glance at Carin. She was completely unruffled by what was going on. A look of idolisation covered her face. She showed no surprise that Merlin knew we had made love. How had he known? He was a symbol of the sixth century, yet he had been updated about something that had happened during the night. A knotted feeling of doubt, that things were not consistent, hung heavily.

Merlin droned on. "I have led you both along a narrow road these past years." Tears rolled down his cheeks. "It has been worth the wait. The two of you will free me from this rock by using the tools that I have given you. I promise that no harm will befall you." Merlin raised his voice. "In delivering me from this stone prison, you will be rewarded beyond your imagination." His face took on a grim look. "I would describe these rewards as awesome. Lord Madrog is hatching a plot against me. He plans to snatch me from my prison and strip me of my powers. Even as I speak, one of Madrog's followers is breaking into your home, Milner. He is taking one of my stones from your sleeping quarters." His voice thundered around the bedroom. "Why did you leave the stone in your room? It should have been hidden in a place of safety. Your carelessness angers me. You should be punished, but I forgive you." Merlin sighed in resignation. "With my stone in his possession, Madrog can release me from this rock. It makes it more important that you free me, to give me the chance to recover my powers before Madrog does his worst. I will show you what will happen to me if you fail me. Look well at the images, and learn from them."

The picture faded away. Carin glared at me, and clicked her tongue. "You idiot. Did you leave one of the Merlin stones in your bedroom?"

"Alright. There's no need to rub it in. How was I to know it was one of his stones? I wasn't thinking straight at the time. I had other things on my mind."

Her mood changed. She was back to her usual perky self. "Never mind. It means that we're duty bound to help him. "I'm prepared to take on the task. What is there to lose? Merlin says that we'll come to no harm and I believe him. So why not?"

She was going too fast for my liking. "Hold on to your horses. Don't you think there's something phoney going on? How did Merlin know about us making love? It's barely happened, yet the joyful tidings have travelled through the ether, and landed up at his rock. He says his powers are fading, yet he's still capable of picking up gossip, as well as transmitting a televised message to us, through the centuries. Is Merlin really the prisoner that he's making himself out to be? And who's this deity he mentioned? It could be the devil, for all we know." It was a powerful argument, backed up by what her father had tried to tell me. Otherwise, what was the holy water, and crucifix, all about? "I'm not happy. And, there's something else. How did Merlin know about the stone being stolen? And how's Grodam going to get it to Madrog? It's bound to be him who stole it."

She threw a wobbly. "You bloody well annoy me with your endless questions. Pull yourself together, man. I know Merlin better than you do. I've spent hours reading his manuscript. He was baptised into the Christian faith, and he's followed this creed all his life. He's a warlock, but he's not evil. Trust me. I've got a feel for the man. He's all good. Merlin wouldn't mislead me. Take things one step at a time instead of jumping ahead of yourself."

The wall began to light up, and the rock came into focus. Madrog stood in front of it, with his two sons. He held a stone vessel in one hand. I whispered to Carin. "The evil looking sod is Madrog. The Grodams are descended from him. The other two are his sons."

She flapped her hand at me. "Quiet, man. I know that. Let's see what they are up to."

Madrog loosened his clothing, and peed into the vessel. He raised it towards the rock. "The powers that were endowed in me, by drinking the blood of my wife, are made more powerful by this Merlin stone, that spawns the magic of Merlin." He held a stone against the rock face. "I command that this rock, which conceals Merlin, bring his soul into my charge." A trail of thick vapour seeped from the rock face. With a deft wave of his hand, he induced the vapour into the neck of the vessel. He applied the stopper, and barked an order to his sons. "I have him trapped. Light me a fire. I have need of the flames."

It wasn't long before a fire crackled away, leaving a trail of smoke drifting towards the sky. Madrog shook the contents of the vessel, and threw it into the flames. He let it lie there, as he bellowed at the fire, "Hear me, flames. I command you to dissolve the vapour of Merlin into my body fluid."

As if at his bidding, tongues of fire leapt around the vessel. Madrog dragged it from the flames with his sword. He motioned to his sons to urinate on it. The madman filled a goblet with the liquid from the vessel, and drank the cocktail with relish, before tossing the goblet away. He sank to his knees, and extolled the heavens. "Master, I have carried out what you asked of me. Come to me, and share in my triumph."

The picture vanished from the wall. Carin leant against the headboard, a smile playing on her face. She licked her lips. "That Madrog certainly has a way about him, doesn't he?"

Her attitude annoyed me. "You're not thinking straight. Are you falling for all that twaddle? Merlin is trying to put us under pressure by scaring the daylights out of us. Can't you see that?"

"You're wrong. You saw the Merlin stone in Madrog's hand. It's the one that was stolen from your bedroom. It's a true prediction of what will happen to Merlin if we don't help him."

Merlin's voice interrupted us. His lived-in face gleamed on the bedroom wall. "You are right, my dear. My prophecy does not lie. What you saw is what will happen if you decide to abandon me." Merlin's eyes bored into mine. "Your words of doubt did not escape me. You disappoint me, and I won't forget your warped words. Never speak such words again or you will be punished." His face softened. "Time does not allow any further delay. Tell me that you have accepted my mission."

Carin made an immediate decision. "We will help you, Merlin. Won't we, Kit?"

She looked at me with pleading eyes. This was the spider and fly syndrome, with me as the fly. I was in a no-win situation. I loved the girl and wasn't prepared to lose her. That had nearly happened, yesterday. The pain came flooding back. The blunt fact is that I am bound up in a state of affairs which has been moulded by destiny. Irrespective of my ever growing misgivings I conceded that I couldn't fight it. My feet have walked too far down that road.

I let out a sigh of resignation. "Her feelings are more fervent than mine, but I will support her."

Merlin's lips twitched. "Your words please me. Listen to what I say. It is foretold that my life will be threatened, on the last day of the month that you call October." Merlin stroked his beard. "This is what you must do. On the twenty ninth day of October, you will travel to Llalogan. This place can be found in the northern part of the country that you call Wales." He smiled wistfully. "I built me a castle there, where I spent many contented years with my queen. On the thirtieth day, you must stand within my castle walls just before the sun sets. You will call on me to conduct you back in time. Further orders will be given to you when you join me. I will provide you with clothing for my time. Do not bring weapons with you, or other trappings of your time. You must wear my stones, at all times, to protect you. Without them, you could die. Mark these instructions well." He pointed a finger at me. "Do not fail me boy, I am watching you. May the deity who controls us all be with you."

The face of Merlin vanished from the pink painted bedroom wall.

CHAPTER SEVENTEEN

Thursday, October 11th to Sunday, October 28th, 2007.

CARIN'S REACTION WAS NONCHALANT. "WELL. That's that. We're agreed on things. I'll get back to the bathroom."

I have a sneaking admiration for how she has taken Merlin on board. I thought she'd be terrified at the things she'd seen. Not Carin. She wasn't all beauty. There was a tough side to her.

My repose was violently disturbed. Carin burst into the room. She looked radiantly beautiful, with that wonderful thatch of auburn hair floating round her shoulders. Her smile was dazzling. She grabbed my face and planted a huge kiss on my lips. "That's for last night." She sat down by my side. "I know you're not happy about rescuing Merlin. Look. When all this is over, you and I are going to start living. The past weeks will be behind us. What do you say?"

"I have reservations. But that's my problem. If you're determined to help him, then I'll go along with the idea. That won't stop me from keeping my eyes peeled every step of the way. I'm going for one reason, and it has nothing to do with Merlin. I want to get this over with, and lead a normal life, where people don't get hurt and apparitions stop appearing on bedroom walls. I don't want to spend the rest of my life looking over my shoulder, to see if Grodam's low-life are around."

She was unmoved. Her tinkling laughter floated through the air, as she swept out of the room. Carin left for work, saying that she'd arrange some holiday for the end of the month. She promised to tell me more about Merlin when she got home.

I passed the day away by driving to Linmere to check the flat out. The door was open. I made my way upstairs. The place was a real mess. Drawers lay on the floor, their contents strewn about in a confusion of unsightliness. The intruders had embarked on a high ratio of wanton damage. Everything was trashed or smashed. The remains of furniture, clothing, pictures and mirrors lay in distressed confusion. Even my bed had been pulled to pieces. Not content with their trail of devastation, the carpets were smeared with human faeces. The hand of spite was at work, enjoying the vandalising of my home. There was no sign of the rock that I'd left on the dresser. I couldn't be sure that it had been taken. That was, until I walked into the bathroom. This was the only room that had not suffered from the hand of maliciousness. A message was scrawled on the back of the door in felt tip pen. *'Sorry about crapping in the lounge, but we didn't want to dirty the toilet. I found Merlin's stone. What a careless boy you are.'*

I swore to myself. Who had told Grodam about the piece of rock? I still couldn't handle the notion that Merlin needed this over-complicated drama to help him. There was a very good reason why he shouldn't be imprisoned in the rock. If I had the gift of time travel, then so must he. I was becoming more sceptical by the minute. Merlin could shove his mission. I was going to sort him out, once and for all. I willed myself to Merlin's time, on the day he'd been banished to the rock. The wind whistled around my face, but nothing happened. I tried again. My second effort was wasted. I had a stab at travelling back three days, to get my hands on the piece of rock before Grodam did. The same wind caressed me, but my powers of time travel had deserted me. It only added fuel to my doubts about the whole Merlin saga.

I drove back to Lovington, just before Carin arrived home. I told her what I'd found at my flat, but didn't mention my time travel failures. She laid the law down. "There's no way you're going back to that flat. You're moving in with me. We're an item, now. It's a pity about the stone, but don't blame yourself. I'm glad it's worked out this way." She pulled a face, and ruffled my hair. "Come on lover-boy. Everything's going to be fine."

I hugged her. "Thanks for the offer of bed and breakfast and anything else that might be included. I'll move some of my things in while you're at work."

"That's settled then. I've arranged a week's holiday for the end of October."

After dinner, we pored over a map of Wales, to see where Llalogan was. It wasn't a good map. We couldn't find the place. Carin suggested checking out the internet. She led me to a small room at the back of the cottage, which doubled as her office.

She typed the word 'Merlin' into her computer. We were quickly rewarded. Some unknown expert had kindly transposed Merlin's kingdom onto a modern day map of Wales. The name 'Llalogan' had disappeared from modern usage. According to the map, the ruins of Merlin's castle nestled off the old B5831 Roman road, a few miles south of Abergele.

Carin was full of herself. "We'll drive up on the Friday, to make sure we arrive in plenty of time. We can find a hotel when we get there."

"Don't you think we ought to book before we go? I don't fancy sleeping in the car, if the hotels are full."

She shook her head. "There's plenty of room, this time of year. That'll give us the time we need to find Merlin's castle on the Saturday."

"You said you'd fill me in about Merlin. How about it?"

"Why not? It all started at the British Library. God only knows why I applied for the job. I'd always wanted to be a doctor. My position allows me access to any book in the building. One lunchtime, on an impulse, I wandered down to the room where we store the rarer books. I wouldn't have minded, if I'd known why I was there. I was on the point of leaving when I had this urge to clamber up some steps to a top shelf of books. A particularly large volume caught my eye. On a whim, I picked it up. It slipped from my grasp and fell to the floor. I'm not in the habit of dropping valuable books, and scrambled down to check if it was damaged. It didn't seem to have suffered from the fall. To make sure, I opened it. A middle part of the book fell out. I knelt down and picked up some brown sheets of delicate looking parchment in what I thought looked like animal skin. They weren't part of the volume at all. I could just about make out the faded words on the front sheet. They were written in a language that I've never come across. Strangely enough, I didn't have any problem in translating it. It turned out to be a handwritten account of Merlin's life.

"I knew that I'd stumbled on something out of the ordinary. These parchments had first seen the light of day in the sixth century. I took the book back to my desk, and hid it in a drawer."

I felt as excited as her. "Where's the manuscript? Can I see it?"

"We're not allowed to bring books home. Don't worry, I can recall everything that's written in it."

I wasn't daft. I'd been fobbed off. She gave an excited laugh. "The parchments cover over ninety years of his life. You'd love the manuscript. It's full of his spells." Her face glazed over. "With the help of my stone, I might be able to invoke some of them. It shouldn't be too hard for me. Who knows what I could achieve." Her face came to life. "I won't bore you with all the detail. It's his last twelve months that make the best reading."

Her mood had changed. There was a touch of hysteria in her voice. And why was she referring to *herself*, and not *us*? It bothered me.

"By the time Merlin was ninety, he'd gone off the rails after his wife's death. He fled into the forest, living the life of a hermit." She squirmed with pleasure. "Merlin is a great man. A visionary. He even looked into the future and foretold a beautiful woman coming into his life, who would be his downfall."

I was getting edgy. "You're wasting your words on me. That's what I told you last night. If Merlin knew he was going to be upstaged by this woman, why didn't he do something about it, instead of ending up in a lump of stone?"

She sighed. "You do go on, even though you've got a fair point. He writes of a woman who would use witchcraft to overpower him. He was old, and confused. For goodness sake, man. Merlin was over ninety when this girl entered his life. He wasn't to know she was a powerful sorceress. Merlin fell in love with this woman, thinking that she was a simple maiden. That's enough to addle any man's brain."

"Believe what you like, Carin. That's up to you. I smell a rat and it's a dead one. Some wizard he's proved to be. He gets himself trapped inside a lump of rock, and his huge powers cannot release him. He waits fourteen hundred years for a knight in shining armour to come to his rescue. Come on. It takes a bit of swallowing." I let my words sink in. "I've promised to go with you, but there's a better way out. Let's walk away from this whole affair. We'll keep the stones, and buy our happiness with them. We can go back in time, and save your mother and father." I found her hand, and kissed it. She didn't react. "We could even get married and have children."

She looked down her nose at me. "I'm the only person who has read Merlin's story. I know everything about the man. He's real to me, and I believe in him. Your dreams for our future are lovely, but you're forgetting one important thing. Your utopian ideas are too late. It doesn't matter what you think, any more. We're both destined to live out a life that was chosen for us. We can't escape it. Can't you feel a tingle in your body?" Her forehead furrowed. "You're scared, aren't you?"

This woman was showing a strength of character that I hadn't seen before. She was acting like Merlin's self appointed chief disciple and go between. Her unwavering determination to keep me on the straight and narrow road to Merlin was worrying.

It was my turn to bristle. "Yes. I should be scared, and who can blame me? But I'm not." Frustration took over. I spat my words out. "For Jesus Christ's sake. Can't you read my smoke signals? I love you and want to make you happy. Is that a sin? Sod Merlin. Can't you forget him?"

She pulled a face. It wasn't pretty. "Lovely sentiments, darling, but there's no need to be profane. Love doesn't come into it anymore. Running away isn't an option. We're the missing pieces in Merlin's jigsaw puzzle. Your eagerness to make me happy has muddled your brain. You've forgotten about Grodam. He's got a Merlin stone, thanks to you. Are you really prepared to let him loose with that stone? There's no telling what evil he'll get up to."

Julius Milner had been right about his daughter. She's shown her worth. I'd learned nothing new about Merlin, or the mission, but she had cottoned onto the run of things. The way her mind coped with each new situation was astonishing. I kidded myself that her brain power complemented my inner strength of character. Without her, I knew I wouldn't have gone through with whatever was expected of me. She had a coping mind, whereas mine probed, and analysed every facet of what was happening.

Her words sounded like a threat. "We're going to help Merlin, no matter what you say. Period. It's as well that I'm here to guide you. By the time I've finished with you, you'll be thanking me for taking up Merlin's challenge. Don't forget. Mister. You were hand-picked for this mission."

I reluctantly gave in. "Alright. Cut out the battle speech. You don't need to build up a case for the defence. I'll go, but I'm doing it for you and our future life, not Merlin."

"You've got an attitude problem. You're still not thinking straight. Merlin's going to be disappointed."

"OK. I own up to being sceptical, but why have *we* been chosen? Didn't he have kids of his own?"

"No, he didn't. At least, not with his wife." She chuckled. "Merlin was a bit of a rogue. He writes that he fathered a couple of children with two different women. He prophesies that one of his progeny, a virgin, will be the saviour of the world. That lets us out." She banged the arm of the settee. "Stop whittling, and accept the fact that he needs our help."

"OK. OK. I'm sorry. I know all about Merlin's later years. What about his earlier years?"

"Thank God. You're showing an interest in him, at last. For a start, he had nothing to do with King Arthur, or the Round Table. He's a king in his own right, and ruled his kingdom for forty five years. Merlin is a good man, a Christian man. He was converted by Saint Blaise. There's no evil in him." She gave me a funny look. "Do you believe in God?"

The question caught me on the hop. "Well, yes, I think so. There's certainly a superior deity. But we're not talking about me. Get back to Merlin. Did you come across anything to suggest that he's alive, in the twentieth century?"

"Of course he's alive. He's immortal. But, he's an old man, for goodness sake. He's still trapped in that rock, but his powers have waned. You keep asking me questions. What do you think?"

I fended off the question. "Your father once told me that Merlin was directing my footsteps. I can't imagine him telling a lie. If I think about it, my answer is yes. If Merlin possesses only half the powers you reckon he has, then he could be alive. That's where the negative side of me kicks in. I'm sorry to labour the point, but if his powers are failing him, how can he be coordinating things from a rock, in the sixth century?"

She rolled her eyes. "You obviously don't believe a word that I've said about him."

My questions were getting too near the mark. We spent the rest of the evening speculating on what might happen when we met up with Merlin. I couldn't resist bringing my negative thoughts to bear on him. "If Merlin comes out on top, how is he going to reward us? He's not going to let us return to our own time, knowing what we know."

Carin snapped. "Questions, questions, questions. With the gifts at your disposal, you're ready made for this mission. We'll find out when we get there. Stop going on."

She glanced at her watch. "It's been a long day. I'm going to bed. Don't wake me when you come in."

The days are running out, before we meet up with Merlin. It is now late Sunday evening on the twenty eighth of October. While Carin has been at work, I've spent my time completing the outline of my life story. I finished on Friday, and I've locked the papers away in my security box, at the Standard Bank. Carin doesn't know that I've put my thoughts down on paper. I don't want her to read about my suspicions of her. Don't run away with the wrong idea. Even though she's not being straight with me, I love her with all my heart, but I can't come to terms with the way her mind is thinking.

We journey to Wales tomorrow, but Carin wants to see her father before we go. That's if the Merlin stones will allow it. I've got no idea why I couldn't time travel to save Merlin, or stop Grodam from stealing the stone. If we do manage to drop in on Julius Milner, I have a feeling that he won't be surprised to see us. A sixth sense is warning me that the only reason for visiting her father is so that he can convince me that everything is above board. We shall see.

I enjoyed unbroken sleep, when I finally got to bed. My dreams have dried up, thank God. I'm going to need all the sleep I can get.

CHAPTER EIGHTEEN

Monday, 29th October, 2007.

I couldn't contain Carin, when she woke up. She's over the moon at the prospect of seeing her father. We've both become blasé when we talk of time travel. To us, it's the norm, in the same way people jump into a car to visit their relatives. It's also a damn sight cheaper.

I'd no sooner finished breakfast, than she was at me. "I can't wait to see him, Kit. Let's be on our way."

I calmed her down. "How far back are you planning to go? I don't want a younger Carin opening the door."

"No problem." She rummaged around in a drawer, and found a small book. She shuffled through its pages. "This is my diary for two thousand and four. We'll go back to the nineteenth of September."

"OK. Ready when you are. Think about the nineteenth of September, 2004. What about eleven, in the morning?"

She nodded and put her hand in mine. Seconds later, we were standing in front of Lovington Rectory. Strange that time travel had kicked in today. Cairn patted at her hair, and adjusted her coat. She rang the bell. Reverend Milner opened the door. "Carin, my dear. It's lovely to see you." I noticed no genuine trace of surprise in his voice. He embraced her, and planted a kiss on her lips. He turned to me. "Good to see you, Kit." He shook my hand. "Come in, the pair of you." We were shepherded into the lounge. He grasped his daughter's hand and grinned. "You're at work, today."

Carin put her arms around her father. "I've missed you so much. I do love you."

He planted a kiss on her head, and stroked her hair. Julius whispered in her ear. "That's in the future, darling. Don't forget your younger version shares my life. Come and sit on the settee with me. Make yourself comfy in the armchair, Kit. Now. Tell me about yourselves."

She told him how we had met, and about Merlin's most recent vision. Carin confirmed that we were off to North Wales, before going back to Merlin's time. She made no mention of the fact that we were an item and had slept together.

Julius Milner beamed. "I'm so happy that you've accepted the assignment, my boy. There were times when I thought you weren't up to it."

I was truthful with him. "I've accepted, but I'm not happy." I goaded him. "I'm only going because your daughter is hell bent on setting off on a wild goose chase. Someone has to look after her."

A look of displeasure crossed his face. He raised his voice. "You are an annoying person. How many times do I have to tell you that you were put on this earth for one reason? You are the key to unlocking the secret of life, as well as heaven itself. Get a grip of yourself." He calmed down. "I'm sorry. I got carried way but I meant what I said."

He wasn't overstating his position. There was a moment when I thought he was going to explode. His whole attitude had changed since I'd last seen him. Then, he'd been hell bent on warning me not to go on the mission. The malarkey about unlocking the secret of life and heaven was something new.

Carin stroked his face and planted a kiss on his lips. I cringed. Her affection was too intimate for my liking. She gazed into her father's eyes. "I'm going because I trust Merlin. He can't do without us."

The Reverend gazed at her lovingly, before throwing

me a dirty look. "Thank goodness someone trusts him." He kissed the palm of her hand, "We must convince this young man that he's wrong. How can we knock some sense into his head?"

I put my oar in. "You can't blame me for the way I feel. At least, I'm being honest. Life dealt me a duff hand of cards during my childhood, Since then, I've been knocked from pillar to post and pushed around the houses not knowing what the hell was going on, until I was told that all the fuss is about a trip to the past, to supposedly save some old sorcerer. I've suffered pain, and mental agony, as well as an attempt on my life. Your own daughter was nearly raped. There had to be a simpler way of finding out what this game is all about."

They stared at me, the same condescending look on their faces as if I was some kind of cretin. It was Julius who spoke. "This isn't a game, young man. Merlin's peril is real. He's a powerful wizard who has been tricked into imprisonment. He's waiting for his chosen people to help him. That's you two." He let out a sigh of exasperation. "You've got the wrong end of the stick, and not for the first time. Magical powers have been around since the world began. You're the only person who's been gifted the knowledge of how to use them. You will have to use some of those powers, when you go back in time, otherwise what's the point of having them?"

Carin nodded her head. "Daddy's right. Get real, and go along with the flow. I know Merlin has a plan."

They smiled at me like a pair of Cheshire cats. I wasn't convinced. I was also flummoxed by this over-cosy relationship that father and daughter were displaying. "I hear what you say, but nothing gels with me. If Merlin is as powerful as you're making him out to be, he must have access to time trekking. Why hasn't he used it to escape from the rock? Where does he get his food and water from? I'm trying to make sense of something that's beyond me, but all I've done is stumble from one problem to another. Why?"

Julius clicked his tongue. "You keep asking the same questions. How many times do I have to tell you! You've been subjected to a period of training, and adjustment, to make you use your brain and encourage you to make decisions as preparation for accepting the powers that you have taken on. How would you have reacted if all your powers had been revealed to you in one fell swoop? What if I'd told you that you had killing powers in your fingertips and you could fly through the pages of time? Or that you have the knack of taking over people's bodies and slowing down time? Your mind wouldn't have coped. You'd have been shut away in a secure mental facility. The visions you've seen are a backdrop to what you can expect, when you travel to Merlin's time. You have to get used to blood and guts. His time was a period of man's inhumanity. We have to be satisfied that you are the right person for this life-changing mission. That's why obstacles were put in your way." He became exasperated. "Of course Merlin can move through time. The witch's spell created a force field around the rock. He's trapped in his prison. As for food and drink, he has no need of it." The Reverend kissed his daughter. "Thank God Carin is around, to hold you in check. Merlin must be wondering if he's chosen the right man."

His explanation about Merlin was codswallop. "Merlin can think what he wants. How do you know that there's a force field around the rock? Did he tell you personally?"

The Reverend became flustered. "There's no need for sarcasm. I saw it in one of Merlin's visions, years ago. It's not important. He's too weak to break out of his prison."

I was being side-tracked. "There's something else I want

to know. Who's my father?"

"Sorry, my boy. Can't tell you. You will find out when you return to Merlin's time."

I gritted my teeth and didn't pursue the argument any further. What was the point, with the judge and jury sitting opposite me? Julius Milner had changed, and the girl's behaviour was becoming weirder by the day. I put on a placating show. "Don't worry. I'll see things through."

They both looked relieved. Julius nodded to his daughter, and the subject was dropped. When the time came to leave, Julius whispered a few words to me. "Carry the mission through, so we can meet in a better world."

CHAPTER NINETEEN

Monday, 29ᵗʰ October, 2007.

WE MATERIALISED IN CARIN'S FLAT. I wasn't allowed to rest. She was snapping at my ankles, like a Jack Russell, with her boundless enthusiasm. "Come on Kit. Let's be on our way."

What an astonishing woman she is. We are about to stray into unknown territory, using the medium of time travel, to consort with magicians and bad guys. She's treating the whole affair as if we are planning a trip to the cinema. Carin's displaying no visible trace of fear, and certainly no worry. And how do I feel? If I'm honest, most of me is prepared for what lies ahead, even though it still bugs me that everything is too timely, too opportune. Carin knows more than she's letting on.

Suitcases packed, we set off for Wales. We used the car. Although time travel was mentioned, we decided against it. The journey was uneventful. We reached Abergele at half past five.

Carin pointed out a hotel in the High Street. "Try there. It will save us searching around."

I strolled into hotel reception whilst Carin waited in the car. The young female said they had a room, and asked my name. She gave me an old fashioned look. "You're already booked in for the night…" she checked the register… "for two people." I tried not to show my surprise. The receptionist, or someone else, was one step ahead of me. I blustered my way through, trying not to look a complete idiot.

Within minutes I'd parked the car and we were signing in.

The girl told us that dinner could be taken from six o'clock. We made our way to a first floor room. I unlocked the door, and let rip at Carin. "What the hell's going on? This room has been booked in our names for weeks. I felt a right prat. You know about this, don't you, otherwise why did you choose this hotel? It's about time you were straight with me."

"Don't shout at me. I didn't know the room was booked. I keep telling you how influential Merlin is, even though he's locked up. Perhaps you'll believe me now. Let's unpack, and get ready for dinner. I'm starving." She walked across to the wardrobe, and flung the doors open. "Someone's left a parcel in here."

I grabbed hold of a bulky package. "The last occupants must have left it. I'll take it down to reception."

Carin grabbed my arm. "Hold on. How do you know it hasn't been put there for us? Merlin said he'd provide suitable clothing."

I managed a laugh. "For crying out loud! Did he get Eddie Stobart to deliver it?"

She let out a huge sigh. "There you go again. For the great white chief, you're displaying all the naivety of a five your old. Even in his prison, he's retained some influence. We know what the stones are capable of. They're probably acting as a catalyst, increasing what reduced powers he has."

I didn't argue. If Merlin could communicate with us then why shouldn't he control other things in our time? I threw the parcel on the bed. "I'm not being naïve, just attentive to the situation. You could be right about the clothing. There's one way to find out."

The parcel was secured with string. I turned it over and pored over a label. 'Kit and Carin Milner. You will have need of these.'

Carin touched the label, tracing every word with her

215

finger. "I told you so. Merlin did arrange for someone to deliver it." She pouted. "You've got to start taking things seriously."

I was in a conciliatory mood. "I give in. Needs be when the devil drives, and all that rubbish. You'd better open it."

The duvet cover was soon hidden under pieces of torn up brown paper. The contents came to light. Clothing. Very smelly clothing. Two sets of smelly clothing. One piece of cloth was designed, in the widest sense of the word, to be worn next to the skin. Made of some course woven material, the garment had three holes cut in it. One for the head and two for the arms. An animal skin cloak was intended to be worn over this garment. The outfit was completed with a rope-like belt, that drew the whole outfit together, plus a crude attempt at headgear, fashioned from what looked like rabbit pelts. A pair of makeshift, animal leather crafted shoes completed the outfit.

We packed the clothes away and dressed for dinner. On the way to the dining room, I asked the receptionist if she knew anything about a parcel being left in our room. She couldn't help. A young waitress showed us to a table in the corner of the dining room. It was all subdued lighting, candles and cosiness. I glanced round the room. Three other couples were dining at candlelit tables. The food didn't disappoint us. We also managed to consume two bottles of wine. Our conversation ranged between personal small-talk and what the morrow might bring. Cheese and biscuits arrived, and we decided to have our coffee.

I turned around to summon the waitress. My eyes settled on a table in the far corner of the room. Someone was gawping at Carin. That's when my mind, under the influence of too much Merlot, started playing tricks with me. An inkling of recognition filtered into my brain. I squinted through the wine inspired tiredness in my eyes. An old man with a wickedly hooked nose and white hair was definitely staring at Carin. I could have sworn it was Merlin. He was clean shaven, and dressed in a dark jacket and bow tie. I closed my eyes to clear them. When I opened them, he'd gone.

My fixation was broken by Carin. "What's wrong?" I told her what I'd seen. "That's impossible and you know it. You've had too much to drink. Have some coffee, to clear your head. I'm going up to our room."

I spoke with the waitress about the old gentleman in the corner of the dining room. From the disdainful look on her face, my words must have sounded slurred and meaningless. "I'm sorry sir. Nobody was dining at that table this evening, and we don't have an old gentleman staying with us." I pressed her further. She stopped me, in full flow. "I can't help you any more. Would you like to speak with the manager?"

I declined her offer, and wished her goodnight. Knowing that I'd made a complete arse of myself, I made my way upstairs. Carin was in bed and asleep. I undressed and slipped in beside her. She didn't move. I went to sleep hoping that I wouldn't dream, but I did. I kept seeing an image of Julius Milner. It flickered, before disappearing and then returning. The effect was like eating a green pepper. It kept repeating. He was acting in an agitated manner, waving his arms about. He sank to his knees, and put his hands together in prayer. He spoke but no sound came from his lips. I forced myself to wake up. A surge of doubt resurfaced in me. I was reassured by a germ of an idea that flirted with my thoughts. It would help me if things got out of control. Feeling happier in my mind, I nodded off into dreamless sleep.

CHAPTER TWENTY

Tuesday, 30th October 2007.

THE RECEPTIONIST GAVE US DIRECTIONS to the castle. She said it was a popular tourist attraction but the site was closed to visitors from the end of September. She didn't know how pleased we were to hear that. By nine thirty, we had left the hotel.

Carin showed no signs of concern, or stress. Her auburn locks were pinned on top of her head. She looked at me. Her eyes reminded me of two islands, floating in the tranquil calm of jade coloured water. The effect was hypnotic. "There's something I want to know, Kit. Are you still willing to go ahead with this?"

I parried the question. "What about you? Are you as committed as you make out?"

She nodded her head. "I've never felt so sure about anything in my life. We'll come out of this smelling of roses." She put her arms round my neck. "It will be heaven."

My opinion had hardened to the degree that I didn't have much choice. I wasn't going to let my own feelings come between us, even though I felt I was being dragged by a rope that Merlin had tied around my neck. She was hooked on the whole idea, no matter what I said. My reply was measured to her enthusiasm. "If you're in, so am I. Somebody has to look after you, to make sure you don't take a fancy to Merlin."

She wasn't impressed. "OK then, let's go. We'll find the castle and sniff around to see where you can hide the car." We headed out of Abergele, until we reached the B5381. I turned left and drove for about five miles, until we came across a sign pointing to Llalogan Castle. I headed down the narrow lane until the track petered out. The castle ruins stood about seventy metres away, on a raised mound. A high chain link fence encircled the site, probably to stop gardeners from ravaging the ruins for rockery stones. An uncut hedge merging with trees grew along the inside of the fence. I turned the engine off.

"We'll hide the car inside the fence behind the hedge."

"Oh yeah and how are you going to get through those padlocked gates?"

"It so happens that I have the very thing." I opened the boot and reached inside. Walking across to the gate, I cut through the padlock with the bolt cutter. I pushed the gates open.

Carin ran across to me. "You've just vandalised Heritage property."

"I know." I put the bolt cutter in the car boot.

Her voice was laced with suspicion. "What else have you got hidden away in that boot?"

"Our luggage, a spare wheel and my tool box."

"What about the broken lock? It'll be just our luck for someone to report it."

I laughed. "You're asking all the right questions." I peered into the car boot. "I happen to have another padlock with me."

I drove the car into the field, and hid it behind the hedge. I replaced the broken padlock, before we ambled toward the ruin. It had lost its roof, but the walls were mainly intact. Fallen stones littered the grass floor, and a chilly wind blew through the holes that had once functioned as windows.

Carin looked around. "It's not exactly home from home, is it? The place reeks of history. The spirits of its people are dripping down the walls. Can you feel it?"

"Yes, I can." I closed my eyes. History was being played out in the ruins. I could feel the presence of a once mighty king. The smell of smoke, and cooking, mingling with echoing voices set about my senses. I opened my eyes. The sensations shrank away.

Carin held my hand. "Isn't it sad? I felt the happiness of this place. But look at it now."

"I think we've seen enough for the time being. Let's get back to the car."

We retraced out way along the B5381 and stopped at a roadside restaurant. The hours passed quicker than I expected. It was time to drive back to the ruins. I parked behind the hedge, making sure that the gates were locked. Carin changed into her sixth century attire in the car, whilst I dressed in the open air. I delved in the boot of the car, and took out a travel bag. I strapped it around my body, under my clothing, and put a small bottle of mineral water in it. My neck pouch held the phials of holy water and the crucifix as well as the Merlin stones. I left the two containers of CS gas in the boot. I felt no guilt in that I hadn't told the girl.

The aroma sidling up from Carin was awful. I must have smelt the same. Her hair was hidden under the rabbit skin hat. All traces of femininity had gone.

The day, that had dawned with overcast skies, had mellowed into a sunny afternoon. I glanced at my watch. Sunset was less than half an hour away. I locked the car, and hid the keys under a stone in the hedge. We made our way across the field, and walked into the ruins. The setting sun shone through a window recess, its rays settling on the ground. I prodded Carin. "I've got a hunch that we should stand in that patch of sunlight."

The wind moaned as it tumbled through the wall apertures. I strained my ears at its sound. The wind was talking to us. It wasn't my mother. "Can you hear what the wind is saying, Carin?" She nodded her head. "Do what it tells you."

The whispering sounds were soothing: "Prepare to undertake your journey. Close your eyes and I will take you through the ether of time." The wind strength increased, and then it was gone.

We opened our eyes. "We've arrived, Carin. That hut is Merlin's home. The rock over there is where he's shut away." We walked across to it. "Let's see if he's in."

"You're pretty cool about this. What happened to the old cynical doubting Thomas?"

"That's because I know this place." I put the palms of my hands against the rock and jumped back when it spoke to me.

"Welcome, my children. You look upon the prison that you must free me from. Early on the morrow, you will journey to Madrog's camp. I will provide you with a disguise for when you meet him. Tell Madrog that you heard Merlin's voice coming from the rock. Say that I spoke of my powers reaching their lowest ebb, and I will find it hard to resist his efforts to release me. He will come to this place later on the morrow. You will be among his number. Do not interfere, unless I call upon you. There is one command, above all others, that you must obey, on pain of death. You will not remove my stones from your bodies, at any time, whilst you are in my century. Without them you will not be protected. They are also the means of releasing your powers, Azur." There was no reaction from the girl at the use of my real name. "Rest your bodies in my abode this night. Is there anything that you would ask of me?"

He had invited a question, and was going to get one. "I

have something to say. Let me find Madrog, and his kinsmen and I will do away with them by using the killing ray that I possess. It'll be short and sweet. Then, I'll transport myself back in time and stop that woman from casting you into the rock. That'll save us a lot of trouble."

Merlin's response was predictable. He went spare. "How dare you speak to me like that, boy! Our deity has been angered by your rebellious attitude. I know of the gifts you possess. It was I who bestowed them on you. You forget that Madrog also has powers." Merlin paused. His voice dropped to a harsh tone, full of authority. "I am not prepared to take the risk that you might upset my plans. From this moment your powers have been stripped away. I have left you with the ability to make fire, for warmth and cooking this night. I will release your other powers only as you have need of them. If you give me any further trouble, then I will remove your stones from you. You will be left defenceless, and unable to use what powers I allow you. Do you understand?"

I appeased him. "Yes. I hear what you are saying."

"There is one other thing that angers me. You were told not to bring anything from your century. Yet, you have something hidden around your body. Remove it."

I smiled to myself. How had he known about the bag? I pandered to him. "I realise my mistake. There are no weapons in the bag." I threw it to the ground. A sheet of light raged from the rock, evaporating the bag and mineral water into nothing.

"I will be watching you, Azur. Make sure my wishes are carried out. Farewell, until the morrow."

The rock stood silent. The woman snapped at me. "What do you think you are playing at, man? Are you purposely trying to antagonise him? Get your act together. You're beginning to make me angry."

I looked into her eyes. "I wonder how he knew about the bag?"

She couldn't hide her look of guilt. "Don't ask me. How am I supposed to know? It doesn't matter. You shouldn't have brought it with you."

The feeling of disquiet continued to stalk me. The once mighty Merlin had somehow conjured enough strength to destroy the bag, as well as stripping me of my powers, yet he couldn't extricate himself from the rock.

We checked out our sleeping quarters. They had nothing to offer in terms of luxury.

Animal skins were strewn on the bare earth. I picked one up then threw it down. It was teeming with fleas. "Bloody hell! It's bad enough being bitten by the beasts in our clothing, let alone being eaten alive by these little bastards. Get the skins out of here." We threw then into the clearing. Where the skins had lain, small pieces of wood were laid across the ground. I knelt down, and moved the branches, exposing a hole in the ground. "What's the old devil hiding in here?" The inside was covered in dry moss. It was empty. "For a moment I thought I'd found where Merlin keeps those parchments that I never saw, that's if they exist."

Carin bristled. "Of course they exist." She simmered down and changed the subject. "I'm freezing. What about a fire?"

I pointed to a pot in the corner of the hut. "I'll find some firewood. Get some water in that."

Five minutes later a pile of wood lay in front of the hut. She stared at it. "I'm impressed, but what about some heat?" I pointed a hand at the wood. The image of fire flickered in my brain. A searing flame leapt from my fingers and ignited the pile. She wasn't impressed. "I'm feeling hungry."

"Go and sit by the fire. I'll check out the wood." I scouted round, but found nothing. The girl was warming herself when I got back. "No luck, not a creature is stirring in the forest."

She smiled, which confused me. "No need to worry, look what I found behind the hut." She led me by the hand. A brace of birds lay on the ground. She purred. "Merlin has answered our prayers. Isn't he wonderful? They are even plucked and gutted." We stuck each of the birds on the end of a branch, and roasted them over the fire. Water, from the pool, washed them down. The satisfying feeling of being fed was spoiled by the biting fiends in our clothing.

Carin scratched at her body. "Can't you do something about these pests?"

Her moaning was getting to me. "There's no pleasing you, is there?" I dragged her to the edge of the pool. It wasn't exactly swimming pool size, perhaps three metres by two metres, in an oval shape. I dipped a branch in the water. It was about a metre and a half deep. "If I heat the water, we can slip our clothes off and give them a wash. While they dry out by the fire, we'll have a soak."

She nodded eagerly. "I'll do anything to get rid of these fleas."

My self-induced flames licked the surface of the pool. Steam soon rose from the water. I checked the temperature with my foot. "It's about right. We may as well wash those skins that were in the hut." We threw our clothes and the skins into the water, then jumped in. I took the washed skins and our clothes across to the fire to dry and slipped back into the pool. Carin nestled her naked body against mine. My manhood stiffened. She played with the hairs on my chest. "I haven't told you, but I had a vivid dream last night. Merlin was in it. He said we must bond our love in a ritual. Merlin says it's common practice, in his time, and we must do what he says. Our loving union is to be marked by the letting of blood. We each cut our thumb, and let our blood mingle." She looked into my eyes. "You do love, me, don't you? Say that you agree to the tryst."

My nose had been put out of joint. Why was Merlin talking with her, and not me? She saw my hesitancy, and began to rub my manhood. Blackmail came to mind. This was the first time she'd shown any interest in my body since that first night when we'd made love. She guided my manhood between her legs, as her tongue explored the inside of my mouth, before nibbling my ear. "Our bonding is unique. The ritual will strengthen our love. Do it for me."

"I don't know what you're on about, but let's do it."

My semen burst into her body. She pushed me away. "Go and find something to cut our thumbs with, before I ravish you again."

I scrambled from the water, in a state of light headedness, and found a sharp piece of rock. We stood together in the water. "You know bloody well that I love you. I don't need this nonsense to prove it." Her eyes pleaded with me. I relented. "If it makes you happy, let's get it over with."

I scraped the rock across my thumb. Blood oozed from the cut. She did the same. The girl squeezed our blooded thumbs together. Droplets of blood dripped into the water. "Do one more thing for me darling, to complete the ritual. Slip your pouch off, and dip it into the water. The Merlin stones will seal our love."

In my woozy state I did as she asked. She looked towards the rock and threw her arms into the air. "It is done. We have the means of defeating death."

My dizziness vanished "What the hell are you on about? Are you off your rocker?"

"It's what my dream was all about. This water contains

semen, the creator of life, blended with life supporting blood. These essentials of life have been blessed with the magic of Merlin's stones." She scooped some water into the palm of her hand. "This liquid holds the secret of life over death."

"You're talking a load of crap. It's not fit for drinking, let alone anything else."

"That's where you're mistaken man. You don't know anything."

She was way ahead of me. "Whatever you say."

Her enthusiasm was quickly stifled, her passionate feelings switched off. She shrugged her shoulders. "I'm stuffed. It's time I turned in. Don't wake me, when you come in."

She dressed herself, and carried the dried skins into the hovel. I dried myself by the fire, before dressing. The girl was gently snoring when I lay down beside her. I couldn't get to sleep. Everything was badly wrong. The woman had changed. Her thoughts didn't gel with mine anymore. Two things kept beating at my brain. Why didn't she want me to see Merlin's writings? And what was all that nonsense about, in the pool?

I kissed her on the back of her neck. She moaned in her sleep. There was a way of reading Merlin's writings, if I still had the knack. I placed my hands on her head, and tried to locate her memory banks. Nothing happened. The gift of mind-reading had deserted me. A feeling of isolation crept into my mind. The idea of losing my powers and being under Merlin's control didn't sit easily with me. I got up and sat by the fire, in an effort to find some inspiration. The tree branches whispered as they moved in unison with the breeze. I revelled in a feeling of love, as my mother spoke to me. "Your mind is calling for help. That which you crave for is hidden under a fallen tree, on the edge of the clearing. The future of humankind is in your hands. God is watching over you. My love goes with you."

Silence fell, as the breeze ceased blowing. As I walked across the clearing, my feet crunched on the frozen leaves. I had no trouble finding the fallen tree. Merlin's writings were hidden in a hole, under the trunk. I looked at the pages by the light of the flames that flickered at the end of my fingertips.

The strange language didn't bother me. Merlin's spells were written on the opening pages. I was struck by his awesome powers. One spell leapt out from the page. The words were those that Lady Emuline had shrieked at Merlin: 'Urtibo dyon vapo.'

The next spell perplexed me. Its purpose was simple. The words undid the spell that turned people into vapour. Why hadn't Merlin used this spell to escape his fate?

My stomach turned over as I read the next page. My irrational fears came home to roost, in the cold reality of Merlin's words. It also indicted Carin as an unwilling accessory to Merlin:

'Azur, and Kareem, are the key to our victory in the heavens. They will see the light of day in the twentieth century. My father's dreams will be fulfilled by them. Through the union of their bodies, the false God will be defeated. All honour to my father. He will bestow eternal greatness on me.

My plan will right an injustice which has hounded my father for many centuries. Azur will be guided by me. Kareem will be controlled by my woman, at all times. A thought will be implanted in their young minds, to ensure that they retain their virginity until they meet each other.

The boy is the pawn in my father's plans, but he

must prove that he is equipped for his destiny. To prepare him, I will make his childhood unbearable. When he comes to adulthood, I will pit him against an adversary, to test his mettle. I have chosen a direct descendant of my old enemy, Lord Madrog of Rileth, for this task. He is named William Grodam. Whatever happens, Azur cannot perish. He is protected by his own special gifts.

The boy must have a mentor, who can reveal some of the unknown powers that Azur possesses. I have chosen Julius Milner, a man of God. I will control Julius, by setting my thoughts and commands in his head. He will have no idea that I am controlling his mind. I cannot enter Azur's body. He must remain pure. I will convince Julius Milner, and the boy, that they are descended from a young man to whom I gave some stones. They will encounter the young man in one of my visions. This is all make-believe. It never happened.

Azur wears the stones for one purpose. They allow me to control his powers, so that I can take them away from him. I do not wish him to have charge of his natural skills, when he returns to my time. If he removes my stones from his body then I no longer control his vast powers. I'll ensure he always wears the stones.

I will create visions for the boy, which he supposes are dreams, to test his resolve. I have also given him a dream world to shroud himself in, so that he may weave dreams in his younger years, to teach him to use his powers without knowing it. What he thinks are dreams, are reality. His dreams will teach him the means of time travel, but he mustn't learn of this *until he is ready.*

And what of the girl? She will be seen as Julius Milner's daughter. Azur will meet the woman and they shall fall in love. He will not be able to stop himself. That is essential to our plan. The boy must not fail. He is the chosen one. I will make certain that he walks the path that my father has ordained, by using the guiles of his woman.'

I'd read enough to realise that my uneasiness was vindicated. I wasn't cowed by the smell of treachery, or the knowledge that I possessed unnatural powers. From now on, I would trust no one, especially the woman.

I replaced the manuscript in the hole, and threw Merlin's stones away. This was the moment of truth, to check out Merlin's words. I picked up three pieces of rock and held them in the palm of my hand. A single thought caused them to move around, as they moulded themselves into rounded shapes. His writings hadn't lied. A buzz ran through me. They were my stones, not Merlin's. I put them in my pouch. With undisguised eagerness, I willed myself into a state of invisibility. I slotted in a command to time trek back to Merlin's clearing, to the moment when the woman had imprisoned him. My order snapped into place. Merlin was sitting, in the shadow of the rock, kissing Lady Emuline, whilst a smiling Madrog looked on.

Madrog got to his feet. "I will return to camp and prepare myself."

Merlin contented himself with a wave of his hand. "Make sure you carry my plan through, as we have agreed."

Madrog careered away on his mount. Merlin got to his feet and pointed towards the hut. The woman laughed and took his proffered hand. They disappeared inside. They had pleasures of the body to attend to.

I time travelled back to the clearing. Carin was still asleep. I walked into the forest, to test some of my other powers. I fed out a string of mental instructions. The blue killing ray flickered at my fingertips. I made a fallen tree hover above the ground, and moved myself to various parts of the forest without using my legs.

The feeling of exhilaration that passed through me defies explanation. Kit Milner is unique, and scared of no one. I am ready to defend myself against anything, or anyone.

I moved myself forward in time, to half an hour after Madrog released the vaporised Merlin from the rock. Merlin and Carin were standing in the clearing with Billy Grodam. Madrog lay on the ground, with the bodies of his sons and warriors lying around him. Whatever happened tomorrow, Merlin wouldn't be harmed, and Grodam was involved. I transported myself back in time, to the clearing.

One last task remained before I turned in for the night. I concentrated my mind on the CS canisters in my car boot. They were safely carried through the ether from the twentieth century and laid at my feet. I hid them under a tree at the edge of the clearing before returning to the hut. Sleep came easily, in the contented thought that my nagging doubts had been justified.

I was woken by the sound of the woman stirring. She sat up, and nuzzled at my shoulder. "I hope you've got rid of your hang-ups. Are you happier now you've had the chance to think things over?"

Lying was becoming a habit. "Don't worry. I'm taking things as they come."

"That's good." She stretched, and had a scratch, before flopping back onto the animal skins, and yawning. I got up and rubbed at the pain in my back. The rock stood silent and brooding, on a calm and windless morning. I ambled across to the pool to freshen myself. A yawning, empty hole greeted me.

I called to the woman. "Come out here. There's something I want you to see." She joined me. "What do you make of that? Is this something to do with Merlin?"

She gaped into the hole, then stared at me. Her eyes lacked any kind of expression. "You're still stuck with that old obsession about Merlin, aren't you? Give it a rest. Come on. We mustn't fall out over Merlin."

I let it go. I'm nobody's fool, but the girl was taking me for one. I knew the water hadn't drained away on its own.

We ate the last of the meat, in silence, washing it down with some water that I'd found in a hollow tree stump. Her body language was tetchy. I didn't trust her, but I needed a working rapport with her. I broke the silence. "I'm sorry at going on about Merlin. I won't take his name in vain again. Can we be friends?"

The sparkle returned to her eyes. "We're more than friends, you idiot." She planted a non-reassuring kiss on my cheek.

"That's good to hear. We'd better be off. I'd rather we found Madrog, before he finds us." I put a hand on her arm. "Forget what I just said. We've been found."

Two men stood at the edge of the forest. They were dressed in animal skin jackets, covered in light chain mail. Hide trouser leggings were tucked into leather footwear reaching up to their calves. Cloaks of a blue woven material hung over their shoulders.

Their heads were protected by metal helmets. They weren't blessed with good looks. Long greasy hair dangled onto their shoulders, and each sported a beard, below a mouthful of blackened teeth. Their broadswords were pointed at us. I whispered to the woman, "These must be the disguises that Merlin promised us, once I can talk them into letting us use their bodies."

One of them rushed across with bloodcurdling yells to where I stood. He raised his sword above his head, intent on burying the blade in my skull. His eyes betrayed his pleasure at the prospect of slaughtering me. I sensed Merlin guiding me into one of my powers. I fixed my eyes on the sword as it sliced through the air towards the top of my head. The unpleasant swishing sound synchronised with the warrior's shrieking.

CHAPTER TWENTY ONE

The Sixth Century AD.

I WATCHED, WITH A DEGREE of fascination, as the sword swept down towards my skull. The blade should have taken less than a second to cleave my head open. That split second spanned an eternity, as I slowed time down. I'd felt the same sensation when the thug had tried to poke a hole in me. I found time to eyeball my aggressor, and waggle my tongue at him. Bewilderment covered his misshapen features. He chickened out. The warrior threw his weapon away and both warriors fell to the ground in homage.

The woman purred. "That was wonderful. I knew Merlin would look after you."

She wouldn't have been so impressed had she known that I was in charge of my powers. "These two brutes are our passport to Madrog." I pointed to the ugliest-looking one. "He's yours. Think yourself into his body. Once inside him, you'll get the hang of things." She probably knew already, but I carried the pretence through. "Think your instructions to him, and he'll do it. You're in charge. Use his skills. Read his memory banks and feed on his retained knowledge. It's the same principle as a ventriloquist's dummy, but instead of having your hand up his backside, all of you is up his backside. Let's do it."

Seconds later, the warriors were on their feet with us inside them. I looked at the other warrior and laughed. "To think that I used to fancy you. The beard suits you."

Her voice was deep and gruff. "You don't look much better yourself."

"My one's called Barum. You're his brother, Cedrus. That's what we must call each other. And no kissing."

She managed a giggle. "Understood, Barum. I'm picking up a thought pattern that Madrog sent us out to scout around the rock. We're to report back to him."

I'm getting the same message. "Let's be on our way."

We jogged towards Madrog's camp. I smelt wood smoke, then heard the faint babble of voices as we cleared the edge of the forest and walked into open ground. A fire burned in front of four crudely built huts. Several horses were tethered to a wooden post, and I counted seven shields stacked against one of the huts, with an assortment of spears and swords. Madrog and his sons were seated at a long, wooden table, close to the fire. Two other warriors stood around the fire, whilst a handful of women skulked in the background. There was no sign of Grodam.

Madrog roared at us. "Come here, dogs. You have taken your time, I am not best pleased."

The fear in Barum's body gnawed at his brain, as we knelt before our Lord and Master. Madrog raised a foot and kicked me in the stomach. I didn't feel the pain. Barum did. He cried out, and rubbed at his body.

"You anger me." He lashed at my face with his fist. "I am tempted to remove your heads from your bodies, but I need your news. It had better be what I want to hear. Tell me what you found at Merlin's rock."

I took my life in my hands, and stared at his good eye. "Master. Would I dare lie to you? Merlin is weak, and ready to give up the fight. He is yours, my Lord. You have tarried in this place too long. Your time has come. Cedrus will tell you that the rock spoke these words."

My words were good. Very good. They even convinced me. All I got for my troubles was a blow across the jaw.

He shouted to the other men. "We march on the rock this afternoon." He put his face close to mine. "If your words prove worthless, then you will not be returning with us. I will have both of you tortured until you plead to die." He spun round, and motioned to the women. "Prepare food and drink, before we journey from this place."

The women busied themselves. Wine and bread were set before us. Madrog banged the table. "Enjoy this feast. It is a small token of what awaits us. At the end of this day you will be drinking to your true deity."

Steaming dishes of food were served, with endless bladders of wine. Lord Madrog clambered onto the table. Kicking the remnants of the meal away, he raised his goblet. "Lift your cups, and drink the health of your divine Master." He grabbed a bladder of wine, and emptied the contents over us. We stood, to a man, and bawled at the top of our voices. He swayed about, wallowing in our adoration. Our Lord silenced us, with a wave of his hand. "If you follow me this day, then I promise you…"

His rhetoric was broken by a giggle from one of the women standing behind him. He whirled around to face them. "Are my words to be cut short by a whore? Who is the piece of man's fodder who dares to laugh at me?"

The women cringed in terror. One of Madrog's men pointed. "It was that wench who stands there."

An excuse for a smile lit up Madrog's face. He jumped down from the table. Drawing his sword, he plunged the blade into her skull. She sank to the ground, her life blood spurting from the wound. He waved the bloodied sword above his head. "This is how I will deal with anyone who dares speak against me." He wiped the blade on the woman's dress, then sheathed the sword. "Take this bitch into the forest, and throw her carcass to the beasts. Cedrus. Barum. Come with

235

me. I am eager to hear your story, again. Cedrus will speak this time." The madman savoured every word, before he got to his feet, and bellowed to his followers. "Get ready for our journey."

We were soon assembled. Madrog and his sons sat astride their mounts, dressed in chain mail and helmets, each with a sword at their side, and a shield on their left arm. We warriors stood behind them armed with a shield, broadsword and spear.

Madrog turned to us. "You will travel at a horse's pace. Don't fall behind, or I will cut your legs off. We must be at the rock before sunset."

We set off. I sensed the mood of expectancy oozing from man and beast. It was a living awareness that masked the stench of masculine and animal sweat, and the tiredness in our legs. The sound of horses' hooves and men's feet beat a loud tempo on the forest floor. The speed of our journey was well judged. As we broke cover into Merlin's clearing, the last lingering rays of sunlight hovered in the late afternoon air. Madrog noticed the ashes of the fire that I'd lit. "We have visitors. Check out the forest. If you find anyone, bring them to me." Our fruitless search satisfied him that no-one was lurking in the trees. He barked out more orders. "Collect firewood. I must have heat to entice Merlin from the rock."

As the sun lowered itself behind the tops of the trees, the light waned. Tongues of flame, from the fire, lit up the clearing. Madrog strutted around the rock. His pacing came to an end. "The moment I have dreamed of is upon me." He nodded to one of his sons. "Bring me the vessel that hangs on my saddle."

I found the chance to speak with Cedrus. "Are you alright?"

He smiled, and licked his lips. "Don't worry about me. Merlin's moment is close."

Madrog clapped his hands. "The time for Merlin's deliverance is here." He put a hand inside his tunic, and pulled out a piece of rock. He beat it against the surface of Merlin's prison. Madrog picked up the vessel and removed the stopper. He fumbled at his clothing, and peed into the container. Facing the rock, he held the vessel at arm's length.

"Come forth from your prison, old man. You are mine." A cloud of vapour floated above the rock's surface. We all gasped. Madrog whispered, with evident pleasure. "It's happening. I will remove Merlin from his rock." The vapour formed into a small, shapeless cloud. Madrog enticed the vapour into the mouth of the vessel with his fingers. As the last trace vanished into the vessel's neck, he replaced the stopper, shook the contents and threw it into the fire.

It had been wasted time, waiting for a signal from Merlin. It wasn't going to happen. He was being boiled alive in urine, but I knew it was a farce. Madrog's sons dragged the vessel from the ashes with their swords. They peed on the hot vessel to cool it. Madrog picked it up, and pulled the stopper out. Raising the vessel to his lips, he drank the contents. A brief feeling of uncertainty swept over me. What if Merlin *had* lost his powers? I brushed the thought to one side. It was a scam. We were being taken for fools.

Madrog's voice echoed round the clearing. "You are looking upon the most powerful sorcerer in this land. If you pieces of dung need convincing, then I will show you."

He threw his arms out, and disappeared from sight, only to appear on the other side of the clearing. I allowed myself a smile. That was one of my party pieces. His warriors' reaction was mutual. We dropped to the ground and humbled ourselves before him as if he were some god.

I had to speak with Carin, and prayed that Madrog was disposed to being patronised. I crawled across the ground towards him. "Great Master. You are more powerful than our god. Let us gather more wood for the fire, so that we may see you more clearly. Then we can worship you, and indulge you with the reverence that befits your divinity."

He placed a foot on my head. "You please me, Barum. Do as he says. Bring more branches to the fire."

We melted into the trees. I grabbed at Cedrus' arm and led him away from the others. I acted like the complete prat that the woman expected of me. "What's happening? Nothing's gone to plan. We were supposed to rescue Merlin, not watch him die."

A stupid grin appeared on her face. "You worry too much. Things aren't what they seem. Merlin is in command. Can't you feel it? Stop fretting. Wait and see what happens."

It was the answer I'd expected. She knew what was going on. I kidded her along. "I'm really pissed off. You're not squaring with me. If you won't be honest with me, then I'm going to confront Madrog."

Cedrus grabbed at my arm. "You haven't got your special powers so forget it. Merlin took them away. Shove your heroics, and get your thinking hat on. Are you really won over to the idea that someone as great as my Merlin would allow himself to be hoodwinked by Madrog? Have faith in him."

This wasn't Carin speaking. I placated her. "Ok. I'll wait. I hope you're right."

She found it hard to hide the bite in Cedrus' voice. "I'm never wrong, and don't you ever forget it. Get some wood, before we're missed."

I gathered a few branches, dragged them into the clearing

and threw them on the fire. Our Lord and Master ordered us onto our knees.

CHAPTER TWENTY TWO

The Sixth Century AD.

Sparks spiralled into the night air, on their fruitless journey to oblivion. Madrog stood before us, arms folded. He surveyed the scene like a general on the field of victory. His head nodded knowingly, a twisted smile on his face. "Traitors stand in our midst. Two of you are plotting against me. I will unmask these traitors and deal with them."

It puzzled me how Madrog had managed to pick us out. I wasn't worried. My powers would protect me. He yanked his sword from its sheath, pushed by his sons, and made his way towards me. The Lord Rileth took me by surprise. He whirled around with a quickness of foot that belied his size. Two blows from his sword and his sons lay dead. Their severed heads rolled in confusion across the ground. His warriors stood in a state of silent shock. "The traitors are no more. Throw their bodies on the fire, and set their heads on wooden stakes. Plant the stakes at the edge of the clearing."

The bodies were flung into the flames, filling the clearing with the smell of cooking, human flesh. Two stakes were thrust into the ground, with the bleeding trophies impaled on the top. Madrog raised his arms in the air. "It is time to meet your real Master."

He clutched at his chest, and fell to the ground. The other warriors stood rooted to the spot, vacant looks on their faces. Cedrus and I hurried to where he lay. His eyes stared at us, in a look of disbelief. I put my face against his mouth. His breath touched my cheek. The two other warriors' concern for

Madrog had passed. They jostled with each other, to decide who should become leader in his place.

A familiar voice floated through the evening air. Billy Grodam walked from behind the lump of stone. I wasn't taken aback. I'd suspected he was controlling Madrog's body. His repulsive bulk was covered in animal skins. The same pasty face and sneer were in evidence but the wig was missing. Sweat glistened on his bald head. "Good evening, Milner. I know it's you hiding inside that repulsive creature. The other unsavoury looking one must be the girl. I compliment you on your disguises."

The two warriors reacted to Grodam's appearance. They drew their swords and charged at him. He shortened the odds by drawing a gun from under his skins. The weapon barked twice. They slumped to the ground. The odious Grodam nodded towards Madrog. "He's paralysed." He attempted to smile and failed. "I know what you're thinking, Milner. What's old Billy doing here, and has he got one of Merlin's stones? You'd like to strike me down with a bolt of lightning, wouldn't you?" He shook his head and clapped his hands. "Oh. How stupid of me. Merlin has taken your powers away, hasn't he?" He was enjoying the spotlight. "You've got some surprises coming to you, Milner." Grodam turned to Cedrus. "What have you got to say for yourself, my dear?" He rolled his eyes. "I forgot. I can't tell you anything that you don't already know, can I?"

I screamed at Cedrus. "Don't just stand there. You can tell me the truth, now. What's all this about?"

Cedrus pulled a face. "You'll find out, soon enough."

Grodam rounded on me. "Get out of that fancy dress. The woman as well."

We did as he asked. Two shots rang out in the evening air. I glanced at the dead bodies of our hosts. "You're a callous sod, Grodam. Surprise me then. Why are you here?"

He laughed, humourlessly. "I used the stone that you kindly left in your bedroom to get here. You're not the only clever one. It was easy to find Madrog's camp. I broke into his body, while he slept. He's an evil bugger, but not very strong in the brains department. What a team we made. I was the think-tank, while his authority carried my ideas through. I've enjoyed living in someone else's body. But, you know all about that, you bastard. It was after I killed Reggie that I realised you were pulling his strings." He coolly fed more bullets into the gun. "The Milners are beaten. I can't wait to get back to the twentieth century, as a part of the new order." He wagged his finger at the woman. "Didn't she tell you what was going on?"

She was sitting on the ground, a satisfied look playing across her face, showing no sign of worry, or emotion. I tapped her with my foot. "Are you ready to tell me what this is all about?" She looked away.

Grodam gloated, "You've lost the girl, Milner. Pity. You were getting on so well."

He pointed the gun at my head. "I've got lots of reasons for doing away with you. Killing my brother and setting fire to my house are enough. Goodbye, Milner."

I watched his finger squeeze the trigger. What followed should have been old hat for me. It was as simple as slowing time down. I dithered, as I read Grodam's thought waves. I was momentarily surprised to find that Merlin was in residence, and driving Grodam's thoughts. I wasn't going to let Merlin know that I controlled my powers, and played things his way. Grodam pulled the trigger, and the bullet eased itself out of the barrel. It tore into my shoulder, and out through my back. I felt no pain.

Merlin materialised by Grodam's side, and croaked an order. "Put the weapon down, William." Billy's body froze and became motionless. Merlin's words slurred through toothless gums. "Welcome, my children."

CHAPTER TWENTY THREE

In the Sixth Century AD.

ERLIN'S FACE AND NECK WERE corrugated with wrinkled flesh, making his aquiline nose even more prominent. His hair and beard had been trimmed, his gaunt body clad in fine robes, with a red woven cloak thrown across his bony shoulders.

The woman's face lit up. She ran across to Merlin and planted a kiss on his wrinkled cheek. "My Lord, I have missed you. Are you well?"

He put a bony arm around her. "Do not worry, my dear." He kissed her on the lips. "Our wait has been worthwhile." He walked across to me, and put his hand on my wound. "I know you felt no pain. You have learned something else of yourself. My stones do protect you. Look where the bullet struck you. You are healed."

I tore the garment away. The skin had healed, without leaving a scar. I shivered at the realisation that I hadn't needed the Merlin stones to protect me. My inbuilt powers had saved me from harm. I swore to remain calm. I greeted Merlin. "We meet at last. Your stones are powerful. Why did I suffer so much pain when the car ran me down, in my own time?"

Merlin smirked. "I made you feel pain, so that you might absorb the lesson to be learned from changing the past. Even then, you didn't believe what had taken place. That is your problem. You think too much."

"You got me here under false pretences. Was this carnage really necessary, to release you from a prison that never held you?"

He showed no concern. "You're still intent on asking too many questions." He gasped and wheezed. "I have no regret at what I've put you through. That is the way I designed your life to be."

Merlin stared at Grodam, and snapped his fingers. He came to life. "You've done all that was asked of you, in making Azur's life intolerable, and killing off those people I wanted out of the way. You perform your vile trade so well that I am relieved that I had the foresight to only grant you the powers of time travel and to penetrate Madrog's body. Your task is finished. I release you from your bond with Merlin."

Grodam smirked at me. "Goodbye Milner. It's not been nice knowing you. I'm going back to look after Merlin's interests."

Merlin pointed a finger at Madrog's still body "No, you're not. Goodbye, William."

The blue ray crackled as it enveloped Madrog's body. Grodam shrieked, as his body fell apart. Then, he was no more. Merlin looked at me. "Lord Madrog is dead, and so is his line. I have rewritten history. Julius Milner and his wife live in your own time, as do the man and woman that you call your parents. It is one of your rewards for being here today."

I remained unruffled. "Why am I here?" I pointed at the woman. "That's not my woman. What have you done to her? You owe me an explanation."

She stood at Merlin's side, an arm draped around him. It wasn't my Carin. I'd lost her, a long time ago.

He tried to smile. His thin lips barely parted. "You're being over perceptive. But I expect nothing less from you." He pointed a bony finger at Carin. "She's not in charge of her mind." He clicked his fingers. "Come and join us, my dear."

A wisp of vapour trickled down Carin's nose. It swirled around before forming itself into a female figure. Auburn hair tumbled to her shoulders. Her pale features were set off by large green eyes, and blood red lips. It was her head that had landed on my bed. The woman smiled. "Welcome to our time. I enjoyed my bond with you, whilst I was in your woman's body." She lowered her eyelashes. "Your lovemaking was breathtaking."

I felt dirty, and used. I ignored her. My eyes lingered on Carin. Her eyes were frozen, her unmoving body devoid of life. Lady Emuline laughed. "Don't worry about her." She kissed Merlin. "Shall I tell him, or will you, my Lord?"

"You tell him what he should know, my dear."

She moved closer to me, and clutched my hand. I pushed her away. "You poor boy. I have sad news. Your woman has been a pawn in our game. I took possession of her mind years ago. You will come to learn that you don't have to live in a person's body to direct their thoughts and actions. Leave your thought patterns in their mind and they will follow them. When we waken her from her trance, she will not remember you. You never existed in her life." She sniggered. "Kareem didn't fall in love with you. Merlin arranged for that to happen."

The old man butted in. "She does not lie. We have one further use for Kareem, before she returns to her parents. She will remember nothing of what has happened, content to take up the reins of her life, until we have further need of her."

I tried not to show my hurt. "I'm impressed. I want to know one thing, more than anything else. Who is my father?"

"Haven't you worked that out for yourself?" A look of amusement covered his face. "You are the son of Merlin."

This bolt from the blue didn't floor me. My mind training had prepared me well. I played him along. "That's impossible. You can't be my father. This is the sixth century. I was born in the twentieth century. You'll have to do better than that."

He sneered. "You speak brave words, but you've learned nothing these past years. The woman that you call your mother never conceived a child of her own. You were born in my time. I abducted you from your mother's arms, and transported you into that woman's care, in your time. I planted my thoughts in her mind, telling her how you should be brought up. I granted you the memory of being taken from your true mother's arms. You do remember, don't you?"

My coolness forced a pleasing smirk to his face. "You have taken my words well. So you should, as someone who is half warlock." His features clouded over. "I understand your reluctance in wanting to hug your father. My words have come as a shock to you. Damn it boy. It's time you learned everything about your family line. My father is the Devil. That makes him your grandfather. What do you have to say about that?"

I winced, inwardly, as the hard realisation of my forbears clicked into place. The shock hit me hard. The Devil was an evil deity, and his genes ran through my blood. A feeling of shame trickled through me. My grandfather didn't enjoy the greatest of street cred. My reply was casual, and gave away nothing of my inner feelings, "I believe what you say. I'm prepared to listen to whatever else you have to tell me."

He visibly relaxed. Merlin licked his lips, "I am blessed with immortal life, a gift given to me by my father. As my son, this gift has passed to you. That's why your wound healed itself. I invoked my stones to protect you. You have inherited all my powers, even though I have taken them away from you. When I return them to you, you will learn how to unlock them. You have been whining for an explanation, and I am ready to tell you what you want to know."

He put an arm round Lady Emuline's waist. "My preparations for today started twenty-seven years ago, when

I realised that the only way to achieve my father's dreams was to sire a son. My wife was not able to bear me a child, so I sought out a young damsel, who happened to be Azurina, a daughter of the wind in her mortal form." I allowed my face to display pretence shock at the news of my mother. "I planted my seed in her womb. You are the result of my dalliance with that maiden."

A fit of coughing racked his body. The woman patted his shoulder. "Enough, my Lord. You are weary. Rest whilst I talk with your son." Merlin allowed the woman to help him to the ground. She fluttered her eyelashes at me. "Your father has sworn to carry out a grand scheme, which Prince Satan has decreed. Your grandfather will replace the God who reigns in heaven and install himself as deity to the whole of humankind."

This outrageous notion angered me. "Are you trying to tell me that I figure in some weird idea to unseat a God who has been worshipped for thousands of years? It isn't possible. He's too powerful to be taken over."

Merlin scrambled to his feet. "When I saw you through the eyes of Julius Milner, I was always let down by your grave reservations. You have no ambition and you think too much. You certainly haven't inherited the traits of your grandfather. What a pity. I always doubted that you would have the resolve to carry the plan through. I thank Prince Satan for commanding me to play on your one weakness, in using your woman to bring you here."

He wasn't as clever as he thought. I'd already read his manuscript. I acted innocently. "So it was you who controlled Julius. I supposed you invaded my body, as well."

"No I didn't. Your body has to be untainted for your task. I guided you through your dream weaving. I did influence the bodies of your mother and stepfather, Joseph and Billy

Grodam, and their parents, as well as Lord Madrog and the men who were attempting to assault your woman. There were countless others but I have never penetrated your body. I used Julius Milner as the means of initiating you into some of the powers that you possess. He led you along my prescribed path, until he started to get too clever for me. He became aware that I was using his body, and fought against my thoughts. So I did away with him. William took care of that. He also had Julius Milner's wife killed."

Merlin was the worst villain of them all. It wasn't pleasant talking to your own father and hating his guts. "So why does it have to be me who will work the miracle that you speak of?" The old man grunted. "Because it's what Prince Satan has commanded. For thousands of years, he has lived with the injustice of being hurled down from heaven by the Archangel Saint Michael, and his band of Angels. They defeated my father, and his angel band in the battle for the heavens. Prince Satan was thrown out of heaven on God's trumped up charge. His rightful place is in heaven. My father will achieve what is truly his, through the guiles of a man and a woman who are both of his blood line."

My ears pricked up. I hoped I'd misheard what he said. "What do you mean, a woman descendant of Satan?"

He kissed Lady Emuline's hand. "It must have slipped my mind. Your woman is my Lady's daughter." He smirked. "And I am her father."

I was pole-axed. To be truthful, I was mortified. Not only had I fallen in love with my half-sister, but we'd made love. I vowed to hear the old man out. If things went wrong, I'd have to resort to my own scheme. Merlin was getting pleasure from his words. "The girl was conceived before Emuline married Lord Madrog. The child was transported to your own time, to be brought up as the Milners' daughter."

I didn't give him the pleasure of showing my true feeling. "Well, well, well. I suppose you set up the business of the davenport desk, and the letters, as well as arranging the visions?"

He pulled a face at my lack of interest. "Some of the visions that I showed you were make believe, otherwise my Emuline wouldn't be here. They were essential, as part of your learning. Your grandfather hoped that the evil you saw would rub off on you, and the power of temptation lure you into evil ways." He shook his head. "Other than killing Joseph Grodam, and setting fire to William's house, you have failed us." He sighed, as his lips twitched into a semblance of a smile. "But we fed on your misery. Watching your reactions to what we arranged, and sharing your suffering, has provided us with much amusement and entertainment, has it not, my dear?"

She smiled. "Indeed my Lord. Especially their lovemaking. For someone who has never dabbled in the art of manipulating a woman's body, he rose quite readily to my promptings."

Merlin kissed his woman. "You taught him well, my dear. Let me explain things to my son. He has a lot to learn. The Reverend was the first person to possess my stones. Forget your visions of the young man, at the rock. This was all make believe. I induced the Reverend to write letters, using the desk as a means of leading you to the stones. The attack on the girl, and setting fire to your dwelling, were at my prompting. They were supposed to prepare you for this mission except you chose to think too deeply about them, and became sceptical." Merlin scowled. "You thought me cruel in killing Grodam, but it was you who killed his brother."

For the first time I felt fear of this man. "You've taken a

lot of trouble to get me here. So, why am I here?"

He attempted another smile. "It is you who will open the gates of heaven. That's why."

Someone walked across my grave. Merlin was beginning to worry me. "You're talking in riddles. I know there's a God, but I don't believe in Satan."

He tugged at his beard. "My blood flows in your veins, so it sickens me that you are not an advocate of Prince Satan." A look of displeasure crossed his face. "He will be most displeased. Satan is a powerful deity, who has many earthly followers…" he sniggered, which brought on a burst of coughing… "even though most of them do not realise it. What you believe in is of no consequence. You will be the instrument of returning Prince Satan to his rightful throne, in the heavens."

It was my turn to laugh. "I don't believe what you say. In my own time, most people are not convinced there is a God, let alone Satan." My words dripped with derision. "Is Prince Satan going to chant some powerful spell that will make God disappear? Perhaps, he's planning to send canvassers around people's doors to drum up support for him."

Merlin spluttered. "Don't you dare mock my father! He has important plans for the people of earth. You've already put the first stage of your grandfather's grand design in place." Merlin, and his woman, rocked with laughter. "Listen to him, my dear. He scoffs at my father, but this man of God doesn't realise that he's the key to my father's scheme to rule in heaven. We couldn't have done it without him." He spat his words out. "Prince Satan's plan was set in place from the moment you entered the world. You have been walking your earth, for nearly twenty seven years, but it's taken just weeks, since you were born, to finalise his plans today."

I was confused. "I don't understand."

"We couldn't wait all those years for you to grow up." He pulled a face. "As well as a past, and the present, we all possess a future that has been mapped out for us. I travelled into segments of your future life to mould you during those years. I've only needed the last few weeks of your life to achieve what my father demands. On this day, in my time, you were born only a few weeks ago."

He was overcome by another fit of coughing. The woman wiped spittle from his lips. "Are you able to continue, my lord, or shall I explain to him?"

He waved her away. "I shall tell him." He rubbed his hands together, and squirmed in anticipation of what he had to say. "It falls, in the end, to me to tell my son how he fits into my father's plan."

She kissed his hand. "Put him out of his misery, my Lord."

"Listen to me, boy. Your grandfather's needs are simple. He yearns to be worshipped, and adored, by mankind. Your God will be routed, and forced to flee the heavens. The Holy Trinity, together with the teachings of his son, Jesus, will be seized by Satan and shattered beyond belief. Your God's promise of a heavenly banquet in his many roomed mansion, and good for good's sake, has failed. All of earth's people will show reverence to the deity of Prince Satan, in a few weeks' time."

A cold hand clutched my heart. Was he really capable of achieving something so far beyond my grasp?

He raised his hands to the sky. "My father's scheme is so easy, that it cannot fail. Not even your God will find it in his power to undo it." He coughed, and spat phlegm from his mouth. "The failing of your deity is that he hasn't involved himself in the affairs of men. He has left mankind to decide whether it should believe in him, or not, through the teachings of his dead son, and his holy Bible, which no one understands." Merlin droned on. "The means of sweeping your God from the heavens lies in the body of your woman." He smiled to himself. "The woman that you profess to love is carrying a baby - your baby. The boy child was spawned out of evil, the product of an illicit union, and punishable under your own laws."

I was stunned by what he said. What hurt me was that the baby hadn't been spawned out of love. I'd been duped.

Merlin was enjoying himself. "In the eyes of your God, your relationship will be called evil. Satan didn't frown upon your fruitful liaison with your half-sister. The child that lives in Kareem's womb was created by two virgins, both of them from Prince Satan's line. Don't fret at your illicit union. Satan decrees that his followers may tread any path that they choose, so long as they are prepared to recognise him as their only deity." He turned aside and drew his woman toward him. "Lady Emuline will tell you of the child that your woman bears."

She walked across to me and took my hand. I didn't enjoy the experience, and snatched it away. She made my flesh crawl. Merlin had rattled me but I wasn't going to give him the satisfaction of showing it. I stared at her. "I wouldn't have enjoyed our lovemaking if I'd known you'd taken up residence. What's the plan, then?"

Lady Emuline cooed her words at me. "Your son is destined to be Satan's salvation. He will be born of a virgin woman, and extolled as the saviour of the world." She shrieked with laughter. "Your unborn son will be the first coming that your book of religion talks about. The God, who now reigns supreme, will lose favour with humankind."

A fleeting ripple of concern flowed through me. "Hold on. It's already been done. He was called Jesus."

She snapped at me. "Be patient, young man, and listen. In the eyes of the world, your unborn son will be greeted as the first saviour. Your Jesus will never have been born." A hint of their intentions settled in my mind. She flicked her hair back. "Merlin and I will travel to Bethlehem, back to the time of the virgin birth of your Christian saviour. We will remove the bastard child from the virgin's womb and replace him with your unborn son, Satan's great grandchild."

I barely dared to breathe at the boldness of what they planned. The thought that my child was intended to be a tool in the furtherance of a religious coup couldn't rest easily with me. I had to concede that Merlin was capable of doing it.

The woman paused to let her words have maximum effect. "I will have power over Mary's body, and Merlin will live in her husband, Joseph. The child that the virgin carries will be drawn out of her body as she sleeps. I will place your baby in Mary's womb, where he will grow and take on the age of the Christ baby. When Prince Satan's great-grandchild is born of the Virgin Mary, the baby will become the true saviour of the human race. And this time, it won't end with crucifixion on a cross. Our saviour will be truly immortal, performing miracles and extolling the virtues of wickedness. You son will be the mirror image of Prince Satan, the spiritual ruler of the world. All religions in the world will worship him. In time your saviour son will be championed by disciples who will be immortal. His disciples will travel the length and breadth of the world, furthering his name. In time, they will write a book of the virgin birth, proclaiming the teachings of our saviour, and Prince Satan. It will become Satan's sacred book to be read by his subjects, who will obey its teachings."

I wasn't as calm as I sounded. "Isn't God going to have something to say about this?" I couldn't help laughing. "And how are you proposing to make all these disciples immortal?"

Merlin nodded. "You're thinking positively, at last. You have to realize that your God, and Satan, are not persons of the flesh. They are spiritual entities, who thrive and feed on the adoration that is drawn from the love and prayers of their followers. My father will overthrow your almighty God by becoming the more powerful and sacred entity, through the power of enticement. Humankind will enjoy the rewards of succumbing to the temptations of life that Satan created for them. Satan will be loved and adored and will dominate the whole of creation enthused by the massive adoration that is shown to him. Your God will not survive when he is repulsed by mankind. His spirit will be snuffed out, because there is no one left to worship him."

He turned to Lady Emuline. "He dares to ask how Satan's disciples can achieve immortality, when it is he who gave the potion of everlasting life." Merlin's face took on a serious look. "It was not down to chance that the pool waters vanished. In your love tryst with the woman your fused blood and life-giving semen created a potion which provides immortality to anyone who drinks of it. I filled a wine bladder with the water of life, and evaporated the rest, whilst you slept. Lady Emuline will drink of this water, to give her immortality. Your unborn child is immortal, as he is of your blood-line."

I was impressed for all the wrong reasons. "You've put a lot of thought into this scheme, yet it doesn't make sense. Why are you sending my woman back to her own time while she carries our child?"

They glanced at each other. Merlin spoke. "Your brain is working well. She will not be taking the baby with her."

He pointed at Carin. "It is time to complete the ceremony." Merlin waved his long fingers in the air. The bottom of Carin's skins moved, as a cloud of vapour drifted from beneath them. Merlin enticed the vapour towards Lady Emuline. It crept under the bottom of her garment, and disappeared. The woman sighed. "It is done, Lord Merlin. The infant nestles in my womb."

He rubbed his hands with glee. "The woman that you profess to love can now return to her own time." Lady Emuline clapped her hands, and Carin was gone. My heart ached at the realisation that the weeks of happiness I had spent with the girl had vanished. We'd met through trickery, but my love for her was still real.

Merlin bowed to his woman. "Thank you my Lady. Kareem remembers nothing of her former life, including you, Azur. Neither will she consort with other men, in her own time. She belongs to us. Her body will be a refuge for Lady Emuline, when she grows older, and her flesh begins to break down." Merlin put his arm around his woman. "We are nearly done in this place."

I applauded myself for keeping my feelings in check "You haven't told me what you've got planned for me. I assume that I have a further role in this scheme?"

"You have carried out your first purpose, in siring the new saviour. But, you still have a part to play. My woman will drink the water of eternal life, then you shall discover what is expected of you. Stay here, while I fetch the bladder that contains the potion."

Merlin shuffled towards his hut. I delayed him with words that I knew would play on his vanity. "Father, I cannot wait to find out what my part will be in creating a change in the divine being." I hoped that my God would excuse a transgression. "You are wrong when you say I am a firm follower of my God. I admire your talents, father. As your son, surely you will favour me with the answer, before the woman drinks the water?"

He pondered, before coming to a decision. "This is more like the son that I wanted. You have the right to know what is expected of you. Prince Satan commands that you rule in the other worlds as his Lord Protector to ensure that his subjects, even in death, do not stray from the path that your grandfather has set them"

This was something new. "What do you mean, the other worlds?"

He reproached himself. "Of course. You know nothing of them. The followers of your deity believe they go to heaven, when they die, and live in the spiritual world of their God." He shook his head. "There is no such place. The spirits of the dead travel to one of numerous parallel worlds, where they take on the bodily form that they possessed on earth. These worlds are in another dimension. They're in the air that we breathe, but you cannot see them or feel them. They are hidden behind an invisible veil, a mere heartbeat away."

This was all twaddle to me. "What happens in these parallel worlds, once you get there?"

"Under your God, they live out an earth-like existence." He managed a laugh. "All that will change under the rule of Prince Satan. In his worlds, the spirits of the dead will be subjected to torture, torment and perdition. The degree of suffering depends on which world they are sent to. Those of his subjects who were most evil during their earthly existence will depart to the first parallel world, where suffering will be less. Those who sinned less on earth, will be sent to other worlds, where the torment is more severe. My father will feed on their pain and suffering. You will oversee these worlds, in the service of Prince Satan."

This was getting a bit out of hand. "What if I don't like what I find and want to come back to earth?"

Merlin lost his rag. "Yours is the ultimate accolade that can be given, in the personal service of the great and powerful Prince Satan. You will swear everlasting allegiance to him which once given, cannot be broken. You will never set foot on earth again." He clapped his hands. "I have said enough. My Lady can wait for the water of life. Let us make preparation for your journey to the parallel worlds."

I'd heard enough. I lost my temper. "If you think I'm going to let myself be transported to some life hereafter, you can shove it. I belong here and there's nothing you can do about it."

Now was the time to put my plan into action. I didn't get the chance. The rock began to tremble, and a voice of razor-sharp authority rang through the clearing. Merlin and his woman fell to the ground in homage. "I have listened too long to your negative words, grandson. My son has failed to convince you, so I will have to. Prostrate yourself before me."

The implication that he was Satan, filled me with dread. In our ordered daily routine, we casually treat God, Satan, and religion as a small part of our lives. Our attitude is to take it, or leave it. And why not? We're never likely to bump into them, during our lifetime, nor when we die, if you believe some people. It was a shock to realise that someone claiming to be Satan was speaking to me. I lay face down on the ground, if for no other reason than to get my jumbled thoughts into some kind of working order. How does one deal with the anti-God? I was jolted back to reality, by a voice speaking in my head. "Do not be afraid, my son. You asked for my help, when you knelt before me, in my church, and I am here for you. You have been cloaked in courage to fight the evil one." I shook my head, to make sure I wasn't hearing things. I wasn't. "Believe in me, and I am with you. You are the man of God. Deal with the Devil, as my son did."

How many people have had a living encounter with God, and the anti-God, on the same day? It was a life changing experience. I should have been quaking, but wasn't. The voice in my head hadn't lied. I had the resources to counter anyone, including Satan.

I got to my feet, and did my best to sound calm. "Are you telling me that you're Satan?" I stepped up my badge of courage. "If you are, then show yourself." A figure materialised, in front of the rock. I made a gasping sound. I could have been looking at my own reflection. "But you don't look…"

He interrupted me. "…like the Devil. Is that what you were about to say, grandson? As a divine entity, I don't possess a human form. If I have the need to show myself, I masquerade in the bodily form of anyone who has dabbled in evil. I am using your body because even you have carried out acts of wickedness. You have met me, many times, during your life. This is how I looked."

The God of Darkness kept changing his image. My mother and stepfather stood in front of me, then Billy Grodam and his cousins, Joseph Grodam, Merlin, Lady Emuline, the two yobbos who had attacked Carin, Lord Madrog, and Julius Milner. Each of them leered at me, before fading from sight.

The Satan look-alike reappeared, "Any of these people can be called the Devil, because they were happy to follow my promptings. They were lured into wickedness, just as I tempted Eve, in the Garden of Eden. I used the guise of a snake to ensnare her, persuading her to pick an apple from the forbidden tree, that her God had told her not to touch. Even your God's holy book cannot be sure that it was me that tempted her. Her expulsion from the garden brought evil, as well as good, into the world, to her descendants. Evil is much more fun than pursuing your God's path, as the world will soon find out. My vision of ruling the heavens was prophesied in your God's holy book. It says that there will be a new earth and a new heaven. That divine prediction will come true."

Flames flickered in his eyes as they pierced mine. "Perhaps you'd rather see me as people imagine me to be?"

His outline blurred. I trembled at what stood in his place. A giant goat towered above me. Its eyes were wickedly yellow, with smoke curling from his nostrils. Its front cloven hooves perched on the top of the rock. Licks of flame spurted from its body. I could feel the heat from where I stood. Blood red mucus dribbled from its mouth, and ran into its matted hair. The creature's breath was sour and rancid. The goat spoke. "As the offspring of my proud line, you anger me. Not only do you hold the Christian God in your thoughts, but you are insolent." Its yellow eyes bored into mine. "With my blood flowing in your veins, wickedness, and you, should be constant companions. But they are not." He struck the rock with a hind hoof. Sparks showered the clearing "It's not important. You have given me the most essential thing that was expected of you. My great-grandson, the saviour of the human race, lives in that woman's body." The Prince Satan took on my human form. "As for you, grandson, you are a thorn in my side. What must I do with you?"

Merlin was still stretched out on the ground, with his woman. He broke his silence. "I hear your wise words, Master. Shall I deal with this miserable son of mine?"

"No, you fool." He snarled at me, "Down on your knees. Show respect for your Lord and Master."

I did as he asked, for good reason. As my head touched the ground, my hand reached inside my pouch. The crucifix and a bottle of holy water were concealed in the palm of my hand.

Satan thundered his words at me. "Listen to this prayer, which all of Satan's subjects will chant when I reign over them:

> *Prince Satan, who art in heaven*
> *Thou vanquisher of the false God*
> *Blessed be thy name forever.*
> *Your teachings will be abided by,*
> *In this world and your worlds beyond,*
> *Through your blessed Saviour,*
> *Who walks amongst us,*
> *And is blessed with immortality.*
> *We are grateful to you, Lord Satan,*
> *For leading us into unholy malevolence.*
> *All praise to you for revealing to us*
> *The pleasures of the flesh.*
> *Bless you Lord Satan,*
> *For consenting to transgressions*
> *against our transgressors.*
> *We offer you a living sacrifice,*
> *as a mark of our homage to you.*
> *Yours is the Kingdom*
> *The Power and the Glory,*
> *For ever and an eternity*
> *We will worship you, Prince of Darkness."*

Satan finished his ranting. He yelled at me to get up and shouted at Merlin. "On your feet. You have work to do. Freeze his body."

They scrambled to their feet. "I will do as you ask, Master. He cannot use his powers, because I control him through my stones." He screamed an incantation at me. It was meant to paralyse me. My mind spoke the words that reversed his spell. I played along with him, and allowed myself to stiffen.

Merlin bowed to Satan. "He is yours to command, as you will."

Prince Satan waved him away, and looked me in the face. His eyes turned red, and flames flickered from his hair. "You were born of my line, and have inherited great powers from me, by which token your soul belongs to me. What a pity that you chose not to tread my path. You would have been a formidable partner. I had hoped you would reign over my parallel worlds but I have no use for a believer in God. You have failed me. What do you have to say, before I have you killed?"

A breeze blew though the clearing. My mother's voice whispered in my ear. "Do not fret, Azur. Satan cannot hear me. My master, your God, is with you. Hear the Devil out, and then use your weapons against him and the others."

I stared at the flames flickering in Satan's eyes. "I have only one thing to ask. How can you take my immortality away?"

He laughed. "You amuse me child. Your immortality will be stripped away by sacrificing you. Your head will be cut off, then your heart ripped out." He nodded to Merlin. "Use your powers to bind him to a tree. When you have done that, cut his head off."

Merlin wasn't quick enough. My mind concentrated on the cylinders of CS gas that I'd hidden under the trees. I watched the cans as they hovered above the ground. On my mental command they hurtled through the air, and struck Merlin and his woman with great force on their heads. They fell to the ground. A second thought sprayed the gas in their faces. They clutched at their throats, the agony they were suffering etched in their faces. No spell tumbled from Merlin's lips. He was out of action.

Satan was transfixed. I hurled the crucifix at him. He watched in fatal fascination as it sped towards him. It affixed itself in his forehead. The flesh around the crucifix started to burn. I sprinkled the holy water over his body. Satan screamed as his body broke down into dust. He vanished from sight.

I wasn't finished. I propelled my body behind a tree, and sent a bolt of lightning toward the rock. It exploded into thousands of fragments, sending pieces of stone flying through the clearing, and into the forest. They sounded like bullets as they whined through the trees. I walked through the dust that hovered like mist in the clearing. The woman was dead. A large piece of rock had ripped her head from her shoulders. Merlin was a mess. His clothes were torn away by the force of the explosion. Merlin's legs lay in an untidy heap, ripped from his body by the lethal fragments of rock. Blood oozed from a multitude of wounds.

The old magician stared at me with hate filled eyes. His lips moved, but no words came out. I picked up his thought waves. "You tricked me. You have killed my woman and forced the Prince of Darkness to flee. I've misjudged you. You were too clever, even for me. I should have known, seeing you are the son of Merlin. You have won this time."

I picked up a sword. "There won't be a next time." In his decrepit state, he still posed a threat. He was immortal. I bit at my lips at the thought of what I had to do. It took two blows to remove his head from his shoulders.

His head lay on the ground contemptuous of me. He managed a few words. "You haven't won." I was sidetracked by a sound from the edge of the forest. An old stag and a fawn stared at me. The stag pawed at the ground as if it was going to charge at me, then raised its head and let out a loud rasping sound. With a contemptuous shake of its antlers it turned around and they both vanished into the trees.

The horror hadn't finished, nor was Merlin. To end his immortality, I dragged the point of the sword across his chest. More blood added to the carnage. Merlin's head coughed, and his eyes slowly closed. I pushed my hand into the gaping wound. My fingers gingerly felt around inside his chest, until I located his heart. It stopped beating. I dragged it out, and chopped at it with the sword to free it from its arteries. I tossed my father's heart into the fire, where it jumped about, as if it was still alive. It popped and burned away. The hairs on the back of my neck stood on end, as I heard a child's voice call me. "Daddy, I'm afraid. Please help me."

I pulled back the hem of Lady Emuline's dress. A naked baby boy lay on the ground, looking up at me, his umbilical cord still attached to the dead woman. I was confused. This couldn't be my son. He'd only been conceived a few days ago, yet this was a fully grown, talking baby. He pushed himself into a sitting position. The baby held out his hands to me. "Father. Don't leave me here. Pick me up and take me with you. I'm your son, your flesh and blood. You have a duty to look after me. We belong to each other."

I looked into the baby's eyes. They were dull and lifeless. The baby stared back, and opened its mouth. It had fine pointed teeth like a cat. I shivered. This was my child, but he was the spawn of the Devil. He clutched at my hand. His fingers felt like ice.

"Take me home with you, Father." The child was changing before my eyes. Hair started to sprout, where he'd been bald, and he was gaining in size. The colour of his eyes changed to deep dark brown. The child gripped more tightly at my fingers, and smiled. He spoke. "You killed my woman, so you must look after me. I've nobody else in the world. I need you Father."

I twigged why he needed me. He was drawing strength from my body, through his fingers. In a matter of minutes his body went through the phases of toddler, young child, and teenager. He became the spitting image of me. He sneered. "Surprised are you. My grandfather is dead, and I intend to carry on the work of my great-grandfather, whether you like it or not. Are you with me, or against me?"

The world wasn't prepared for my child. I sent out an unspoken spell, which bound his limbs. I pushed him over, and picked up the sword. "You're no son of mine. The Devil possesses your body."

I cut the youth's head off. It landed on the ground, where it continued to shriek and curse me. My blue ray obliterated it into nothingness. I pierced his chest, took out a beating heart, and threw it into the fire, together with his body. Red smoke filled the air, as my dead son burned in the fierce flames that were induced by my blue ray.

Feelings of doubt emerged, that really shouldn't have been there. Not only had I murdered my father, but also something that masqueraded as my son. Perhaps, I should have felt sadness, and a little pity. I couldn't.

I took the second phial of holy water from my pouch and screamed the words that turned what was left of Merlin and the woman into vapour. Their bodies fell apart, breaking down into a gaseous mist. I beckoned the vapours towards me, and guided them into the neck of my bottle, before replacing the stopper.

The fire still burned brightly. I found the bladder that was filled with the water of life. It was going back with me together with the parchments, and the bottle that held the ethereal vapours.

Dead leaves blew across the clearing as a shadow moved across me. I looked up. My mother was watching me. Her eyes lit up, as I hurried to her, and smothered her in my arms. She whispered in my ear. "Have no misgivings for what you have done. Merlin was an evil man, as would your son have been. Go home, Azur, you are finished in this place."

Tears ran down my cheeks. "Will I see you again, mother?"

She kissed me on the forehead. "I cannot say. You should never have cast your eyes on me. Remember me every time you feel the touch of the wind on your cheek. I love you."

I took one last look at the clearing. It held no good memories for me. I gathered up my possessions, and instructed my mind to return me to my own time. The gift of time travel carried me safely from the clearing, to where my father's ruined castle stood.

CHAPTER TWENTY FOUR

Wednesday, October 31st 2007.

I CAME TO MY SENSES, with the stench of death trapped in my nostrils. The images of mutilated, dying men battered at my brain, and all because of the whim of an evil deity, in his desperate bid to rule the heavens. The red mist permeating the passages of my mind gradually receded, just as warm autumn sunshine burns through early morning pockets of fog. I allowed my weary eyes to open. It took them time to focus in the bright sunlight which streamed through the windows of the ruined castle, that had once been my father's proud house.

My heart pounded at a frantic rate. It threatened to burst through the wall of my chest. Muttering a brief prayer towards the heavens I thanked him for being alive.

Without thinking, I pinched the top of my leg to make sure that I was in the land of reality. The pain proved that I was awake. It made me wish that the events of the past few weeks could have been a dream, instead of the real thing.

My body was covered in sweat. It had soaked into the fabric of my clothing. The warmth of the sun created a perceptible cloud of steam, rising like mist into the chill morning air. The mental and physical agony must have been etched into my face. Painful spasms ebbed and flowed through every muscle in my tormented body. My mind engaged in agitated turmoil, even though the demons had long departed.

Unashamedly I wiped away the tears that trickled down my face. I caught sight of my father's handwritten manuscript lying on the ground.

A wistful smile tugged at the corners of my mouth. No one will ever believe what is written in those pages, even though I am the walking proof of his words. I thought about the girl. She should have been with me this morning. I was struck by the realization that she was no longer a part of me. The girl was only a memory in the pages of time. I pictured her auburn hair, hanging in ringlets about her face, and those green eyes, which with one look had the effect of turning my whole body into warm jelly. It reminded me of how much I loved her, and the immense happiness I have derived from her all too short presence in my life.

My love for her is so intense, that if she had asked me to die for her, I would willingly have done so. Such is the measure of the deep unshakeable affection in which I hold her. I can't begin to imagine a future without her.

The girl has gone, and the love we shared during our brief relationship is stripped from her mind. Her feelings for me have been blown away like chaff on the wind. I'm a complete stranger in her heart and mind. She's forgotten me as though I had never existed.

I shivered at the images of what has happened during these past few weeks. But, at the end of our brief relationship, our happiness was blighted by a string of evil and moving events. I tried to summon up some inner mental strength to help erase the memories of our relationship. It was a waste of time. How can I wipe from my mind the dangers, the passion and ecstasy that we shared during those weeks of light and darkness?

CHAPTER TWENTY FIVE

Wednesday and Thursday, 31st October
and November 1st, 2007.

I MADE MY WAY BACK to the car. The sun tried its best to raise my spirits, but failed. I changed back into my twentieth century clothing, and stowed everything in the back of the car. Minutes later, I was on the main road heading back to Lovington.

There were chinks of happiness in my sadness. A lot of things have changed in the twentieth century.

Life will go on in the new mode, but only I can remember how it was. My foster parents are alive, along with the Milners. The Reverend's lifestyle has improved, now that Merlin isn't controlling his mind, and thugs aren't hounding him. The Grodams never existed and I still have a job in Martin's company.

I toyed with the idea of reviving my relationship with Carin. It would have been easy to plant a thought in her mind, to make her love me. That wasn't fair. It was unlikely that she'd fallen in love with me the first time round. She was destined to become a sad old spinster, because of Merlin's hold on her mind. If I meddled with her thoughts, and we did fall in love, the law of the land was overtly clear on its view of a physical relationship with your half-sister. We'd already created a monster baby. I made a decision. It was the coward's way out. I could call on her, and take things from there. Destiny could make the judgment. What harm was there in that?

The journey became more bearable. I stopped at a service station, had a wash, and managed to enjoy an unremarkable meal.

It was paid for with my last ten pound note. The money that Julius Milner had left me wasn't in my wallet.

As I walked out of the restaurant into the corridor a noisy crowd was milling around someone lying on the ground. I edged a bit closer, as my curiosity got the better of me. A paramedic was kneeling beside an old lady. Her eyes were closed. He applied pressure to the woman's chest, then carried out mouth to mouth resuscitation. His face reflected a lack of interest. The woman remained motionless.

I've never had first aid training, but that didn't stop me from stepping forward. I patted the paramedic on the back. "Let me have a go." He stepped back. I put my lips against the woman's open mouth, and willed her heart to beat. Her eyes opened. She mouthed "thank you" to me.

The paramedic shook my hand in amazement. "She's alive. What did you do?"

"I'm not sure. You'd better look after her."

As I got up, an old woman clasped my hand. "Thank you. She's my sister. I thought I'd lost her."

An older man put his arms around me. "It's a bloody miracle. What's your name?"

It was all too much for me. How could I explain what had happened? I wasn't sure, myself. As I walked away, people chased after me. I had to get away. I ran around a corner out of their sight, made myself invisible and headed for the car. It didn't please me, what I had done. In helping the woman, I'd managed to broadcast to all and sundry that I didn't conform to their way of life. I hoped no one had taken a photograph of me.

I switched the radio on as I drove down the motorway.

A news broadcaster was already reporting on the incident. His words went something like this: 'Reports are coming in of an elderly woman being brought back to life by an unknown man at the Watford Gap Services on the M1. The paramedic attending the woman said that despite all his attempts, she had died. He went on to say that a young man resuscitated her, which was a medical impossibility. He said it was like watching someone being raised from the dead. The matter doesn't end there. Eyewitnesses maintained that the unknown man vanished in front of their eyes. The report is being treated with some scepticism by the authorities.' A cold sweat covered my body. My powers were beginning to unnerve me. Was there no end to what I could do?

It was too early to call on the Milners. I sauntered down the High Street, to the tea shop with the phallic spouted teapots. The same pleasant lady served me. I ordered toast and tea, and whiled the time away.

The shop emptied, and the lady came to clear my table. "Haven't seen you before. Just visiting for the day?"

I fabricated. "I've got some business to attend to with a Reverend Milner, the rector of your local church. Do you happen to know him?"

"My dear. I'm one of his congregation. He's a lovely man." Her eyes twinkled and she patted her hair. "You're not getting married, are you?"

I winced. "No, nothing like that. Does his daughter still live at home?"

"Yes, she's still there." Her face took on a cheeky look. "I don't think there's a man in her life."

After more idle chit-chat, I wished her goodbye, and made my way back to the car. Within minutes, I was parked outside All Saints' Church. I couldn't resist going inside. It felt strange, walking past the pulpit and standing in front of the altar, where Carin's ravaged body had lain.

I'd murdered a young man in this church. I shrugged my shoulders. What was the point of tormenting myself? Carin hadn't died, and Joseph Grodam had never been born. I stood by the marble slab, where Julius had originally hidden Joseph Grodam's body. A single thought raised it above the ground. I placed the bottle containing the vapours of Merlin and his woman in the hole, together with the water of life and Merlin's parchments, before replacing the slab.

A car trundled by, as I left the church, and turned into the rectory. Carin got out and went indoors. I ambled down the road, walked up the rectory drive and rang the door bell. Carin opened the door. I tried to speak, but nothing came out. She stared at me, without a hint of recognition, sharing my tongue-tied state.

The awkward silence was broken by a familiar voice. "Who is it, Carin?" Julius Milner came to the door. He pulled a face, "Good evening, I know you from somewhere, don't I?"

I found my tongue, "Hello. We met casually in church a couple of times. I've called about your restoration appeal. I think I can help."

His face lit up. "Really? Do come in." He shook my hand and guided me into the lounge. It hadn't changed since the last time I'd seen it. I glanced at the davenport desk that I'd once owned. Carin followed us in. She hadn't spoken a word since I arrived. The Reverend failed in his attempts to hide his excitement. "Would you care for a glass of sherry, Mister...? I'm sorry, I didn't catch your name."

"I'm Kit Milner. A glass of sherry would be fine."

He patted me on the shoulder. "This is my daughter, Carin. What a coincidence that we share the same name."

She held out a hand, which I grasped. "Hello Kit. It's nice to meet you."

I didn't let go of her, until I realised that I was caressing the back of her hand with my thumb. Julius sat us down, and poured the sherry. We sat in front of a roaring fire. He coughed. "You mentioned the restoration fund, Kit." He put his empty glass on a table, and walked over to the fire, where he warmed his backside.

"The church is in dire straits. There's so much work that wants doing but we're barely crawling towards our financial target. Why are you interested in us? Are you from these parts?"

"I'm from Linmere, but Lovington has happy memories for me. I once knew someone very special, who lived here." Carin was hanging onto my every word, her jade green eyes boring into my face. "I'm prepared to make a donation to your fund. How much do you need?"

"We have to find in the region of one hundred and eighty thousand pounds."

I paused for maximum effect. "I can fund all of that, for you." They weren't empty words. The money was coming from a national bookmaker, although they didn't realize it. Knowing the winning horses, before the races started, gave me a head start.

He shook my hand. "I can't believe this. What a most generous offer, Kit!" A look of concern crossed his face. "Is there a catch, my boy? I'm sorry if I'm displaying a tinge of negativity but I've been promised monies before that never materialised."

"No need to worry. You'll have my cheque during the next few weeks. There's one condition. I don't want any publicity."

"I'll see that your wishes are carried out." He scratched

273

his head. "I can't put into words how delighted I am. You must stay for dinner. I can tell you more about the work that needs to be done. What do you say, Carin?"

She put her hand on my arm. "Thank you for helping Daddy. He does worry about the church. I'd love you to stay for dinner." Was it my imagination or had she said love, intentionally?

The Reverend gentleman hopped about with delight. "That's agreed then. I'll pop into the kitchen and ask my wife to lay an extra place."

The girl moved across to the fire. "Daddy looks so happy. You are for real, aren't you? He's been let down before. I don't want him to get hurt." I ached to take her into my arms, and tell her how much I loved her. I contented myself by joining her in front of the fire. "Your father will get the money. That's a promise."

"Sorry, if I had my doubts." A playful smile crossed her face. "Who's this special person from Lovington? I bet it's a woman!"

"You don't beat around the bush, do you? Yes, it is a woman. More correctly, it was a woman. I lost touch with her. But that was in another lifetime. You remind me of her. That's why I stared at you when you opened the door."

"I envy you, Kit." I purred at the use of my name. "Goodness knows why I'm telling you this." She blushed and pulled a funny face. "I've never had a boyfriend."

We'd had this conversation once before. "I wouldn't worry, Carin. There's someone out there for you. I only knew this girl a couple of weeks before we split up. I'm getting on for twenty-seven, and she was my first girlfriend." Another white lie wasn't going to do any harm. She'd already heard this in our previous life. "We didn't have a close relationship. You're looking at a male virgin, first class."

I knew she wouldn't be shocked. She roared with laughter. "That's a relief. I thought I was the only one left."

I shook her hand. "Welcome to the club. I'm saving myself for someone special, when she comes along."

That special person couldn't be Carin, so long as she was under Merlin's spell. I snapped my fingers in her face. She went rigid. I whispered in her ear. "Listen to me. Merlin's hold on you is broken. You will remember nothing of your previous life. You are free to fall in love, with anyone. You won't remember these words when I wake you."

I clicked my fingers. Her face came alive. "I hope you find her, Kit." Her father walked into the room with Mrs Milner. "Kit. This is my wife. She won't mind if you call her Meg."

She smiled, and kissed me on the cheek. "Of course I don't. You're most welcome to stay for dinner." She shook her head. "How typical of a man. He hasn't even taken your coat. I'll hang it up for you."

That evening will live with me for ever. It was a pleasure to be with people whose lives had been resurrected by something that happened in the sixth century. They were leading the lifestyle they deserved, without the spectre of Merlin hanging over them. More importantly, they liked me, and it had nothing to do with the money I'd pledged to the church.

It was time to go home. I bid goodnight to Carin at the front door. As I walked down the drive, I turned around. She blew me a kiss. My feet barely touched the ground as I hurried down the road. The despair of this morning had turned to undeniable elation. My foot caught the edge of the curb. I couldn't stop myself from falling. As I clattered to the ground my head struck the top of the church wall. White lights, and stars flashed in front of my eyes. I struggled to my feet, holding onto the wall for support.

My eyes chanced on the illuminated church notice board. I blinked, to make sure I wasn't seeing things. With a feeling of inner coldness, I read the wording a second time: 'THIS HOUSE OF WORSHIP IS DEDICATED TO MERLIN, THE SON, AND PROPHET, OF OUR BELOVED LORD SATAN.' The church was as I'd seen it, earlier in the evening, but there was no sign of the houses at the end of the road. I went inside, and switched the lights on. It was the same interior that I'd got to know, except a few changes had since been made. Black sheets were draped around the pillars, and woven tapestries, portraying grotesque scenes of devil worship, hung from the walls. A black carpet ran the length of the nave, and through the chancel. The building reeked of death. I made my way to the altar, and checked out the stained glass window. Merlin stared down at me, with Lady Emuline on one side, and what looked like me, on the other. The altar was devoid of an altar cloth and candlesticks. A knife, axe and chalice lay on top of a wooden, bloodstained surface.

I started to run back to the rectory, when everything blurred and went dark. When I came to my senses, I was sprawled on the rectory drive. Dragging myself to my feet, I frantically rang the bell. Julius Milner opened the door. "What's happened, Kit? You're covered in blood. Let's get you inside, so that Meg can have a look at that cut on your forehead."

He hurried me into the kitchen, and sat me down. Carin and Julius fussed around me, whilst Meg bathed the wound. She stopped the flow of blood and put a plaster over it. "That's a nasty cut, young man. I think it needs stitches. Julius had better get you to hospital."

She wasn't to know that it would heal itself. "There's no need, Meg. I'm not in any pain. Let's see how it is tomorrow."

My words won her over. "Alright. But you're not driving home in this state. You can stay here for the night."

I was given a couple of pain killers, and shown up to the spare bedroom. Dressed in a pair of the rector's pyjamas, I fell asleep as soon as my head hit the pillow.

It was gone ten o'clock when I came to. There was a soft knock on the door. I invited whoever it was to come in. The girl's worried looking face peeped round the door. She was still in her pyjamas. "Morning, Kit. Mummy told me to let you sleep in. How are you feeling?"

"Much better, thank you."

"My parents have gone to Ely for the day. Would you like a drink?"

"A coffee would be great. I'll get dressed, and come down."

She put her foot down. "Mummy said you've got to rest. I'll bring it up."

"If you insist. Where's the bathroom?"

"It's the second door on the right, along the landing."

The door closed behind her. I made my way to the bathroom. My face looked disgustingly healthy in the mirror. I pulled the plaster from my forehead. There was no sign of the wound. I put the plaster back on. I'd just settled back in bed, when there was a knock on the door. "It's only me."

"Come in. I'm not used to being waited on like this."

She put the mug on the bedside cabinet. "No problem. I'd better have a look at your head. You might need another plaster."

She leaned over me. I had a clear view of milk white breasts, nestling under her pyjama top. I grasped her hand.

277

"There's no need. My head's fine. Honestly. I'll go and see my doctor later on."

She frowned. "There's no bruising. You're a quick healer. When you're ready, you'll find your shirt in the airing cupboard along the landing. Mummy washed and dried it. I'll cook you something when you come down." When I made my way downstairs, Carin rustled up a fried breakfast. She sat down, whilst I ate. "What happened last night?"

I wasn't sure. The whole thing reminded me of dream experiences I'd come across, during the last few weeks, which had turned out to be encounters in time. I scoffed at the thought. Merlin was dead.

Carin brought me back to reality. "Are you alright?"

"I'm sorry. I was somewhere else. It was nothing mind-boggling. I tripped on the kerb, and smacked my head against the church wall."

After breakfast, we made ourselves comfortable in the lounge. I sat in an armchair, while she hovered in front of the fire, staring at me with those pleasing green eyes. I could see the outline of her body through the thin material of her pyjamas. I felt uncomfortable under her gaze. "Aren't you going to work today?"

She grinned. "No. I've more important things to attend to."

I got up. "In that case, I'd better be on my way. My parents will be wondering where I've got to."

Carin pushed me back and plonked herself on the arm of my chair. She pouted, like a spoilt child. "I don't want you to go."

I tried not to read her thoughts, but couldn't stop myself. She wanted me to make love to her. A further physical relationship with my half-sister was something I hadn't come to terms with. I got up to leave, but knew it was too late. My groin was aching in the expectation of having her body.

She took hold of my hand and slid it inside her pyjama bottom. "I don't care what you think of me, but you're not going anywhere. I've never done this before, but I want you."

I tried to stall her. It was a feeble attempt. "What if your parents come back?"

She laughed. "They won't be home for hours."

We sat on the carpet, in front of the fire. I undressed, as Carin slipped out of her pyjamas. I entered her body, with confidence. At least she didn't have Lady Emuline inside her, pulling the strings.

She sighed. "I'm not a regular man-eater, Kit, but as soon as I met you last night, I knew we were meant for each other."

I whispered in her ear. "I'd already fallen in love with you before I met you last night. The restoration fund was an excuse for calling here. I first saw you, some weeks ago, and couldn't get you out of my mind." I managed the truth. "I even asked the lady who runs the High Street teashop if you had a boyfriend. She said you hadn't. So I came up with the idea of calling on you. I hoped you might see something in me that you liked. The bit about helping the church is real. Your father will get his money." I kissed her. "I didn't expect to get this close to you, so soon."

She put her finger over my mouth. "Less of the talking, make love to me." I knew every inch of her body. She groaned with pleasure as we climaxed. We made love again, before I left.

The rest is history. Our physical bond is something I have to come to terms with. I'm the spawn of Satan, but that's between me and my God. There is one comfort. Being immortal, I won't have to face him on Judgement Day.

I'll tell Carin about Merlin, and Lady Emuline one day. She'll never know that we made a child. As for my special powers, I'll have to tell her, in time. As Merlin's daughter, I wouldn't be surprised if she has hidden powers of her own, which need unlocking. She's probably inherited her father's immortality, but I'll get her to drink some of the water of life, just in case.

And what about my gifts? I'm not bursting to use them, or show them to the world. I will bide my time. Merlin still concerns me, even though I took away his immortality. I'm not underestimating the resolve of Prince Satan. He is a dangerous deity.

As I walked back to the car, I checked the church notice board. This was the Christian church of All Saints'. Something clicked inside my head, which made me go into the building. The church interior was lit by intense light, shining from the chancel. With a sense of elation, I walked to the altar, and knelt down. The light source shone from the Christ figure in the stained glass window. Its brightness enveloped me, shrouding me in a sensation of serenity.

The figure of Jesus floated down through the air. He stepped onto the altar, then drifted to the floor. The Saviour beckoned me to stand. I saw a scar in the palm of each outstretched hand. I put my hands into his. An energy field flowed into my body. He let go of me, and raised his hand in the sign of peace. His kindly features were wreathed in a smile, his brown eyes shining in a swarthy face. "Welcome my brother. I have filled you with the spirit of God, so that you will have no fear of what you have seen here. Our Father is well pleased with you. You are truly a man of God. Should he have further need of you, he will call on you." He smiled at me. "Our Father knows of your conflict with yourself, in the bond that you share with your woman. He commands me to tell you that you are not the son of the evil one, Merlin. You will find your real father, one day. Go forth from this place, with happiness in your heart. Peace be with you, my brother."

The light vanished, and I was left in darkness. One problem had been resolved, to be replaced with another. If Merlin wasn't my father, then, who was? My mind flipped to a bigger worry. Where had I inherited my powers from?

I was strong enough to dismiss these thoughts from my head. Whatever the future might hold, I will be facing it with the woman I love. Life has turned lucky for me. I hope that nothing is going to change it.

CHAPTER TWENTY SIX

ONE DAY IN THE FUTURE (January 20**)

(I won't reveal this date.
I don't wish to alarm my readers.)

CARIN AND I ARE GOING out for a meal this evening. As I drove by All Saints' church to pick her up, my engine cut out. With a curse, I got out of the car. I sensed my mother was close by, as a breeze tickled the nape of my neck. "Azur. My master has sent me. Use your cloak of invisibility and fly with me."

As far-fetched as her request sounded, I instinctively knew it was within my power. I did as she asked, and soared in my mother's slipstream. "Where are we going, mother?"

"Your God has taken you forward, in time. What you will see is All Saints' church, in the future."

I looked down and recognised the church, as it came into view. The only other building of any note was a large, square structure belching out clouds of black smoke from its chimney. The smell of burning flesh offended me as I flew through the smoke. "What is that building, mother?"

"You will learn, Azur. Fly down to the church, and see what is going on. Keep your cloak of concealment about you."

I did as she asked, and landed by the church porch. A group of people, wearing hooded cloaks, were entering the building. The door was closed and barred, as the last one went in. I made my way around to the chancel window, and peered into the church. A young naked girl lay on the altar. Her limbs moved in a slow, lethargic manner, suggesting she was drugged.

A hooded man addressed the gathering, waving a knife in his hand. He pointed to the stained glass window, then at the naked girl. The congregation shouted: "A sacrifice for Satan...a sacrifice for Satan." The man, holding the knife, turned to the altar and casually cut the girl's throat. Not content with that he slashed the knife across the dead girl's chest, and removed her heart. He drank blood from it then threw it to the congregation. His hand alighted on an axe. He hacked at the girl's neck. Blood erupted from the stump, as her head fell to the floor. He collected her blood in a chalice.

The mob screamed with delirious rapture. "The sacrifice has been made to Lord Satan." The executioner removed his hood, and calmed the crowd with his bloodied hands. My heart stopped beating. Julius Milner was wallowing in the adoration of the chanting crowd. He silenced them. "Hear me, followers of Lord Satan. Our own Saviour, the great-grandson of our Lord and Master, welcomes you to this sacrifice. We are not worthy of his presence."

Julius Milner inclined his head, in a show of reverence, and beckoned to someone standing in the shadows. Another jolting blow hit me. A man, who could have been me, stepped up to the altar. The rowdy crowd grew quiet, and fell to their knees. My twin extended his arm, and addressed them. "Our Master, Lord Satan, has decreed that after the act of sacrifice, his true believers should join in our Lord's feast. Swear your allegiance to our Deity, as you feed and drink, in his name."

The crowd filed to the altar rail where they dedicated themselves to Satan by eating the flesh of the dead girl, which their Saviour sliced from her body. Julius Milner offered her blood in a chalice.

The crowd returned to the body of the church, and fell about in acts of wanton fornication. The Saviour raised his arms, and shouted for his followers. "Be silent. You have shown your belief in our Lord Satan, by eating and drinking at his table, and indulging in the pleasures of the flesh. It falls on me to prepare our next sacrifice." The Saviour stepped into the shadows and led a naked girl to the altar. It was my Carin. She made no protest as the Saviour laid her on the altar. "This woman will be sacrificed at the next sacrificial service of devotion to our Lord and Master."

I'd seen enough. I walked around the back of the church, and headed for the building shovelling out the acrid smoke. Through the open doors I caught sight of a pile of mutilated, dead bodies, lying in one corner. Two men were enjoying their inhuman work, laughing and joking as they threw human corpses into two blast furnaces. The sound of crackling spitting bodies carried to where I stood. One of the men cut an ear from a body and munched on it. The other gouged out an eye from the same corpse and popped it in his mouth. The sight sickened me. I pointed a finger at the corpses and with a single thought rendered the two men incapable of movement. The living dead raised themselves up from the floor and stretched their limbs. They jabbered amongst themselves, before falling on the two men. They were torn apart, limb by limb, and thrown into the furnaces.

My mother flew round my head scolding me. "Enough, Azur. Don't get involved. This is a figment of the future; Our Lord commands that you return to your own time."

The next moment I was sitting in my car. The engine was running. I've been confused many times during the past few weeks, but my present mood eclipsed anything that I'd experienced. Had this been a bad dream, or were my efforts of the last two days in vain?

Someone tapped on the window. The passenger door opened. Carin got in and sat down beside me. She had a distant look in her eyes. The girl took hold of my hand. "Forgive me, my son, for talking through the mouth of your woman. You have seen the future. I am destined to lose the battle for the heavens and will be cast out, with my legion of angels. Satan and his archangels reign in my stead. He has captured the spirit of all humankind. Satan's saviour walks on this earth and his subjects practise the dark and occult arts. Your recent battle was in vain. My son, Jesus, was never born. As a spiritual being, I cannot interfere with the course of humankind. I can only hope they will follow my teachings, if they have a love and belief in me. Only you can keep me in my rightful place in the heavens. What you have seen must not become a reality." Then, the voice was gone. Carin got out of the car and walked back to the rectory.

I am the only person who knows when Satan is fated to take over the world. I'm puzzled that Satan's saviour is the mirror image of my son whom I put to the sword. And why are Julius Milner and Carin involved? Have I been tricked? I'll only find out for sure when I try to put this portent of the future right.

Enjoy your God while you can, because if I fail, mankind is faced with the prospect of everlasting purgatory. Whatever happens, never forget that good will always triumph over evil.